Retake

By Tonya Clark

Sandie,
Thank you for your support. Hope you enjoy Adam + Kays story.
Tonya Clark

Cover created by selfpubbookcovers.com/Shardel

Dedication

I would like to dedicate and thank first and foremost my amazing husband, Don. Without his support and his push this book would have stayed in a hand written form and for my eyes only. Him believing in me was all I needed to bring it out for everyone else to enjoy. This is for my two beautiful daughters who through the whole process had to give up a little mommy time but pushed me to finish it because they knew it was a dream of mine. To all of my amazing family and friends who have believed in me from the beginning, this book is for all of you!

Chapter 1

"Hailey, I miss you dearly too, but I don't think with my schedule right now that I can make a trip out. I have too many photo shoots scheduled right now to just up and take a vacation."

I have worked extremely hard the last eight years to build my photography business here in Napa, California. I never considered what I was doing as a job or work. Photography has always been a passion of mine and being able to do something every day that put a smile on other people's faces and is fun to me, could never be considered work. No, I got paid to go out every day, watch children grow up, families being created, love blooming, and couples lives being started and get paid for it. I wasn't stuck in an office all day long. I didn't have someone telling me what hours I had to work. I answered to no one except myself, which for the last eight years I thrived on. I was doing what I wanted to do, not what someone else told me I had to do.

I haven't lived my whole life in Napa. I really wouldn't even call it home. Home would be a little town outside of Nashville called Nolensville in Tennessee. That is where I was born and spent more than half my life growing up with my best friend Hailey. We have been friends since before grade school. I wouldn't even consider her just a friend, we were more like sisters.

My sophomore year of high school was when I moved to Napa, after my father had taken a job transfer. I thought my world was falling apart that day. I had to say goodbye to Hailey. Even though we were hundreds of miles apart we never lost track of one another and still to this day we speak everyday on the phone. Eight years ago my marriage ended, and if not for Hailey, I am pretty sure I wouldn't have even survived physically or mentally. We may be hundreds of miles apart from each other but I know that if I needed her no amount of miles would keep her for helping me and she knows the same about me if she needed me.

Hailey married her high school sweetheart Ryan McComb and together they have a little boy named Bryson who was five now. She still lives in Nolensville with Ryan and their son along with her older brother Adam and their grandmother, who everyone calls Grams. They all run the family ranch which breeds some of the best horses in the state of Tennessee, if not all of the United States.

Hailey and Adam have lived with their grandparents ever since Hailey was about a year old. Their parents had both been killed in a car accident. Their grandfather passed away about thirteen years ago of a heart attack just shortly after Adam had graduated from high school. He felt that it was his responsibility to take over and run the family ranch. Hailey and Ryan got married right after Ryan graduated from the police academy. He is currently working on the force in Nashville but on his days off helps Adam out on the ranch.

Would I love to go back home and visit? Absolutely, I would love to but now wasn't the time. I had way too many bookings right now to drop everything and go visit what I still to this day considered home.

Cradling the phone between my shoulder and ear I walked outside to my mailbox, "All of a sudden I swear everyone in the city of Napa decided they needed some kind of pictures taken. My phone has been going crazy the last couple of weeks. To top it off on Friday I fly down to San Diego to shoot a wedding. She is a sister of one of my brides from up here and she fell in love with her sister's wedding pictures. She said that there was no way she wasn't having me photograph her wedding as well."

"Well when you are the best what do you expect?"

Hailey personally thought I worked way too much, saying it wasn't good for me. Of course, I always tried to inform her that I wasn't working, more like playing.

"I think you are over exaggerating that just a tad my friend," mail in hand, I started walking back towards the house flipping through the mail. I stopped right before walking into my front door. The envelope I was looking at gave me a very uneasy feeling. Why would my lawyer be sending me something? "What is this?"

"What is what?" Hailey asked back.

I hadn't realized I had even spoken out loud and I hadn't heard Hailey ask the question back either. I quickly opened the letter and read it. My hands began to shake, this could not be happening. This had to be some kind of sick joke, "Oh no."

Hailey had known her friend for years she could read her like a book, even if she couldn't see her face. She could tell something was terribly wrong, she could hear it in her voice. She stopped folding the laundry she had been working on while on the phone, "Oh no what? Taylor what is going on over there?"

No answer came, all she could hear was Taylor's labored breathing. She sounded like she was almost crying, "Damn it Taylor talk to me, what's wrong" Hailey asked again? These were the moments she hated being this far away from her friend.

Hearing Hailey's worried words I finally found my voice, "It's Mike."

Hailey jumped up from the couch, "What? Where? I thought he was in jail?"

"For about another two weeks he is still in jail. I just received a letter from my lawyer informing me that they are letting him out early on account of good behavior. He was awarded early parole."

I read the letter over and over again. This could not be happening. Mike and good behavior weren't words you used in the same sentence. I felt my knees becoming weak, I couldn't faint, I wouldn't faint but I did need to sit down. Walking quickly over to a chair I had on my front porch, I flopped myself down, "Hailey I will call you back."

"No Taylor don't hang up. Talk to me. I want to make sure you are alright, please don't hang up the phone," she repeated.

"I promise I will call you back in a minute. I just need to sit here a moment," then without waiting for a response I hung up the phone.

I sat back in the chair my head resting back, my eyes closing a single tear escaped. How could this be real? The moment my eyes closed flashes of that day quickly played through my mind.

Eight years ago I was lying in a hospital bed my family being told by the doctors that they weren't sure if I would live through the night. I don't remember any of that part of the night myself but I do remember my mother's voice when she told me about it and the expression on her face.

Right after I had graduated from high school I decided I wanted to go to school for photography and entered into a couple of classes at the college. My first day of class I walk in and right away I saw Mike. Blonde hair, green eyes, tall and gorgeous. All that semester we flirted with each other. It drove me crazy that he would never ask me out. I wasn't an expert on guys or anything, really, I hadn't even dated a lot in school, but I was pretty sure he liked me and I was too shy to ask him out first. Finally, right before the end of the semester he asked me out to dinner. I was on cloud nine.

Mike was everything a girl looked for in a guy. He was perfect or so I thought. He was always buying me gifts and sending me flowers. He was always taking me out, just the two of us. That's all I needed, just the two of us. I fell in love with him right away, I mean, what was there not to fall in love with? He treated me like a queen. My parents loved him, even my older brother liked him right away. Mike knew how to charm everyone. Everywhere we went girls would stare and guys would come up to us, slapping him on the back.

We had only been dating for six months when he asked me to marry him. I felt that things were going a little fast. I mean, who really gets proposed to after only six months? I remember thinking to myself, "didn't that kind of stuff only happen in the movies?" That thought seriously only lasted a moment because I knew he was the one and we were perfect together! I mean, everyone had always told us that, so I said yes to his proposal.

The two of us did everything together. Any photo shoots we would have we went to together. We never left one another's side. We were even hired by the same wedding photographer to intern with.

Mike had pushed for not waiting too long for the wedding so we were married only one month after he proposed. I had always dreamed of a large wedding and was slightly disappointed when Mike told me something small at the court house was all we needed. He convinced me that since money was tight and that we had decided to start our own photography business that we should just go to the justice of the peace and get married that way to save the money. Sad, but too in love to pay attention to the first signs, I agreed.

Looking back I get so mad at myself for not noticing the signs at the beginning. Right after we were married Mike started becoming very controlling. First the verbal abuse started. He would put me down all the time, he was always yelling at me. Nothing I did in the marriage or the job was right for him. Slowly he worked into not allowing me to hang out with friends and then he started to slowly push me away from my family. He would even monitor my calls from Hailey, either telling her I was unable to talk to her or he would stay on the line during our conversations. Mike knew everything I said and did and, I am sure, even thought.

Every job that we would go to we would shoot together. He never allowed me to take one alone. He was beside me at all times, even at the weddings. When we would shoot, he would stay right at my side and then at the end, on our way home, he would be angry with me, telling me that he couldn't believe what a tramp I was flirting with all the groomsmen.

Things really started getting bad about a year into our marriage. He began to get physically abusive. Pushing, nudging, hitting, and the sex was on his time, when and where he wanted it and so help me if I ever tried to refuse him. I became very good at hiding the bruises. I refused to allow my family to find out because it was all too embarrassing.

After about a month of not feeling very well, I managed to convince Mike that I needed to make a doctor's appointment explaining to him that I was due for my yearly "womanly physical." Surprisingly, he allowed me to go alone. That was when I found out I was pregnant.

I remember that drive home like it was yesterday. I had been so happy. I wanted a family and I was sure this would change Mike and having his baby would make him happy. I was sure of it. The drive home had seemed endless. I was so excited to go tell him the news.

Walking into the house I found him sitting at the kitchen table cleaning some camera equipment, "Hon, you won't believe what I found out today," I was smiling from ear to ear. I waited for him to look up but he didn't so I continued on with my news, he would look up then I was sure of it, "I'm pregnant! We are going to have a baby!"

I remember the smile on my face quickly fading as he looked up with so much anger in his eyes. I was sure he would be happy about the baby. I couldn't figure out what he was so angry about.

"Are you not excited?" I asked my voice was already shaking. I knew that look. I knew what it meant, but what I couldn't understand is. Why he was giving me the look?

"You bitch," he started to stand, "how dare you betray me," now he was coming around the table.

I slowly started backing up into the living room. I had never seen him this way. "Mike what are you talking about? I thought you would be excited about us having a baby?"

He grabbed me by both arms, his grip was like steel, "You want me to be happy that my wife is carrying another man's baby?"

I had no idea what he was talking about and I had no time to ask either. All at once everything happened, his fist connected with the side of my face. I remember that punch very well. Even to this day I swore I could feel the blow to the side of my face. My hand went up to trace the scars around my eye. I even remembered the two blows that followed. I remember watching him take a step back then kick me with all he could right into my stomach at the same time saying, "You will never see this baby I promise you that." As I fell back my head slammed against the coffee table knocking me out.

A little over a week later I woke up in a hospital room, my mom and Hailey sitting in two of the chairs both asleep. Hailey had flown to California the minute she had gotten the call from my mom explaining what had happened.

After being told the story of how my mother and father had stopped by to try and see me, since Mike very rarely allowed them to visit their daughter, he always had some excuse as to why I was not home or why they couldn't come over at that time, they had decided not to call this time. They were just going to stop by. They told me how they came up to the front door finding it wide open and as they walked in they found me laying lifeless on the floor, blood everywhere, and Mike nowhere to be found. Bringing a mirror to me, my mother and Hailey showed me the injuries to my face. The stitches that now went from my forehead to my eye and then down my cheek. Then the news came that I would never forget for as long as I lived, I had lost the baby and to top it all off, I now had a large gash where Mike had taken a knife to me from right below my breast to about where my belly button was. Every time I looked into a mirror or found someone starring at my now scarred face I am reminded of my ex-husband and my weakness to protect my child and myself.

The police had found Mike downtown, drunk at one of the bars. They said he never denied that he was the one who had done it but he never said he did either. He even told them straight out that I deserved to die for cheating on him. His lawyer was able to twist my testimony around and the knife that he used was never found so the jury came up with not an attempted murder charge but an spousal abuse charge which gave him ten years in jail with bail and probation being considered after eight years depending on his time and his attitude while in. Of course knowing Mike's temper, I would never have guessed he could keep himself and his temper in check for one month, let alone eight years, so I fully believed he wouldn't be released early.

My phone ringing in my lap brought me out of my thoughts. The screen on the phone told me Hailey was calling me back. Actually, I was a little surprised she waited this long to call me back. I knew if I didn't answer it she would just keep on calling, "Hello."

"Don't hello me. Why did you hang up on me? I told you not to. Taylor I am going crazy here. What do you mean they are letting him out early? This must me some kind of joke. He only received ten years for almost killing you and now they are letting him off of that as well?"

"Hailey, I wish I was kidding but I'm not. My lawyer just sent me a letter letting me know they are releasing him in two weeks."

I couldn't believe this was happening. I was just starting to get my life somewhat back together. I figured I had a couple more years before I had to worry about him being around me again.

"Hailey, what am I going to do? I'm not ready for this at all?"

"Taylor, I know you just said you were busy with work and all but I think you need to come to Nolensville. Come and visit for a while at least, stay long enough for him to get out and hopefully move on with his own life."

"This isn't fair. Why do I have to keep changing my life for him? I'm not sure if I want to keep running from all of this," Of course I wasn't sure if I wanted to face all of this either but how was I supposed to just drop everything for who knows how long and leave? "I can't leave anyway, I have a full book of appointments for at least the next month or so," I tried to talk myself into not leaving.

"I'm sorry but you need to cancel them. Taylor, you have no idea how Mike is going to be when he gets out. Your safety is far more important than a family getting their pictures taken."

I thought about it for a moment, "I am not even sure he will try anything once he gets out. He may leave me alone. I mean, think about it, why would he risk doing anything that will put him back in jail?"

"Taylor don't make me fly out there, pack your things and drag your ass back here. You are right he may not, but then again, he very well may come after you again. You survived him once please don't allow him to have a second chance. I'm begging you."

I thought about it for a minute and I found myself tracing the scar on my face rubbing it as though it hurt. I would admit I was scared along, with all the nightmares I had about that night my worst nightmare had been the one where Mike is a free man again.

Hailey waited knowing her friend was thinking about what to do, "Taylor you said you have two weeks. Well cram in what photo shoots you can in a couple of weeks then cancel and reschedule the rest."

I squinted my eyes as I looked out over my front yard. Almost like I was looking for the answer to just appear in the street. As I listened to Hailey, I thought,"It would only be for a couple of weeks". Just long enough to collect my thoughts and courage, then I could return and pick up where I left off. The clients I couldn't fit in would understand if I explain to them that I have a family issue that needed to be dealt with, "Alright," I said before I changed my mind again, " I will come out and stay with you for a couple of weeks."

Hailey took a deep breath and slowly released it. If Mike had any ideas about going after Taylor then he was going to be a little disappointed when he finds her not there, what were the chances he would figure out where she went? She travels a lot with her job and all they had to spread around is that she was off on another photo shoot.

"Well I have a lot to do now. Lots of phone calls to make and schedules to rearrange, flights to book that kind of stuff. I will give you a call with all the details of my flight and the day I will be arriving," I looked over the letter again, how could one person affect another person's life so much?

"I know this isn't exactly what you want to do Taylor but I am glad you are coming. I will talk to you later," she hung up the phone.

Grams walked into the living room just as Haley hung up and leaned back against couch, "What is the matter hon? You have that look in your eyes like something is bothering you?"

Hailey didn't want to spill all the details so she forced a smile, "I'm sorry Grams. Nothing is wrong, the opposite really, Taylor is coming out to visit, finally, so why should anything be wrong?" She wasn't going to tell the family why Taylor was coming and all the details about Mike, it would only scare Grams and worry her for no reason. The whole family knew what had happen between Mike and Taylor but the least amount of people who knew what was going on the less chance of any information landing on the wrong ears.

"I am glad you are going Taylor. I don't think Mike is going to just leave you alone. He isn't that smart."

"Mom, I can't hide forever, I'm going to have to come back. My job can't stay on hold for too long."

Sandy knew her daughter was right but some time away was better than none, "Yes honey I know and your father and I have talked about that as well. Mike just might wait until you come back but hopefully after a couple of weeks he will just move on. Honestly, I'm hoping he just moves on the second he is free but something tells me things aren't going to be that simple."

I grabbed a few more things from my closet and folded them into my suitcase as I held my phone between my ear and shoulder. My flight was leaving early in the morning and my brother was taking me to the airport. My family agreed with me leaving once I told them about Mike's early release. To be honest, I was a little surprised my parents didn't try to talk me into moving out of the country once they found out the news.

"Don't worry about anything everyone who knows you around here will think you are leaving on another photo shoot. Even if he asks around some, no one knows where you really are. We will keep an eye on things for you, check your mail, that kind of stuff."

"Thanks mom I will call and let you know when I plan to come home once I figure it out. I only plan to be gone for a couple of weeks," I hated everything that was going on. I was completely exhausted right now. All I had done in the last week and a half was fit in as many photo shoots as I could. Surprisingly, I had managed to reschedule all of my appointments but two and they were alright with waiting until I got back home so at least something was working out. I almost felt like I needed this vacation, if that was what you wanted to call this after how busy things had been.

"I know this may sound odd at a time like this but honey, try and have fun. You have needed some time off. Try and enjoy your visit with Hailey and her family."

"I will mom. Love you guys. Tell dad I said bye and I love him," I hung up my phone and finished packing.

I was very excited that I was finally getting a chance to see my friend, I would admit that, but I hated the circumstances. I wish I would be able to enjoy it a little more and not worry about what was going to be going on at home. I hated that I was running. This was my life and I was running from it. What was I thinking? I sat down on my bed looking down at my suitcase. Was leaving for a couple of weeks really going to change anything? If Mike wanted to do something he was going to wait for me to get back, especially if everyone figured I was only on a photo shoot, he would wait for me to come home. Why drag it out two weeks? Maybe I should just stay home and face things now, I wasn't going to be able to run my entire life. I looked around my room, in the last eight years I had worked hard to make a name for myself doing the thing I loved, photography. I had to look at this as though I wasn't running but taking the time to figure out how I was going to not allow this man to run my life now that he was out. I needed a couple of weeks to get my nerves up to face him which is why I needed to leave. I would give it a couple of weeks so that way I could figure out how I was going to deal with him. I stood back up and finished packing.

Chapter 2

"Honey calm down," Ryan laughed as he watched his wife sway back and forth as the passengers filed off the airplane.

"Where is she? What if she missed her flight? What if she changed her mind all together about coming? I don't see her. What is taking so long?" Hailey continued to weave back and forth as the passengers filed off the plane.

Ryan placed both hands on her shoulders and stopped her from swaying, "I'm sure she would have called and told you if any of that had happened."

Hailey nodded, "You're right I'm sorry, I guess I just can't believe she is finally coming. I'm afraid somehow she won't make it.

She looked past her husband's shoulder just in time to see Taylor coming through the door. Pulling out of Ryan's grasp she ran to her best friend, "You are here, finally," throwing her arms around Taylor in a bone crushing hug.

I stumbled back a little as my friend embraced me, laughing, I hugged her back, "I have missed you girl."

Hailey pulled back, "I have missed you too."

I watched as Hailey looked me over like she was trying to make sure I was real and not just her imagination. We hadn't seen each other since the whole issue with Mike. When she left I was just getting my stitches out so I knew that she was looking at all the scars. I saw the sadness in her eyes even though she was trying very hard to hide what she was thinking. I was kind of use to all the looks and the pity in everyone's eyes.

It was the look that said “this girl would be pretty. It’s a pity she has all those scars”. At first it was hard not to make a comment to those people but I did finally realize they weren’t being mean they felt sorry for me it wasn’t a whole lot better but it would be too much work to make a comment to everyone who looked at me this way I just started ignoring it the best I could. Finally she took a deep breath and smiled, “You look great Taylor.”

I smiled, “Thanks so do you, it feels like forever since the last time we've seen each other.”

Nodding her head in agreement Hailey hugged me again, “Eight years to long.”

Someone cleared their throat. I looked over Hailey’s shoulder to see Ryan, “Do I get any "hello" guys, or was I brought to be the chauffer only?”

Laughing, I pulled away from Hailey and walked over to Ryan, wrapping my arms around his neck, “Hey Ryan.”

Ryan was just as good looking, if not better looking, than he was in school. Sandy blonde hair, brown eyes, not more then maybe five feet ten inches tall. I would admit Hailey was a very lucky girl. “You look great Ryan.”

“Same goes for you girl,” Ryan tried not to stare at the scars. He didn’t want to make Taylor feel uncomfortable but he had to control a feeling of anger. How could any man treat a woman like that? "Even though her face was scarred, Taylor was still a very attractive woman" Ryan thought to himself.

“Where is Bryson?” I asked as I looked around.

“He stayed with Grams. It was just easier than worrying about him running all around the airport.” Hailey grabbed my hand, “Come on let’s go get your bags and get out of here.”

I watched as the city of Nashville turned into the rural ranch town of Nolensville, man, how I have missed this place. I would admit, Napa was beautiful, but nothing compared to Nolensville. This was home. It still felt like home and I knew it would always feel like home.

"It hasn't really changed has it?" I commented from the back seat, "It still looks like it did the last time I was here."

Hailey turned around in her seat and smiled at me, "You actually miss this place? I love it here and couldn't imagine living anywhere else, but, Napa is gorgeous all those vineyards. It's so green."

I nodded my head in agreement, "Yes, Napa is beautiful, but there is something about this place. I will always consider this home over Napa."

The drive from the airport in Nashville to Nolensville was maybe thirty minute, if that, so before I knew it we were pulling into the driveway of the ranch. I jumped out of the truck and took a deep breath, it even smelt the same as I remembered. The sound of the front porch door slamming open and a little voice booming, "Mommy! Daddy!" caught my attention. I looked towards the house and watched a little boy run down the porch and right into Ryan's arms.

"Hey buddy! Were you a good boy for Grams," Ryan asked?

The little blonde head nodded up and down. He looked just like his father, "Yep, I sure was."

Hailey walked over to her son, "Excuse me? Where is my hello?"

Bryson leaned over and gave his mom a kiss and then looked over at me, "Who are you?"

"Bryson, remember that picture of Aunt Taylor you always ask me about? You have talked to her on the phone a lot," Hailey answered him.

"Hello Bryson."

"I'm five," he said holding up his hand and showing his five fingers, "I get to start school pretty soon."

"Wow! School already? That is exciting! You're a very lucky boy."

"You want to see my horse," Bryson asked all excited?

"Buddy, why don't you and I go find Uncle Adam and see if he needs help feeding the horses? It's supper time for them," Ryan asked his son.

"But daddy, she hasn't seen my horse," Bryson protested a small pout on his face.

"You know what? After dinner you can take me to see your horse," I suggested to Bryson.

The three adults watched as Bryson thought about it for a moment and then nodded his little head, "Okay, you promise?"

"I promise."

Ryan started heading for the stable, "We will be in soon. I'm sure Grams will have supper on the table soon. We're going to help Adam while you get Taylor settled."

I watched as Ryan and Bryson walked over to the stables and disappeared inside. I turned to my friend, "Hailey, Bryson is adorable." I couldn't help but feel a little jealous over what Haley had in her life. A loving husband and a child that was as adorable as they came.

"Thanks, we think so too. I'm pretty lucky to have the men in my life that I do," Hailey frowned, "I'm sorry Taylor, I didn't mean."

"Hailey stop it! I know what you meant. You don't have to worry about saying things that may offend me. I know there are good men out there, I just happened to find the wolf that was hiding in sheep's clothing I guess you can say."

Hailey picked up one of my bags and started up the stairs of the porch, "Come on. Let's get you settled in before Grams calls us for dinner."

I followed Hailey into the house. Everything still looked exactly like I remembered it. Hailey hadn't changed a thing in the house, of course, I was sure that if Hailey changed things it wouldn't be until after Grams passed. The house was now considered Hailey and Ryan's but I don't think Hailey saw it that way. I followed Hailey up the large staircase and into one of the spare bedrooms.

"There are towels in your bathroom. If you need anything let me know. You know where everything is so of course you can help yourself. I'm going to let you get settled and while you do that I'm going to see if Grams needs any help with dinner," she gave me another hug, "I am so glad you are here. I have missed you like crazy."

I hugged her back, "I have missed you too. It feels good to be back even though I almost changed my mind I don't know how many times but I'm glad I decided to come."

Hailey started to leave but stopped just before she closed the door, "Oh just to let you know, I haven't said anything to anyone on why you really came out. They all just figure I finally talked you into it."

I nodded, "I understand thank you," I waited for Hailey to shut the door and then I plopped down on the bed and took a deep breath, the first real breath since I had read the letter from her lawyer. Everything was going to be fine. I was going to enjoy my time with Hailey and the family and try my best to forget about Mike. At least for the next couple of weeks because once I went back home I knew everything was going to change.

I got up from the bed and walked over to the window that looked out over the stables, some of the arenas, and a house that was Adam's. I remembered Hailey showing it to me when I was here for the wedding. The house had been built for Hailey's brother right before Hailey and Ryan got married. My eyes scanned the area outside. I missed all of this. The open area, no neighbors around, only open land and the horses. I had to admit, I missed riding more than anything. If things weren't going so well in Napa I would consider moving back. I turned away from the window and went back to the bed where my bags were. I needed to unpack and then I would go down and see if they needed help in the kitchen. Plus I couldn't wait to see Grams.

I knew this house like the back of my hand. I made my way to the kitchen. Going through the doorway, I found Hailey pulling plates out of the cabinet and Grams putting mashed potatoes into a bowl, "Is there anything I can help with?"

Grams turned wiping her hands on her apron, "Taylor my girl, look at you! You haven't changed a bit. You are still as beautiful as ever," she gave me a hug.

I missed Grams hugs. They were always filled with a grandma's love, "Hello Grams! I've missed you and your hugs."

"Wel,l while you are here you may have as many hugs as you like," Grams searched Taylor's face her heart ached as she noticed the pain in Taylor's eyes, those beautiful crystal green eyes were missing the life she use to see in them. The scars on her face almost told the story themselves.

I watched as Grams looked at my face. I was used to people's shocked expressions when they first noticed my scars. Ryan, Hailey, and Grams all tried to be discreet about noticing them and staring but I knew they were looking and each of them cringed a little the first time they looked at me today.

I knew that people thought the same thing I did when I looked into the mirror every day, "what a shame. She would be pretty if it weren't for the scars." My heart twisted a little. Mike had taken so much away from me and upon my face were the marks to remind me every day of it.

"Is there anything I can help with?"

The question brought Grams out of her stare, "Everything is done in here you can help carry it out to the table if you like."

Out at the stables Ryan found Adam feeding the horses, "Hey you need any help in here?"

"Uncle Adam, we came to help feed the horsies," Bryson jumped out of Ryan's arms and ran to his uncle holding his arms out waiting for a flake of hay.

Adam smiled down at his nephew, tore a section off the flake he had in his hand and handed it to Bryson, "Come on buddy follow me."

Adam threw the hay into the stall. Bryson followed his every move even wiping his hands on his jeans just like Uncle Adam. He also took the same stance when Adam stopped in front of Ryan. Adam laughed at his nephew and shook his head.

"I am done but thanks for offering. Actually I expected you guys a couple of hours ago."

Ryan nodded, "Yeah well Taylor's flight was about an hour and a half late."

"So she made it?"

"Yep," Ryan looked down at the ground and played with a piece of hay with his foot.

"What's wrong?"

Ryan looked up at Adam and shrugged, "In my profession, I see abuse all the time on calls but seeing those scars on Taylor's face makes me want to jump onto a plane, fly to California and beat the crap out of her ex-husband."

"Wow, that bad?" Adam asked. He remembered the last time he had seen Taylor. She had been out for Hailey's wedding. She was a beautiful woman and he remembered thinking when he first saw her again, how strange it was that he had never noticed that before. She had moved away when she was just a teenager and he was three years older than them. He had always looked at her like his sister since he had watched her grow up with his own sister. When she came back for the wedding she was a woman and she was with her now ex-husband. They had just gotten married themselves.

"Actually they are faint. There are two of them but all the same, they are there, and knowing how they got there makes my blood boil."

"Ryan, Bryson, Adam come on! Dinner is on the table," Hailey yelled for the boys from the porch of the house.

"Come on Uncle Adam, I will race you," Bryson called out as he started running to the house.

Adam and Ryan followed at a quick walk. Bryson ran up the steps and turned to wait, "I beat you Uncle Adam!"

Adam walked up the steps and grabbed Bryson up into his arms, "Yes you did buddy. You are just too fast for me."

Adam holding Bryson and Ryan walked into the dining room, "Sit down boys, we are bringing out the rest," Grams then disappeared back into the kitchen.

Adam placed Bryson into his chair and then sat down himself just in time for the door to the kitchen to open. He looked up and there was a vision. There was no way this was his baby sister's friend Taylor. Before him was a woman. She had long, almost waist length, blonde hair and jeans on that hugged every curve of her slender body perfectly and a blue V-neck t-shirt.

She sat the plate that she was carrying onto the table and looked up at him with the most memorizing crystal green eyes. He didn't remember them being so green, "Hi Adam it's good to see you again."

Adam heard her speak but was not sure if he knew what she said. His eyes roamed her face and noticed the two scars. They were faint scars, Ryan was right about that, but still noticeable. He had to admit, they added mystery to her beautiful face.

I waited for Adam to respond and when he didn't, I took the opportunity to look him over. Same dark wavy hair and yes, those almost clear blue eyes. Both Hailey and Adam had those eyes. It was a color not many people had. His chest was broader and his arms bigger than the last time I had saw him. I had always thought Adam was good looking but I had always seen him just as Hailey's older brother. We had grown up together, but with a three year age difference, which was a big difference when you are kids and teenagers, not so much of a difference when you were adults, he would hang out with his own friends and Hailey and I with ours. Now I'm seeing him in a whole new light. He was all man, and a good looking man at that.

I felt my smile fade as I noticed his expression and where his eyes were looking. Strangers staring I had gotten use to and could ignore. Adam staring made me feel like I had to cover my face and should leave the room. I looked down knowing it should angle my face enough to pull him out of his trance and it did. He looked away.

Adam realized he was staring so he quickly looked away for a second to collect his thoughts. When he looked back he realized she was looking down at her plate like she was trying to cover or hide herself. Damn, he had been staring and she must have thought he was staring at her scarred face, which he had to admit he was, but not like she thought he was. It wasn't the scars he was staring at but the woman.

Grams and Hailey brought in the rest of the food and sat down, "Bow your heads please," Grams announced and followed it with the prayer and then began passing the food around.

"So Taylor how has the photography been going for you, dear? Hailey says you are pretty busy?" Grams started the conversation at the table.

I took a bite of my food trying to calm my nerves before I looked back up and at Adam's staring eyes. I swallowed and looked up directly at Grams, "Everything is going well. I have been very busy. I can't remember when the last time I had a day off was."

"You probably needed some time off then, we are so glad you were able to finally come visit." Grams passed the plate of chicken to Ryan.

Hailey looked at her friend, something was wrong, but what? Just a minute ago in the kitchen she was fine. Now she seemed like she was pulling back, almost like she was trying to hide.

I nodded my head in agreement with Grams, "It has been a while since I have had a real vacation. Hailey has been asking me forever to come and visit, so I decided it was finally time for me to come back. I've missed this place."

Adam took this opportunity to try and lighten things between Taylor and himself. He'd noticed she was trying very hard to ignore him. "Hailey is always talking about all the traveling you are doing with the photography."

Now what was I supposed to do? I had to look at Adam to answer him. I took a deep breath and closed my eyes for a moment then turned my attention to Adam. Opening my eyes, my breath caught in my throat, those blue eyes were going to be my undoing. I shook my head. What was I thinking? For one, I didn't need to be attracted to any guy, especially Adam. He had always been like another big brother to me. I had promised myself no relationships. I needed to get my life in order first. Anyway, there was no way Adam would be interested in me. I could tell just by the way he was looking at me that my scarred face bothered him.

"Umm, yes, work kind of pulls me in a lot of different directions. I may travel a lot but you really can't consider it a vacation when you spend the entire day at someone's beck and call. A wedding is a sun up sun down kind of work day sometimes."

She was answering him but he noticed she wasn't really looking at him. She was keeping her eyes more down then up. It bothered him that she was uncomfortable around him. Of course he didn't know why it bothered him so much but, all the same it did.

Hailey watched the scene in front of her with her best friend and her brother. Why didn't she think of this herself? They were attracted to each other. Hailey had been trying to find someone for her brother forever and of course she would love to see Taylor find someone who would treat her right. This was too perfect! She smiled to herself. She was going to somehow find a way to make her brother and best friend figure out they needed and wanted each other. "Why don't the four of us go out tomorrow night? Have a drink or two, maybe some dancing. What do you guys think?" she suggested.

"Honey, I have that over time tomorrow night but I have the next day off," Ryan reminded her.

"So what do you say Adam? It's about time you go out and have a little fun. We haven't been out in a while," Hailey pushed.

Adam looked over at his sister, she had that look in her eye which meant she was up to something. He looked back at Taylor who was still looking down at her plate. Going out would give him a chance to spend a little time with Taylor, on the dance floor sounded especially nice. Of course if she wouldn't look at him now what made him think she would dance with him?

He looked over at his sister, "If you guys want to I am in. You are right, we haven't been out in a while."

Taylor looked up to find all eyes on her, "Um, sure. I can't say that I'm busy so I am up for whatever." Adam watched as she looked around the table but she never looked at him and that was starting to really bother him what had he done to have her ignoring him.

Taylor wasn't sure if she really wanted to go. In all honesty she had not really been out in years. Now that she thought about it, probably not since before Mike and her got married. They would go out all the time before they got married, but as soon as they said "I do", Mike stopped wanting to go out and so did she. Every time they would go somewhere he would accuse her of flirting with someone.

"Good I have been looking for a reason to go out and what better one than to celebrate Taylor visiting." Haley speaking pulled Taylor out of her thoughts and her attention back to the table.

Ryan looked over at his wife, "All you have to do is ask. You make it sound like I never take you anywhere."

Hailey grabbed her husband's hand, "Not what I meant. We just go out a lot less since we have responsibilities now." She looked over at Bryson who was shoving a spoon full of potatoes into his mouth.

"Aunt Taylor, can you please give me some more mash potatoes," Bryson asked?

I was taken back by him calling me Aunt. He seemed as though he had known me his entire life. For a five year old his manners and speech were great, "Of course," I picked up the bowl and spooned some potatoes onto his plate.

"Thank you. How did you get hurt?" Bryson asked suddenly then scooped another spoonful of potatoes into his mouth.

I was surprised at first. Pain knifed through my heart for a second and then I remembered his innocence. Of course he would eventually ask, he was a kid.

"Bryson don't be so rude. Finish you dinner," Hailey scolded her son, a little embarrassed.

"No, it is alright Hailey." Of course Bryson would ask about my scars now. Adam was already staring at me like I had two heads why not bring more attention to my deformities.

I looked down at Bryson. How do you explain such abuse to a child of innocence? Honestly, I was at a loss for words. I didn't want to lie to him but I didn't want to tell him the ugly truth either.

"Did you fall off a horse? I have done that and got marks like that but mine are not on my face," Bryson asked when I took too long with answering him.

No, not a horse I thought to herself, I met up with a jackass though, "No I didn't fall off my horse."

"Oh. So what happened then?" He asked again.

I looked up at Hailey for some help. I didn't know how much information she wanted her five year old to know.

Finally Ryan came to the rescue, "Aunt Taylor met up with a bad person who hurt her."

Bryson's eyes got big and round when he looked up at his dad, "Did you take him to jail daddy?"

That broke the tension a little everyone laughed. For kids it was that simple, answer their question and they will just move on to the next.

Ryan shook his head, "No buddy, I wish I had, but I wasn't there when she got hurt."

Bryson looked back up at me, "My daddy puts bad people in jail so if that person ever hurts you again you call my daddy."

I felt a tear threaten to escape. I smiled down at Bryson, "I will, thank you."

I looked up at Hailey then Ryan. If he only knew how possible it could be for that man to hurt me again. No one here knew Mike was getting out of jail except Hailey. I looked back at my friend who seemed to know exactly what I was thinking, "It will be okay," Hailey mouthed to me. I tried to smile I hoped Hailey was right.

Adam caught what his sister had mouthed to Taylor and wondered what she meant by it? He looked from his sister to Taylor and then back at his sister. Hailey looked at him and then knowing she was caught she looked away and back at her dinner again. That brought my eyes back to Taylor. Something was going on between his sister and Taylor.

I felt Adam's eyes on me. I didn't really want to look over at him but my head turned anyway and my eyes looked right into Adam's. He gave me a small smile then looked back down at his plate.

Dinner was completed with little small talk. I helped with the dishes then used the excuse that the days travel had exhausted me and excused myself to my room.

I sat down on my bed my hand tracing the scar that ran from the corner of my mouth up half my cheek. I thought back to the first time in the hospital when I finally got enough courage to look at myself in a mirror. I couldn't believe what kind of damage a fist could do. Both of my eyes were black and blue and swollen. My nose broken and there were stitches above my eye and more running from mouth to cheek. My lip was split open and there was a bandage around my head where more stitches were placed from where I had hit the coffee table.

I remembered my broken ribs, my slashed and bruised stomach, and worst of all, my empty belly where my baby once grew. The pain physically and mentally was so bad that at the time I thought often of how I wished I had died. I had no reason to really want to live anymore.

I divorced my husband as soon as I was able to sign papers but I had never recovered my old life completely. Sure, I was doing great in the photography world but personal life, well, I didn't have a personal life. I had lost what friends I had while married and once everything was over I was too embarrassed to go back and beg them for forgiveness. The only real friend I had was Hailey and she lived hundreds of miles away. I didn't date, although I had been asked out a couple of times, but I hadn't been ready for all of that yet.

I thought of Bryson. He was adorable. I had looked around the table at dinner, a mom, a dad and child and of course, in this family, a few extras but still a family. Something when I got married I thought I would have. Then there was the day I found out I was pregnant. I was so happy I was getting my family. Then as quickly as I got that family Mike took it away from me.

I took one of the pillows and hugged it. Tears rolling down my face. What had I ever done in my life to deserve all of this?

"Taylor are you alright in there," Hailey's voice came from the other side of the door?

I quickly wiped the tears from my face, "Yeah I'm alright," I watched as the door opened.

Hailey stuck her head in right away noticing I had been crying, "Taylor," she entered quickly and sat down on the bed next to me, "What's wrong?"

I shook my head how silly would my excuse for crying be to Hailey?

"Come on, if you can't talk to your best friend then who can you talk to? Did Bryson's questions about your scars bother you?"

I shook my head, "No I'm use to the questions and I'm getting use to the stares. Trust me, I know what I look like. Seeing your family around the dinner table, seeing Bryson and the way he looks at you two, how happy he was when you guys got home today. I should be living that life right now," I jumped up off the bed and walked over to the window my hand once again going to my scarred face.

"I married a guy who controlled my life. Almost took my life and who took my child's life. What do I have? The scars to look at and remind me every day of what I don't have," I turned again to look at Hailey tears once again rolling down my face, "I don't think I will ever have what you have here."

Hailey got up and walked over to me, "Why do you say that? Taylor not all guys out there treat women like Mike treated you. You will find that right guy and you will have your family."

"Who would want to look at this every day," I pointed at my face, "I don't even want to look at this every day. It's disgusting."

"Now you hold it right there young lady," Both of us looked over at the doorway in surprise and watched Grams entering the room.

"I am sorry to eavesdrop but the door was open and I happened to over hear your conversation," Grams walked over to me, her hands going to my face, "You are far from disgusting to look at. You are beautiful inside and out," Grams fingers traced the scar on my cheek.

"You need to walk with pride. You couldn't have known what kind of man Mike really was. Those kind of guys never show their real sides until you are in too deep. What you need to do now is know you survived it. He did take some very precious things from you and I am not telling you to forget that but you move on and prove to him that he didn't destroy you. Taylor, I once knew a girl full of life, her eyes almost twinkled, and while you are here you find that girl again. Don't look at yourself in the mirror and see disgust, but see strength and pride. See again that beautiful young lady you are."

I threw my arms around Grams neck. This is why I loved this woman so much. Grams kissed my cheek and started back for the door Hailey right on her heels, "Now get some sleep."

Just before Hailey followed Grams completely out she turned, "Tomorrow we are going to go take a ride."

I didn't say anything, I just nodded, "Oh and Taylor you will have that family but first you have to heal yourself. You have to learn to accept yourself before anyone else can."

I stared at the closed door for a moment and then I turned and looked back out the window, my reflection staring back at me. I tried to look past the scars but that was all I saw. The ugliness of my past staring straight back at me.

Hailey and Grams walked back downstairs. Once Hailey knew they were out of hearing of Taylor she turned to Grams, "I am worried about her Grams. I knew she was having a hard time still but I never would have thought it was this bad. She hates herself."

"I know but that is where friends come into the picture. Back home she did nothing but work. Every time you talked to her you would tell me about how much she was working. She doesn't go out. You have even told me her mom tells you she pushes away from them. She is ashamed and embarrassed. She doesn't only have scars on her face but she had them inside as well. We will have to try and make her see while she is here that her scars show strength not weakness."

Hailey nodded in agreement with her grandmother, "You are right like always."

Grams smiled, "I have many years of experience and wisdom my love, now, go get Bryson into his bath. Tomorrow we will start things over. She will heal Hailey. She is around family."

As Hailey went to find Bryson she thought back to dinner. Taylor and Adam would make the perfect match but maybe she shouldn't try and push them together. Taylor was not ready yet for that. First she was going to help Taylor find herself and heal and then she would play a little match making. She smiled to herself.

Chapter 3

Horses in full run, I couldn't believe how much I had missed riding. The wind in my face, I felt free. I could ride like this all day.

Hailey pulled on the reins of her horse to slow them down then brought the horse to a complete stop. I came up beside her, "How are you doing? I know it's been a while since you have rode?"

"Great! I had almost forgotten how good it felt to ride but I don't think I would ever forget how to ride no matter how long I have been away."

Hailey laughed, "I will bet you are going to be sore tomorrow though no matter how good you feel now."

"I don't care. I love the feeling of freedom like there isn't a care in the world. I could ride all day," I looked around, "I should have brought my camera though, I could get some amazing pictures out here."

"No working just yet. The cameras can stay packed for a while longer, there will be plenty of time for that," Hailey was determined to have me relax, no work of any kind. I couldn't seem to make her understand that taking pictures wasn't considered work to me it was like breathing.

"Fine but before I go back home I get to take some real family pictures for you. No more of that studio stuff you have hanging on the walls," I made a disgusting face like I had smelt something bad.

Hailey laughed, "Sorry my pictures don't meet your approval but when the best photographer lives hundreds of miles away you kind of need to work with what's available."

“I’m not the best but thank you,” I looked around. How I missed this place, this kind of life.

“You can always move back you know,” Hailey suggested.

“What are you talking about?” It was almost like she could read what I was thinking. Of course we've always made jokes about how we could read the other’s thoughts. I would love to move back but I had made a career for myself in California.

“Come on Taylor, I can read you like a book. I know what’s running through that mind. You miss it, you love this place, and you always have. What keeps you in California?”

I agreed. I wouldn’t deny it. I couldn’t deny it if I tried. “Alright so I miss it. That is no big secret but my life and my work are in California now.”

“Your job can follow you anywhere and you know it. You travel all over the place. Where you live is not going to stop people from calling you,” Hailey challenged me.

“You’re right. I’m sure I could pick up the photography anywhere although I already have set clients back in Napa plus my parents and brothers are there,” I found excuses.

Hailey knew excuses would be by the hundreds so she gave up on the conversation for now. She would think a person would want to run from an area of their life which held such bad memories but Taylor wanted to stay for some reason.

“Come on I’ll race you back to the house,” I yelled as I turned my horse back towards the direction of the house. I was done with the conversation. It was too nice of a day to ruin my mood with all the talk about why I wouldn’t leave California.

After turning the horses loose to run and cool down in the arena, Hailey went up to the house to get Bryson and feed him his lunch. I stayed to watch the horses. I watched as they played around a little, and grazed a little, how simple a horse's life was in some ways. How simple and quiet life seemed here at the ranch. I hadn't felt this relaxed in a long, long time.

Adam walked out of the stables finding Taylor one foot up on the rail, arms crossed on the top rail, chin resting on her hands. She almost looked like a little girl or more like the young girl he once knew. He remembered Taylor standing there a lot when she would come over to the house. She loved to watch the horses. He remembered Taylor out here watching their grandfather train the horses, standing there just as she was right now, only difference was now he saw a woman, a beautiful one at that.

"You know you use to stand right in that spot, the exact way you are now all the time when you were younger and watch grandfather train the horses."

I jumped at the sound of Adam's voice. I had been so deep in thought I didn't even hear him walk up. "Adam you scared me!" My hand came up to my heart.

Adam's smile faded. He actually saw real fear in her eyes, "Taylor, I am sorry I did not mean to scare you!" My god, that ex had done a real number on her! Anger bubbled deep inside him.

I watched as once again I saw Adam stare at my face. Was I that repulsive to look at? His eyes even took a different look in them, almost like he was mad or disgusted. I started to walk away. I couldn't handle the way he was looking at me. What was starting to bother me more was the fact that Adam staring at me like that was bothering me like it was. Sure, I never felt easy when I caught people staring but for some reason knowing that they bothered Adam and seeing the look of disgust in his eyes was really bothering me. My chest even hurt but why, why was Adam any different than anyone else. As I walked past him he grabbed my arm to stop me, "You don't have to leave."

I felt the strong grip on my arm and froze. I looked at the hand then up at Adam. Adam released my arm quickly when my eyes came up to look at him, fear was etched in them, "Taylor what is wrong?"

I could still feel where his fingers had been on my arm. Why was I afraid? I knew Adam would never hurt me? Being man handled was something that did not settle well with me though.

Adam watched as emotions played in Taylor's eyes. Hailey had never really told Adam exactly what Taylor's ex-husband had done. He knew he beat the crap out of her and they were not sure if at first she would even live through it but Hailey never really talked about it to him. He had never really asked any questions about it either.

Finally I found my voice but I wasn't sure why I asked the question, "Does my face repulse you that much?" Once the question was out I wished I could have taken it back.

Adam was so shocked by the question he didn't know what to say.

I, on the other hand, only wanted to run. Why would that come out of my mouth?

Adam stood there staring at her for a moment. What had brought that question on? As he thought about it, he did notice she wouldn't look at him. "Do you honestly think I am repulsed by you?"

"Sorry. I don't know why I said that. I am going to go now," I turned to walk away, again more embarrassed then anything.

Adam stopped me only this time he didn't dare touch me, "Taylor, wait, we need to talk about this."

I wanted to keep on walking, no, I wanted to keep on running. I stopped but I didn't turn around.

"Please look at me Taylor."

Again my mind screamed no but my body was not listening. I slowly turned around but I kept my eyes at the ground. I couldn't handle him staring at me. For some reason my heart tore a little every time I found him staring.

Adam lightly placed one finger under her chin. She flinched which almost caused Adam to remove his hand but determination made him continue to lift her face until she looked up into his eyes. He searched them for a moment. She had so many emotions running through them. A feeling of protectiveness over whelmed him. He wanted to wrap his arms around her and protect her from all the fear he saw in her eyes. "Again I am going to ask why you asked me if you repulse me?"

It took everything I had not to completely loose myself in those ice blue eyes. He wanted an answer then fine I would give him one, "Adam, I see the way you stare at my face," I pointed at my scars, "actually you stare more at my scars," I pulled away from his touch and took a step back.

"You think I am repulsed by the scars on your face?"

"I don't think it Adam, I see it. Every time you look at me or should I say every time you stare at me. Honestly, all I want to do is run and hide my face." I fought the tears that threaten to escape. Why did he bother me so much? Why couldn't I just ignore him like I did everyone else?

"Taylor I am sorry..." he was stopped before he could finish.

"I don't want you to be sorry Adam. I know how hard it is to look at them, trust me I see it every time I look in the mirror."

He grabbed her by both arms and he watched her face go white. She looked as though she was going to faint, Adam was about to release her but something made him hold on. He wanted her to trust him, "You are far from being repulsive Taylor. Honestly, I can't stop staring at you because I can't get over what a beautiful woman you have become. You are no longer that little girl who would stand here and watch my grandfather and I train horses. You are a woman, an amazingly beautiful woman."

I couldn't believe what I was hearing. Did Adam just call me beautiful?

Adam waited for her to say something but she just stared wide eye at him. He pulled her closer to him, "Tay don't be scared of me, please. Not all men hurt women."

Tay, no one called me that. If they tried I would correct them. I never cared much for the nickname but when Adam said it, it sounded nice. He pulled me closer. Oh god, was he going to kiss me? Was I ready for that? No, I didn't think so, "Adam please don't." I pulled out of his grasp and took a couple steps back.

Adam's arms fell to his side, "I'm sorry," was all he said.

Surprisingly I wanted to go back into his arms and I wanted to be held by him. What surprised me more was I wanted to kiss him. I just wasn't ready for all of this. Before I could change my mind and throw myself back at him, I turned around and left.

I stood in front of my closet and stared at my clothes hanging in front of me. What to wear... we were going out tonight and now I was having serious second thoughts about all this. I heard the knock at the door but I ignored it

"Taylor are you ready yet?" Hailey came in when she got no answer from me. She found me in my robe, hair done and makeup done, "Why aren't you dressed yet? Everyone is ready to go?"

I turned away from my clothes and walked over and sat down on the bed, "You guys go ahead without me. I don't want to go, I have nothing to wear."

Hailey walked over to the closet, "Don't give me that," she flipped through my clothes, "you would look great in a potato sack if that was all you had." She pulled a shirt from the closet and tossed it at me. She then pulled out a pair of jeans and tossed them to me, grabbed my boots set them down in front of me and walked back to the door, "Get dressed and hurry up about it. We will meet you down stairs in five minutes," then she walked out of the room before I could say a word.

I stared at the door for a moment then down at my clothes that Hailey had thrown at me. I really didn't want to go, but there was no way Hailey was going to allow me not to go. I took a deep breath, rolled my eyes. and then admitted defeat. I stood up and got dressed taking one last look in the mirror, I decided it wasn't going to get any better and left the room to meet everyone downstairs.

The dancing was in full swing and there were tons of people on the dance floor. The couple of pool tables the place had were full, music was loud and so were the people. They managed to find a table for all of them to sit at.

"Wow this place is busy tonight! Do you ladies want anything to drink," Ryan asked after they settled at the table?

"Beer for me please," Hailey answered and looked at Taylor, "Taylor, beer for you too?"

I nodded, "Please that would be good." I looked around. I hadn't been around this many people in years and a beer would hopefully calm my nerves a little.

"I'll go with you Ryan," Adam stood up and left with Ryan.

Hailey looked over at me, "You look like a lost child what is wrong with you?"

I looked over at Hailey, "Honestly, I feel like a lost child right now."

"Haven't you gone out at all?"

I shook my head, “No.”

“Are you kidding? In the last three years you haven’t gone out at all? Taylor that’s crazy?” Hailey knew her friend didn’t have much of a social life any more but not going out at all, that was crazy. She was now realizing exactly how much her friend had changed.

“I had lots of work to do. I don’t have time to go out a lot. I lost all of my friends right after Mike and I married. He slowly pushed all of them away,” I knew how pathetic my life sounded.

“Ma'am, would you care to dance,” I heard behind me? I looked up to find a young guy blonde hair and brown eyes standing behind me, “Um,” I looked over at Hailey for some help.

“Sorry buddy, this lady already has a dance partner,” Adam announced. He sat down the two beers he was carrying on the table then held his hand out to me.

I didn’t want to dance but dancing with Adam was better than dancing with some guy I didn’t know. I looked up at the guy, “Thank you for the offer though,” I politely responded then accepted Adam’s hand and followed him out to the dance floor.

The song was now a slow couple’s song. Adam smiled to himself, at least he would have a good excuse to wrap his arms around her waist. He found a spot on the floor, twirled Taylor around, and brought her close into him, wrapping one arm around her waist and taking the other hand into his.

I inhaled deeply when our chest came together and his arm tightly went around my waist. My whole body tingled and he smelt so good.

“Taylor, breathe, it will look a little funny if you pass out right here on the dance floor.” Adam was smiling down at her. He knew he affected her just as much as she affected him. He also knew that she was trying very hard not to let him affect her but it wasn’t working well for her, he would bet.

I exhaled and looked up at him. His smile could melt me to the ground. The rhythm of our bodies dancing to the music caused my heart to race.

"I won't hurt you Tay. I wish you would stop looking at me with that deer in headlights look," he didn't like the idea that she would put him in the same category as her ex-husband.

I looked into his eyes, "I know you won't hurt me Adam. I will be honest, I feel like a school girl doing and feeling everything for the first time."

"Well, tonight you look nothing like a school girl. All I see is a beautiful woman. Why don't you give me a chance to show you how a woman should be treated," he almost begged her. From the moment he had seen her at the table the other night he had decided he wanted her.

I looked away from those blue eyes of his so I could collect my thoughts for a moment. When I thought I had the strength to look at him again and not melt, I looked back up. "Adam why get anything started? I'm only here to visit. I will only be here for a couple of weeks. I am not sure if I am ready for a relationship."

"Tay, I'm the king of staying away from relationships. I have no time for a relationship with running the ranch and all but something hit me like a ton of bricks the other day when I saw you."

I laughed, "Yeah it is called male hormones."

He liked to hear her laugh and her smile was beautiful. No woman had ever affected him like this. He stayed away from relationships and never even thought about one, until now that is. There was something pushing him towards her. "That may be, so I won't deny that when you walk in front of me, my blood shoots up in temperature. It is not just male hormones."

"What would Hailey say?"

Adam looked over at the table where Hailey and Ryan were sitting, "Well from the expression on her face I don't think she would mind."

I looked over at Hailey. She sat there watching Adam and myself with a huge smile on her face.

"So what do you think? Do you think they will get together," Hailey asked Ryan as she sat there and watched her best friend and brother dance.

"Hailey, don't get into the middle of it. If it is going to happen then allow it to happen on its own," Ryan warned her as he stood up and grabbed her hand, "come on, stop starring at them and come dance with me," he lead her out onto the dance floor.

"So what do you say?" Adam asked again when she was quiet.

I have to admit, I am attracted to Adam, of course, who wouldn't be. I could see how the women in this place were staring at him like a pack of wolves ready to pounce. I looked back up at Adam who was waiting for an answer.

Adam took this opportunity to do what he had been dying to do since yesterday at the arena. He leaned in slowly, his eyes never leaving hers. Taylor wanted to run, he could see it in her eyes.

I wanted to stop him but not one muscle in my body was listening to my brain. I watched as he leaned forward his face coming down to mine.

Adam lightly brushed his lips across hers. He heard her inhale sharply but she wasn't pushing him away or trying to pull out of my arms. He wrapped his other arm around her waist and pulled her to him as close as he could. This time there was no brushing of the lips he fully claimed her lips with his own.

Taylor stood there for a moment not responding to the kiss. She was in too much shock to react. Then she realized she was starting to kiss him back. Feelings she had not felt in years, if ever, started to awaken inside of her. Before she knew it her arms were going up around his neck and she wasn't sure (but was almost positive) that she was the one who deepened the kiss.

"Oh Ryan look they are kissing!" Hailey couldn't contain her excitement.

Ryan grabbed her chin and turned her face to look back at him, "You know if I remember right, you said you never get to go out anymore so why don't you pay attention to your husband instead of them and kiss me."

Hailey smiled up at her husband, "I'm sorry. I'm just excited for them both."

"Hailey, you have to stay out of this whole thing. If something does happen between the two of them then it will have to be between them not with you included. Alright?"

Ryan was right. Hailey knew that, "I will stay out of it. I promise," she pushed up on her tippy toes and with her arms around his neck pulled his head down and claimed her husband's lips.

The truck pulled up into the front of the house and Adam quickly jumped out of the front seat and opened the door behind him for me. "Take a walk with me please?" he whispered when I jumped down and stood in front of him.

The whole night Adam had been very attentive. We danced with only each other. Many women had asked him to dance and he would tell them no very politely and then lead me back on to the dance floor. "I should go inside Adam."

"Look, I just want to talk to you for a moment, please."

I tried to look away from those pleading eyes. His eyes were going to be my undoing that I was sure of. "Alright, for a minute." I looked at

Hailey who was standing on the porch with Ryan waiting for me, "I will be right in."

Hailey smiled, "Take your time," she turned with Ryan and the two of them went into the house.

Adam took my hand and led me over to the arena. "Adam I had a nice time tonight. Thank you."

"You are welcome but I didn't do much," he leaned up against the rail, one foot up on the bottom rail he wrapped his hands around my waist and pulled my body up against his, "So have you decided to give us a try?"

I about melted to the ground when my body pressed against his. He was all male and right now I felt every part of him against me, I locked my knees so that they would not give out on me. My eyes watched his lips move as he talked. I could still feel them on my lips and I fought the temptation to claim his lips in another kiss. Then his question registered, are you ready to give us a try? Was I ready? Honestly, I wasn't sure.

Adam watched the play of emotion in her eyes. He could tell everything she was thinking just by looking into her eyes, she wore her feelings in her eyes. He reached up and was just about to touch her cheek but Taylor quickly turned her face, "Adam, don't please. Don't touch my face."

Adam's hand suspended in air for a moment at her words then dropped to rest on his knee his other hand though never left her waist.

"I am sorry. Please understand it's not you," I explained quickly.

Adam shrugged his shoulders acting as though it was no big deal. He would get her to trust him, he just had to move slowly at it, "I understand it's alright."

"Adam I am not going to lie and say I didn't feel something when we kissed earlier and I am not going to say there isn't a part of me that wants to give us a try, but to be honest I am not sure of myself. I don't know if I am ready for all of this yet."

Adam looked away for a moment. He wasn't quite sure what it was about Taylor that made him want her like this. He hadn't been with one steady woman in a very long time. He spent way too much of his time with the ranch. Although from the moment he saw her, something inside of him was set aflame. He wanted her. He also had this need to protect her from anything and everything that could possible harm her again in her life. She always has this look of pain and fear in her eyes, her confidence was no longer there. If there was one thing about Taylor he did remember from when she was young, it was her ambition for life. She was always smiling, always positive. He looked back down at her, "Alright so how about this, we take it one day at a time and see where it takes both of us? No pressure of any kind we will take it slow. Tay, I have stayed away from any kind of relationship for years. This ranch is my life but when I saw you for the first time the other night something snapped inside of me. You feel right to me. I wish I could explain it, trust me I have thought about this a lot. How could the young girl I used to know now be the woman I want? I have told myself to walk away. You are only here for a short time. Again, it didn't work. Something inside is strongly telling me to go with this and I don't want to fight it. This isn't a normal reaction for me, but it feels right. Just kissing you feels right."

I was shocked. Here was Adam Kageen, her best friend's older brother, admitting to wanting me and from the sounds of it not giving up until I gave in. I did have to agree with him on one thing, kissing him did feel right to me as well. I looked down at my hands that were on his chest, I had to look away from those eyes. Did I really want this? I was only here to visit. What if we did find out that we liked being together? What would happen when it was time for me to go home? All he was asking for was for us to take it one day at a time. What excuse could I come up with to fight that? Better question was, did I really want to find an excuse? Yes, part of me did but then again, part of me didn't. I looked back up at him, "Alright, one day at a time." Wait, did I really just say that out loud?

Adam laughed. She looked just as shocked as him with her answer but he wasn't going to give her time to change her mind. He bent his head and claimed her lips for the second time tonight. He felt her body relax against his and she kissed him back.

I had to admit one thing to myself, I was excited to think that I could now kiss this man as often as I wanted but for now I had to slow things down just a little. With my hands on his chest and every ounce of will power I had I pushed slightly away parting our lips. "I should be heading back in now."

"Alright," he pushed away from the rail, "I will walk you back to the house."

"No," I stopped him, "you don't have to. I will see you in the morning," I turned and started back for the house. I needed the distance from him and that body. Everything in me was aching to turn around and place myself back into his arms and against that chest, but I had to think a little. I had to figure out how this was supposed to work. Maybe once I was alone I could think straight but up against that man my brain was mush.

Adam watched as Taylor walked away. He watched until she disappeared around the corner of the stables, then he looked up into the sky full of stars, "Alright gramps, you were right," he said as if his grandfather was standing next to him.

He remembered back to graduation day, right after the party that night with all his friends, he drove his girlfriend home and she turned to him just before getting out of the car, "Adam, I am breaking up with you. I am leaving for college in a couple of weeks and I don't think it is fair to either of us if we stayed together," she than leaned across, kissed him on the cheek, and then got out of the car and ran into the house without looking back. Adam thought he was in love with her and she just broke him into pieces.

That night his grandfather found him in the stables sulking. His words that night were still fresh in his mind, just like his grandfather had just spoken them yesterday, not years ago. "Son, I know it hurts but she was not the one. When the one shows up in your life it will be like lightening just struck you in the heart. You won't even have to think twice about it. Love at first sight really does happen."

Of course he looked at his grandfather at the time like he had no idea what he was talking about. A short time later his grandfather died from a heart attack and from that day on Adam's whole life has been the ranch.

Adam couldn't honestly say he was in love with Taylor, love was a powerful word, but he would admit to feeling something he had never felt about any other woman before. Something was pushing him towards her. He looked around the sky, what a beautiful night, "It's you gramps, I understand."

Taylor walked into her room closed the door, and went and sat down on her bed. What a day! Waking up this morning she would have never imagined the events that would unfold through the day. She touched her lips, they still tingled. A knock at the door startled her but she knew who it would be. It was probably killing Hailey to wait for her to come back into the house, "Come on in Hailey."

Hailey opened the door and poked her head in, "So are you going to tell me?"

I laughed and patted the mattress next to me, "What would you like me to tell you about?"

Hailey came in and sat down next to me, "What do you think I want to talk about?"

I thought about giving my friend a hard time but I decided not to torture her tonight. I felt like we were back in high school and we were talking about some boy at school, only this time it was not just some boy, it was Adam. "Is this going to be weird for you? I am not saying anything is going to actually happen but all the same we have decided to take it day by day."

"Of course it's not weird for me! I'm totally excited! I want you to find someone and I have been dying for Adam to find someone to make a life with...."

I threw my hands up to stop Hailey, "Slow down a little. We are taking it slow so don't marry us to each other yet. I am not sure how ready I am for all this relationship stuff."

"I know. I am just excited that's all. So, does this mean you are going to stay awhile?" Hope filled Hailey's voice. The longer Taylor stayed here, the longer she was away from Mike, the more time her and Adam would have together, she thought to herself.

"I really don't know what any of this means. I can't stay away from home and my job for too long." I got up and walked over to the window and looked out. My life was back in California, my family and my job. Adam's life was here at the ranch. He would never leave the ranch and she would never expect him too, actually, she would never allow him to. She knew what this place meant to him. Was she willing to leave her life in Napa?

"I don't want to jump to any quick conclusions," I said turning back to my friend sitting on the bed, "nothing may come of this. Who knows, but I am wondering if we should tell the guys why I am really here."

Hailey shook her head, "Taylor I really don't think it is necessary for them to know. Like I said if you and I are the only ones who know then Grams won't find out. If she was to find out she would just worry about it all the time and that would not be good for her."

I stared at Hailey for a moment. I really thought we should tell the guys why I was here, but I understood why Hailey didn't want Grams to find out, "Alright if you think it's best. Thank you for tonight. I am glad you made me go. It has been a real long time and I have to admit I had fun. It was good to go out again."

Hailey got up from the bed, walked over to Taylor, and gave her a hug then started out of the room, "Have a good night sleep. I will see you in the morning." Then she disappeared out the door.

I turned and looked back out the window again. There was Adam walking back to his house. From my window I had a straight on view of Adam's house. I watched as he walked up the steps of his front porch then disappeared into the front door. Hailey told me the house was built right around the time that her and Ryan got married. It was supposed to be as large inside as the main house was. Adam designed the house himself.

My fingers went to my lips. I swore I could still feel Adam's lips on mine. I thought back to the first time Mike and I had kissed. Wow, I couldn't even remember what it was like, but, I knew I would never forget the feel of Adam's lips against mine. I would admit, I thought Mike was good looking, but put him next to Adam, and I couldn't figure out what I ever saw in Mike. Of course, my opinion may have changed a little since Mike almost took my life.

I thought about the Adam situation. What was I really thinking agreeing to this day by day thing? I knew I was only here to visit, not stay. What if this whole relationship did work out? What then? Would a long distance relationship work? Maybe for a short time. Again, I had to ask myself, was I willing to leave Napa and everything I had worked so hard to put together? If I had to be honest with myself, I knew my job would not be hard to move. I traveled a lot for weddings and I had a great clientele in Napa but I knew I could just as easily start a new one here. Was that really what I wanted to do? Was this something I really wanted or better yet something I was really ready for? What about my family, they were all in Napa?

On the other hand, was this something I should really be worried about right now? We weren't even in a real relationship yet. We may never be in a real relationship. Maybe I shouldn't worry about it so much for now, like Adam said, take it one day at a time.

Adam watched Taylor as she stood at her bedroom window. He had gone straight to his room not even turning on any lights and when he looked out his window he'd seen the glow from the light in her room and her standing at the window, with his room in darkness she couldn't see him. He thought back to when he tried to touch her face. She had turned away pretty quick so he didn't push the issue. She was embarrassed, he was sure of it. Maybe one of these days he would get Hailey, or better yet, get Taylor to tell him exactly what had happen that day with her ex-husband.

He watched as she turned and walked away from the window. Now all he could see was her shadow moving around in the room. He figured she was getting ready for bed. He could imagine her getting undressed her jeans sliding down her perfectly shaped legs, her shirt coming off to reveal her flat stomach, her breast. Damn he had to stop imaging this. He was going to drive himself crazy with wanting her. The last thing he needed was to want her more than he already did and then push her to fast. He needed to build her trust in him. He wouldn't be getting too far with that if he only tried to have sex with her. Taylor's room was now dark, she had gone to bed. He had an early day tomorrow so he needed to do the same.

Chapter 4

"They were kissing? Well now, doesn't that beat all?" Grams finished the last pancake, placing it on top of the large pile on the plate. "I can't even recall the last girl your brother was with." Actually, that was one of the things she had worried about for years. Adam had put his whole life into this ranch when her husband died. His grandfather would be very proud, but she knew he would not want him to find someone to share his life with and have a family with.

"That is because the last relationship he was in was in high school. Sure when we go out he dances with girls who are more than willing to go further than just a dance but Adam never shows any interest other than dancing. He is always saying he is too busy with the ranch to worry about keeping up with a relationship." Hailey grabbed the butter and syrup out of the refrigerator.

"Young lady, you remember to stay out of it! If something is to happen it will be their doing not, yours," Grams grabbed the plate of pancakes and placed it into her empty hand.

"Trust me, Ryan has already lectured me about staying out of it," Hailey commented before disappearing through the kitchen door into the dining room.

Grams followed her out with her hands full with plates of scrambled eggs, bacon, and biscuits, "Good, I love the way that boy keeps you in line."

"Who keeps Hailey in line? Is that even possible?" I came into the dining room just in time to see all the food already on the table. I really had to get up earlier to get down here and help.

"Ha-ha very funny." Hailey disappeared back through the doors leading to the kitchen to grab a couple more things.

"Good morning dear. I was saying that Ryan keeps her in line, well, more like he attempts too. Could you please go and let the boys know breakfast is ready?"

Bryson came running down the stairs, "Taylor, Taylor, sit next to me please?"

"Ok, just save my seat for me while I go and get your uncle and dad," I turned to walk out just as
Adam walked into the dining room, Ryan following behind

"What if I wanted Taylor to sit next to me," Adam asked his nephew?

"She already said she wanted to sit next to me. Why would she want to sit next to you Uncle Adam?"

"Here, why don't I do this," I walked to the other side of Bryson and sat down in the chair, now putting myself between Bryson and Adam, "Now I am sitting with both of you."

"Better watch yourself Adam, you may have a little competition," Ryan took his seat next to his wife.

"Taylor can I show you my horse today?" Bryson asked as he watched his mother dish him some food.

I felt bad, I had promised the little guy the first night I was here that I would go see his horse, "I would love to have you show me your horse today."

"Maybe after you and I help Uncle Adam with the chores that we need to get done the five of us can go for a ride," Ryan suggested, "I have been promising you I would take you out and today is my last day off for a couple of days."

"Really daddy?" Bryson's excitement almost sent him and his chair over backwards! Lucky for him I had quick reflexes. I grabbed the chair before it fell back. He settled himself for a moment then looked over at Uncle Adam, "Can we go please?"

"Well buddy we have some work to do first but I am sure if all three of us work hard we should be able to go for a ride before dinner tonight." Adam then leaned over to me and whispered for my ears only, "You look great."

I looked around the table to find everyone looking at us, I could feel my cheeks turning red, "Thank you," was all I said then turned my attention to my pancakes. I was not used to this kind of attention. I almost forgot what it was like to get compliments from a guy, however I didn't like to be the center of attention, and I almost felt like climbing under the table to escape the eyes.

Hailey felt Taylors discomfort at being center of attention, "Well if you want to go then I suggest you all get to eating so that you can go get to work."

My phone ringing saved me. I pulled it out of my pocket the screen informed me it was my mom. I got up from the table, "Excuse me it is my mom, I will be right back," and I left the dining room. Once out of hearing distance from the rest of the family I answered it, "Hi mom."

"Hey sweetie, I just wanted to call and let you know they released Mike yesterday."

My blood started quickly pulsing through my veins. I could feel my heart beginning to beat faster. I was hoping he would do something stupid before they released him and keep him in there, but of course, no such luck."

"Honey, are you alright?"

"Yeah mom. We knew it was coming, I just don't know what to do now. I hate that my life is at a halt because of him."

"Honey, I know you don't like all this hiding but it is worth it I believe, for your safety. Are things not going well there?" Sandy knew her daughter didn't want to be away from her work, but she was happy that she decided to go for more than just Mike getting out. Her daughter needed to get away for a while, take a little break from her work. Plus, she knew her daughter would be safe there and not in Napa.

How much should I tell my mom, is what I was trying to decide? Adam and I may have kissed a few times but nothing more so for now she would keep it to herself, "Everything here is great! It is nice to be back. Hailey's little boy Bryson is adorable. We even went out last night and had a lot of fun. All the same, my life back there in Napa can only stay on hold for so long."

Sandy was happy to hear that they had gone out and even more happy to hear Taylor say that she had fun, "I understand, but, you need to stay there at least until we find out what Mike is thinking. If you are lucky he will have smartened up in jail and will leave you alone. Then you can come back and pick up your life where you left off. Do not worry, you will be back to working way to much again soon. In the meantime enjoy a little time off."

"Alright mom, love you."

"I love you too honey. I will keep you posted. Please try to enjoy you visit and don't worry about things here."

"Easier said than done, but thanks mom. Bye." I hung up my phone. Sitting on the porch steps I looked out to the ranch. How did my life turn out like this?

"Everything alright?" Hailey sat down next to me on the step.

I shrugged my shoulders, "Mom was just letting me know they released Mike yesterday."

"Has he tried to contact anyone about you?"

I shook my head, "Not yet. He would wait anyway and see what he could find out first without making it known he was trying to get any information."

Hailey studied Taylor for a moment. There was more she was not saying, "Taylor talk to me. What else is on your mind? What are you not saying?"

I shrugged, "I don't know," a single tear rolled down my cheek.

"Taylor, you do know. You don't just cry for no reason. What is wrong," Hailey pushed.

"These days trust me, I cry all the time for no reason. What has happened to me? Hailey I don't know who I am anymore. I remember being carefree, loving life. I could talk to anyone and took challenges head on! Now look at me. I am hiding from my ex-husband. I hate being in public places because I fear everyone is looking at the scars that show my weakness. How did I manage to screw my life up so badly?" I stood up and walked down the steps, turned around throwing my arms up, "Then there is your brother. He wants us to try and have a relationship. How am I supposed to do that if I can't give my all to him? He doesn't need a messed up person like me."

Hailey watched as tears streamed down Taylor's face, her own tears springing up into her eyes. She hated all that her friend had gone through these past few years, "I know you must feel lost right now but everything will be fine. We will get you through this. We will find the old Taylor."

"What if I am too far gone? I need a little time to think. I am going for a walk. I will be back later." I turned and walk away.

Hailey sat there staring at Taylor's retreating back. She felt helpless, Taylor was still in more pain than she ever figured and she had no idea on how to help her. What kind of friend did that make her? She could also see the fear in Taylor's eyes. She was scared about Mike being out, and she was scared about things with Adam.

“Everything alright out here? Where is Taylor?” Adam asked as him and Ryan walked out of the house.

Hailey decided this situation was much too big for just herself to fix or help with so she decided it was time to let the guys in on exactly why Taylor had decided to come and visit. “I need to talk to you two. Where is Bryson?”

“In with Gram. I didn’t know where you were so he is attempting to help Grams with the breakfast clean up.” Ryan went and sat down next to his wife, “So what is going on?”

“I will tell you but we have to keep quiet about this around Grams. I don’t want to worry her.”

“Hailey what is going on,” Adam was losing his patience. He knew there was more to this story with Taylor visiting.

“A couple of weeks ago Taylor received a letter from her lawyer. Mike, her ex-husband, is getting released from jail. The call from her mom just now was her telling Taylor he was release yesterday.”

“Hailey, why didn’t you tell us earlier?” Ryan demanded.

“Because I knew if only Taylor and I knew then there was little chance of Grams finding out. She would only worry that he was going to show up here and I know he won’t. I'd be surprised if he even knew where she lived before she moved to Napa. If he starts asking around trying to find out where she is everyone believes she is gone on a photo shoot somewhere. She only agreed to come because all of this happened.”

Adam thought back to when Hailey told them all about the trial being over. Taylor’s ex had gotten off very easy but he could have sworn he got more years. “How did he already get out? Didn’t he get like ten years or something like that?”

“They released him early because of good behavior. The jackass should have gotten life in prison for what he did to her, but instead some evidence gets thrown out. They couldn't find the knife that Mike used but they did agree on spousal abuse. He only received ten years and now he gets out in just eight. Taylor is going crazy."

"How long can she stay away from her job and everything," Ryan asked?

"Well, that's part of the problem. She had no idea on how long to stay away or what will happen when she goes back. She knows she can't stay away forever and coming here was only a way for her to more prepare herself. It was such short notice and she needed time to figure things out. It is driving her crazy that she has no control of her own life right now and she is completely terrified of the whole situation." Hailey didn't mention that Taylor was also terrified of the relationship thing with Adam. She didn't want Adam to back away. She still thought they would be perfect for each other.

"Where is she now?" Adam asked concerned.

Hailey pointed in the direction that she last saw Taylor walking in. "She went that way. She said she needed some time and was going for a walk. I am sure she hasn't gone too far."

Adam started down the stairs, "Where are you going? "Ryan asked.

Adam didn't stop, "To see if I can find her and make sure she is alright."

"Adam, wait." Hailey stopped her brother. She waited for him to turn and look at her, "She may need some time to herself to think."

Adam shrugged his shoulders, "Fine. Then after I find her and I know she is alright then I will leave her alone if she ask me to leave." He turned back around and went to find her.

Ryan watched Adam walk away, "Your brother has never shown this much interest in a woman. I wonder why he pays so much to Taylor. I mean, yes, she is beautiful, but, he has had a chance at a lot of beautiful women. What is so different about Taylor?"

Hailey shrugged. She had no idea what caught Adam about Taylor but she was very happy it did. "I have no idea but I am not going to try and stop it. I would love to see them get together."

"Honey don't get your hopes up. It is something new right now and Taylor is just visiting. Adam will never leave the ranch and Taylor's life is in California."

"We will see, we will see," Hailey got up and walked back into the house to go help Grams.

Adam checked around the corrals, inside the stables, and then finally he found Taylor sitting on a bale of hay over where all the hay was stored. Her legs pulled up to her chest, her chin resting on her knees, he walked over to her, "Are you alright?"

I nodded my head but I didn't look up at him.

Adam knelt down in front of me. "Taylor, Hailey told Ryan and I about the real reason why you came. About how your ex-husband is being released from jail early. You two shouldn't have kept that from us."

"It was Hailey's idea, I just went with what she wanted to do. She didn't want to scare Grams and I completely understand that." I explained but never looked up at him.

"Well Ryan and I should still have been told. What if he was to show up here and we didn't know anything about all of this?"

I finally looked up at Adam. I knew we should have told them. I had even asked Hailey about it again last night, "Don't worry. Mike doesn't know where I am and no one back home knows except for my parents and my brother. Everyone else thinks I am off working. I wouldn't let anything happen to this family, which is one of the reasons why I am leaving."

Her eyes were all red from crying. Tears were still escaping from her eyes and rolling down her cheeks. He wiped her face with his fingers, "Calm down Tay. No one is worried. We just felt that we should have been told the whole story, and you aren't leaving."

I threw up my arms in exasperation, "Why do you want to get tangled up with me Adam? If you were smart you would run and fast."

Adam laughed, "Trust me, I have asked myself why. I don't have time for a relationship and I know you are going back to California, but Tay, I don't have a good reason. Only that I know I want you and trust me I would love to get tangled up with you." he gave her a mischievous smile.

I smiled, "Oh you would, would you?" My smiled faded. I once again looked down, "Adam, I am scared. I am scared about Mike being out. I am terrified of you and what you make me feel. Mostly though I am terrified about never finding my true self again."

Adam placed a gentle finger under her chin and lifted her face so that she had to look at him. "Tay you will find yourself again. I think you are there you are just scared to bring her back out. It's easier to hide but please don't be scared of me."

There was pleading in his eyes. "I am not scared of you physically or mentally. I am scared of these feeling you are creating in me. I'm not sure if I'm ready for them."

Adam leaned forward just inches away from her lips, "Please give in to those feelings Taylor. Give us a chance."

I wanted nothing more than to close the space between us and take his lips, "I am trying Adam. Be patient with me." Then to my surprise I found myself leaning forward and claiming his lips.

Adam was shocked at first, she kissed him first! He wrapped is arm around her waist and pulled her over to sit on his knee, his lips never leaving hers. He followed her lead when she tilted her head to deepen the kiss. He felt her tongue hesitantly began to enter, as his met hers, he heard her moan. This woman was born to know how to drive a man crazy with just a kiss.

I felt his tongue meet mine and I could feel all those barriers that I put up so carefully beginning to crumble away. I heard myself moan and was a little embarrassed but that feeling was quickly lost in the heat of the kiss. Senses in my body were beginning to awaken. Ones that had been asleep for a very long time.

Adam was about to lose his mind. He wanted nothing more than to sit here and kiss her all day, but, there were feeling beginning to make themselves known that he needed to get under control. The hardest thing to do was pull away from this woman's sweet lips.

I felt Adam end the kiss. I had to admit I was glad he found the strength to pull away but then again I was disappointed I wanted him. I was very surprised at that moment, to admit to myself, that if he would have pressed on further, I probably would have been more than willing to give him whatever he wanted.

"I want nothing more than to sit here with you and kiss you all day but I made a promise to a little boy, we would work hard so that we can all go on a ride today. I need to get going and do some work."

I nodded stood up and almost had to catch myself. My knees were weak and this man was driving my body crazy with need. I caught my balance before I fell over and embarrassed myself. "We cannot disappoint him either."

Adam stood up and wrapped his arms around her waist, pulling her right up to his chest, and gave her a small kiss, "Are you going to be alright?"

"Yes, I'm not going to say I am still not scared a little but I will be alright," I felt protected in his arms, almost like I knew nothing could touch me.

"Everything will be alright. I have to go. I'll see you in a little while." He gave me one more small kiss, then released me, turned and walked away.

Adam knew if he was to stay any longer he would be way to tempted to pick her up and carry her back to his house and give into those feelings her kisses were starting to ignite. As he walked back he thought how strange it was that he had spent all these past years ignoring relationships all together, never even going on dates with all the women that would ask him out. Sure, if they went out dancing he would dance with a couple but it never went any further than that. He didn't need that distraction from the ranch. He had his family to look after. Yet Taylor shows up and something just strikes him right in the chest. He knew Taylor knew how important the ranch was. He knew she would never be one of those women who asked him to walk away from it or complain that he wasn't spending enough time with her. Maybe that was one of the reasons he was so drawn to her. The first moment he walked into the dining room and her eyes looked up at him something slammed into his chest and now he felt like he had someone standing behind him pushing him towards her. Everything just felt natural with her. Now that he knew the real reason for her visit he swore he would do anything to make sure she stayed safe. Taylor was his now and nothing was going to take her away from him. There was only one small thing is the way and that was her home. He couldn't leave the ranch and he knew Taylor knew that. If she agreed to try this then maybe there was a small chance he could convince her to stay. He knew she missed it. You could see it in her eyes. Now all he had to do was convince her.

I watched as Adam walked away. I still didn't know if this was a good idea but I did know that I haven't had the feelings that I have when I am with Adam in a very long time. I liked the way I felt when I was around him. For now I decided I wouldn't worry about the "what if" and just take it one day at a time. Only problem with that is there was going to come a time here real soon when I would have to make a choice. Maybe I did need to think this over a little more. Was it right of me to let this move forward if I was planning on going home soon? Sure I could play this off in my mind as "just a little fun while I'm here" sort of thing. What's the saying? Enjoy it while you have it? I knew my mind was already past that. I was already developing feelings for Adam. I couldn't even sit here and be mad at myself for falling for a guy I had only met or haven't known for that long. I have known Adam all of my life. I was here when their grandfather died. I watched Adam change overnight and take on the large responsibility of this ranch and taking care of his Grams and Hailey. Remembering all of my conversations with Hailey in the past years, she was worried that he was never going to allow himself to find someone to build a family with because he was too busy with the ranch, so what changed him with me? What makes him want to try a relationship with me? Maybe they should talk this through a little more before feelings became too strong.

Chapter 5

A week had past and there had been no sign of his ex-wife. Mike sat in his room at his brother's house staring at the wall. Everyone who he had talked to told him as far as they knew she was out of town on a photography job. No one knew where that job was or what kind of photo shoot it was so of course no one knew when she should be back. He didn't even bother to ask any of her family. He knew they wouldn't tell him anything. He didn't really believe she was on a job. She had left to close to his release date for him to believe for one minute she just happened to get a job out of town. He had heard she had been traveling quite a bit but something told him it was more than that. She was hiding and he knew it. How long did she think she could stay away? Her family was here, her home was here and her business, no wait, his business was here. His business, everything he had put together. He spends eight years in hell because of her and she was able to live and thrive on everything he had put together and from what he had heard, she was doing very well.

He looked around his room. Nothing but a bed, dresser and a chair. Not much more than he had in jail, the only real difference was he was free to leave when he wanted. He had nothing, she had it all. He did have a little money thankful for being smart enough to start an account that Taylor had no idea about. When he had gone to the bank he had found that the account he had opened had not been touched at all in the eight years he was gone. It made him believe she must have doing alright with the business because she no longer lived in the house they had rented. She was now living in a condo on the other side of town.

"Mike, are you in there?" he heard his brother ask from the other side of the door.

Mike stood up and walked over and opened his door, "What's up little brother?" He walked over to the bedroom window and looked out.

"I am heading out with a couple of buddies. Do you want to come with us?" Kevin stood there staring at the back of his brother. He needed to get out of this house. He rarely left his room and when he did it was brief. He would only be going out to see if he could find out any new information about Taylor. When Mike didn't say anything Kevin tried again, "Come on, you should get out a little. You need to move on with your life. Give up this thing about Taylor. It's only going to get you in trouble again."

"No, this time little brother Taylor will get what is coming to her. She cheated on me, got herself pregnant and then put me in jail. To top it off, she took over my business and took everything I had." He turned away from the window and glared at his brother, "Hell no, I'm not giving up!" she would pay and pay dearly just as soon as he figured out where she was.

"Whatever. I will be home later." Kevin didn't know why he even tried. His brother hadn't learned one thing in the past eight years.

Kevin remembered the night his brother was arrested. Taylor was in the hospital holding on for dear life. When he confronted his brother, he had told him the whole story. He admitted to beating her but only after Taylor came home from a doctor's appointment and told him she was pregnant and that she was leaving him for the father of the baby. Mike had told him the only reason he had hit Taylor was because after she told him she was leaving him, he had refused her request of a divorce, and became extremely angry and began throwing things at him and hitting him. It was all out of self-defense according to Mike.

Kevin was not sure exactly what to believe of the story his brother had told him. He knew his brother was controlling of his women. Mike had always had a very short temper, it had gotten him into trouble a few different times. Growing up with Mike, Kevin had learned to just stay away from him, it was a lot less painful. It was hard for him to believe

Taylor would stray off and get herself pregnant by another guy. He had liked Taylor. He actually felt sorry for her for being tied up with his brother, and Mike didn't deserve a girl like Taylor.

In the last eight years Kevin had not spoken to Taylor. He had seen her a couple of times, had seen the scars on her face which made him ashamed of his brother. Even if it had been out of self-defense, those scars were a little more than self-defense. He was embarrassed by what his brother had done and had no idea what he would say to her, so he always made sure to stay clear of her. He had heard a couple of different stories about that night from different people, one even said Mike had slashed her stomach open but Kevin tried to ignore the fact that his brother was that full of hate. Deep down he knew the stories were probably right and that his brother had lied to him about what really happened.

When Mike had called him and told him they were releasing him early Kevin didn't know what to say. Then he asked if he could come stay with him for a little while until he was able to get enough money to get his own place. Kevin didn't know how to tell his only brother no, so he said that would be fine. He knew now that was a mistake. His brother was not the same man at all anymore. Honestly, he scared the hell out of him and couldn't wait for him to be gone, but, one thing Kevin was pretty sure of was that when Mike left, it would not be to his own place. Kevin would bet his brother was going to end up back in prison.

"Fourth of July is in a couple of weeks. You haven't been to a Fourth celebration in Nolensville in how long? Are you thinking about staying around for this years?" Hailey asked Taylor as they sat in the diner they use to go to all the time in high school eating lunch.

I shrugged my shoulders and I dabbed my fry into some ranch dressing, "I have a business to get back to. I cannot stay away for too long."

"Have you talked to your mom at all? It has been what a little over a week now. Has he asked around about you that they have heard?"

I pushed my fry around in the bowl of ranch not looking up at my friend but nodding my head. "I talked to her yesterday and yes, he has been asking questions. I guess he is living with his younger brother right now." My stomach had been in knots ever since talking to my mother yesterday. I had really hoped I would hear that Mike moved out of town and on with his life or something, but finding out he was staying and that he had been asking questions was only confirming my worst fears.

"What kind of questions has he been asking?" Hailey pushed.

"I really don't know. I am assuming he is trying to figure out where I am and when I am coming home but Hailey, I can't stay in hiding forever I have my life to get back to in Napa."

Hailey shook her head. Was Taylor out of her mind? Why would anyone want to go and put themselves into that kind of danger again? "No, you can leave there all together and move back here. You can move in with me. Your name in wedding photography is so large you can move anywhere and still be busy Taylor. Why go back and give him a second chance at killing you?"

"I am not going to allow him to push me away from my life Hailey. That is like telling him he has won. I won't allow that to happen. I promised myself I wouldn't allow another man to control my life again. If I leave Napa that is exactly what I'm allowing to happen."

"What about Adam?" Hailey challenged. She had been watching the two of them the last couple of days. There was a connection between the two of them, no one not even Taylor could deny that.

Again, I shrugged, but didn't look up from my plate, "What about Adam?"

"Come on Taylor. You two like each other. Are you saying you can just leave and go home now and not have a second thought about him?"

“Hailey, I didn’t come here to get into a relationship. That is the last thing I wanted to do. I can’t just pack up and leave my home. Honestly, maybe I should leave now, that way nothing major happens between your brother and I and then we can both get on with our lives and jobs.”

“What about Mike?” Hailey was not ready to let Taylor go home yet. She loved having her friend here and she knew she was safe. She didn’t trust Mike at all and if Taylor went back to California something bad would happen.

“I can’t worry about Mike. I will deal with that if and when something happens.” I pushed my plate away, I was no longer hungry. Maybe it was time to get my life back and under control, starting with not running and hiding but going home and dealing with Mike if I had too. Yes, my mom had heard he was asking around about me, but that was no surprise. I figured he would. I was a grown woman and I needed to start acting like one and taking back my life was a good start.

What about Adam, Hailey had asked? I myself couldn’t answer that question. I wanted to run and hide from the feelings Adam was making me feel. One major issue between them was where they lived. Yes, I belonged here, I wouldn’t deny it. I loved being back in Tennessee. It was home, but my life now was in California. My family and my job were there. You don’t just pick that up and move.

Hailey watched as her friend fought with herself and her feelings. She knew she had to stop pushing Taylor or she would just leave just to prove a point. “Stay one more week, please. We talked about two weeks to begin with. It would give Mike a little more time to calm down and I would feel a lot better about it, plus, I’m not ready to give you up yet.”

I looked up from my plate into the pleading and hopeful eyes of my best friend. Another week wasn’t too much of a request. Hailey was right, they had planned on a two week trip anyway. “Alright one more week but I am not making any promises for after that. We will just have to play it by ear.”

Well, it wasn't a moving back decision yet, but it was another week for her brother to get a little closer to her and Mike nowhere near her. She would accept that for now, "Deal, now we better be heading back," Hailey grabbed the check the waitress had just set down on the table, but I grabbed it quickly out of her hands.

"This is on me. You have done too much as it is. At least let me buy you lunch."

I pushed the porch swing back and forth slowly with my tippy toes. It was still hot outside but I didn't care. It was peaceful. I leaned my head back and closed my eyes. I had to admit, taking a break felt great. Not worrying about the next photo shoot or the next appointment of the day, just relaxing. I had even made myself leave my phone in my room. My message explained I was on an important job that would require my full attention, to leave a message, and I would return calls in a couple of weeks. I had told my mom I would periodically check on my messages but if it was important to call the house.

I loved my job. I never really considered it work. I loved photography and I loved capturing special moments in people's lives for them to look back onto for the rest of their lives. I had to be honest with myself, I had been pouring so much time into photography I was becoming tired. Maybe once I got back home I would slow down a little enjoy some free time in my life as well.

"Are you asleep?" I heard Adam's voice close to my ear, his hot breath on my face gave me chills.

I liked opening my eyes to the vision of Adam standing with his face only inches from mine. I fought the urge to lift my head just a little to claim his lips. "No I am just relaxing." Adam stood back up to his full height in front of me, looking down, "Good, go get your camera. I just found the wild herd. You mentioned wanting to get some pictures of them and they are at the perfect spot right now."

"Really?!" I shot up out of the porch swing so quickly the back of my leg somehow caught the front of the swing sending me forward. Adam with his quick reflexes, had his arm shooting out and grabbed me around the waist before I ended up face down on the porch.

"Slow down before you hurt yourself!" He made sure I had my balance before he released me then he gave me a small kiss. "Go get your equipment and I will go and saddle one of the horses for you. Meet me out by the stables when you are ready."

"Alright, I will be right back," I turned quickly, ran into the house and up the stairs almost colliding into Hailey as I reached the top.

"What's the hurry?" Hailey followed me into my room.

"Adam found the herd! He is taking me out to go take pictures. He is saddling a horse while I grab everything." I shot around my room gathering everything I would need. I quickly went into the bathroom, threw my hair up into a ponytail, and then came back out. I grabbed my backpack full of equipment and started back out the door.

Hailey watched her friend as she flew through the room. She was about to ask if she could go but then changed her mind. This was perfect for the two of them. They could use the alone time. She moved aside as Taylor came back out of the room, "Well you two have fun! I can't wait to see the pictures when you get back."

"Ok thanks! See you later." I didn't even stop, I quickly went back down the stairs and out to the stables. I didn't want to miss this.

Hailey headed down the stairs and over to the large window that looked out into the front yard from the family room. She could see Adam out with the two horses ready to go, "Do your magic Adam and make her fall in love with you."

"Look over there Tay. They are still there." Adam stopped his horse once he spotted the herd.

I came up alongside of him and looked in the direction of which Adam was pointing. There I saw the stream, tons of trees, and the herd of horses. Some of them drinking from the stream, others grazing on the grass that grew around the area. "They are beautiful."

Adam looked over at her. He didn't know about the horses but the woman mounted on the horse next to him was beautiful. Her eyes were shining as she looked over at where the herd was. "Come on! We'll go this way a little. I don't want to get our horses to close to them, we need to keep a little distance between them."

My eyes never left the herd but my horse followed Adam's to the location that Adam felt was a safe distance from the wild herd. I slid down off the horse quickly and handed the reins to Adam then pulled my equipment down and began assembling my camera.

Adam tied both reins to a low branch, but allowed enough length for the horses to graze. He turned to find Taylor already moving closer to the horses on the other side of the stream. He leaned up against the large Oak tree and watched her. She had on a pair of jeans that hugged her curvy legs and hips perfectly. She had on a black tank top and a pair of cowboy boots. She'd worn a straw cowboy hat on the way up here but he now found that forgotten, on the ground. Her golden hair tied up in a ponytail hanging almost down to her waist, shined like silk with the sun hitting it. His fingers itched to run through that hair and over those curves. He could feel himself getting hard just standing here looking at her. He looked away from her and at the horses across the stream for a moment to get some control of himself.

I turned to say something to Adam, my breath catching in my chest. What a vision my eyes were taking in. There was Adam leaning up against this huge oak tree, blue jeans and white shirt, boots and cowboy hat. His arms crossed on his chest, the two horses creating an amazing background to this very good looking cowboy in front of me. I brought my camera up and focused in on him. My knees about gave way under me.

I have photographed models, men who were considered gorgeous, but they held no comparison to the man in my lens right now. I took a couple of different shots. My blood began to heat up and pump faster through my veins. I wanted nothing more than to go up to him and pull that shirt up over the chest. I could only imagine what was hiding under there and run my fingers up and down his chest. I zoomed the lens in closer, his face filling most of the frame. Just as I was about to take the picture, Adam's attention was back on me. He smiled, my heart melted, I took the shot.

"I thought you wanted to take pictures of the herd?" Adam was surprised to look back at Taylor and find her taking pictures of him.

"I am but if another opportunity arises for a good picture, you always take it," I explained, a little embarrassed that he caught me taking the pictures.

"So you're saying you like what you see?" Adam pushed. He wanted Taylor to admit she was attracted to him. He knew she was though, every time they kissed her reaction alone spoke loud and clear.

I knew he was baiting me but I would play along. "You know I am attracted to you Adam. I don't go around kissing every guy I'm around."

I watched as he pushed away from the large tree and walked over to me. "Well, I have to admit to being happy to hear that." He grabbed the camera from my hands and unwound the strap from my neck, "So, can I take a picture of you since I like what I see?"

Shaking my head my smile faded, "No Adam, please, no pictures of me. I don't have my picture taken," I tried to grab the camera back from him but he was not allowing it.

Adam stretched his arm back holding the camera away from my reach, his other arm going around my waist. The feeling of his body up against mine about had me melting to the ground I now found talking very hard to do, "Please Adam no pictures give me the camera."

"Tay, how fair is it that you got to take one of me and then not allow me to take one of you? Just let me take one and then you can print it for me and destroy any other proof of the picture. It's only fair for me to have one of you if you have one of me." He knew she was going to say no. He could see it in her eyes along with something that looked a little like pain. He brought his arm down and placed the strap of the camera around his shoulder, his hand coming up to her face, he traced her scar that she had on her cheek. "You are a beautiful woman. Why do you have such a hard time realizing how beautiful you are?"

"Adam I am scarred by meanness and violence." I tried to pull away from him but he was not letting me go. "Adam let me go please." I begged.

Adam didn't say a word. His lips touched the scar on her forehead. I again tried to pull away from him but his arm tightened around my waist. His lips followed the scar then kissed my temple catching a tear from my eye.

That one tear almost did him in. Knowing she was crying made him almost release her but something told him to hold her even tighter and he did. He found the scar on her cheek, it was wet from her tears as well, he could taste the salty flavor of her tears but he continued to trace the scar with his lips.

I didn't know which emotion running through me was greater. One part of me wanted to demand he let me go, hop on my horse, and race back to the house, pack and leave on the first plane back to California. The other side of me wanted to enjoy his embrace and melt into him, allowing him to lead me into places I hadn't been to in a very long time. Then there was the emotion scaring me the most. The one that made my heart beat fast, my veins come alive with fire flowing through them. An emotion I swore I never wanted to feel again.

"Tay please don't cry. Let me show you how beautiful you are. These scars," he touched the one on her cheek again with his thumb, "they just show what a fighter you are! How strong you are. You fought for your life and you won Taylor. Be proud of what you over came and what you have become. Let me take your picture please, one for me only."

His eyes pleaded with me, those eyes could make me do and say just about anything he wanted me to. The feeling in my heart scared me but I decided to listen to it. "Alright," was all I said. The reward from that one word was amazing.

Adam's lips claimed mine in a heated kiss like no other. His lips were warm, his tongue darted straight into my mouth, his one hand on the back of my head crushing us together. There was force and strength but neither scared me, it only aroused every nerve in my body. I was feeling things I was pretty sure I had never felt in my life, nothing could compare. Not even when Mike and I were first together and I thought he was the most amazing man alive, did I ever feel what I was feeling now. Mike always tried to dominate over me. Adam, on the other hand, was trying to make sure I was right alongside of him, if not before him.

My hands went from his chest to up around his neck my body seemed to mold perfectly to his. It was like they were created for each other. Every curve and every muscle seemed to fit perfectly together.

Adam was trying very hard to not want Taylor but it wasn't working. Every time their bodies were together like this, every time she kissed him, he didn't want to stop. Right now he definitely didn't want to stop. He didn't want the clothes in between them. He wanted her skin against his, he wanted to be inside her, to feel her all around him. He had been trying to keep himself from getting these feelings around her, taking things slow not pushing her. When he would feel his body beginning to heat up he usually used that as the sign to stop things and breath but right now, he had messed up, he hadn't pushed away and now he wanted her.

I felt his hand move up and down my back and then very slowly I felt his hand move around and cup my breast. I moaned, or was that him? I wasn't sure. Was I ready for this? I wasn't sure but it felt good. As his fingers brushed across my nipple I realized it felt great, not just good.

Adam realized she was not stopping him and he was trying to take it slow give her the opportunity to stop him but the moment his hand touched her breast and she moaned he knew he was gone. He deepened the kiss, she moaned again, and his hand moved down to the edge of her shirt and pulled it out from where it was tucked into her pants.

Adam's finger rubbing against my skin was like a splash of cold water to me, I wasn't ready for this. I pulled away from Adam quickly but realized that wasn't a good idea, I lost my balance and began to fall back. Adam's arms once again were around my waist keeping me from landing on my backside. "I'm sorry Tay," he said as he brought me back up against his chest.

I kept my eyes down. I was too embarrassed to look up at him. "Adam, I'm sorry. I should never have teased you like that. For a moment I wanted.....," she stopped mid-sentence, she felt the red in her cheeks.

"Tay, don't ever be embarrassed to talk to me. I should be the one apologizing. I promised to take things slow and I jumped ahead to fast."

I looked up. He was taking the blame for what just happened? He wasn't blaming me? There was that feeling in my heart again. "Don't apologize Adam. I should have stopped before it got to this point but when you kiss me, I lose myself and that scares me."

He placed his hands on either side of my face and lightly kissed me, "I love that I have that effect on you." He smiled down at me. "How about you let me take that picture of you now?"

I smiled up at him, "How about I set up the camera and we take on together? One with all those beautiful horses behind us."

"Here is the deal, one of just you and then as many as you want with the two of us."

I was finding I couldn't say no to this man, "Alright, where do you want me?"

Glancing at all the pictures on my computer I had taken for the day, I stopped on one of Adam that I had taken. All I could do was stare at the amazing male form in front of me. He belonged out in the open, horses all around him. It was a picture that I would have posed, but he did it all naturally and it looked right. I thought back to our kiss. I could have easily lost myself with this man, given all to him, but I wasn't ready for him to know all of me. I wasn't ready to uncover all of my scars. Why was I dragging this out? Why do this to him or myself? I would never allow him to leave this place, not that he would, this ranch was his life. I wasn't ready to pick up my life and move from Napa, but why wasn't I, I had to ask myself? What was in Napa for me? Yes, my family was there, but if I was honest with myself
I knew I would always visit and so would they. My mom talks about how much she herself, missed Tennessee. Hailey was right all the times she said I could move my photography and be fine. Sure I wouldn't have the clients in Napa, but I was becoming very requested all around for weddings. I could travel no matter where I lived. So what was holding me there? I had no answers to that, but I knew I was not ready. Maybe I should leave now, not drag this out for another week. All that was going to happen was I was going to continue to get closer and closer to Adam, and when it was time to leave it was going to be all that much harder. Every day I was falling a little harder for this cowboy in front of me.

"You guys are back already? I expected you to be gone most of the day." I jumped almost knocking my computer to the floor at hearing Hailey's voice in the room. I hadn't even heard the door open.

"Do you knock?"

"Actually I did," she held up two fingers, "twice as a matter of fact but when you didn't answer I figured maybe you were in the shower and I wanted to hear how the day went so, I let myself in and decided I would wait."

I watched as Hailey came over and sat down on the bed next to me. "Wow that is a great picture of
Adam! How did you manage to get him to pose for you? He hates having his picture taken."

"I didn't have him pose actually. He wasn't aware that I was taking them at the time. I was taking pictures of the horses, turned around, and he happened to be standing there perfectly so I started taking pictures." I tapped on the arrow key of my computer to move back to some of the horse pictures.

"Taylor, those are amazing!" Hailey watched as I flipped through the pictures.

One came up of me, "We don't need to look at those," I quickly pushed the arrow key passed the photos of myself.

"No, wait, I want to see them." Hailey tried pushing the arrow key back to see the picture.

I attempted to push Hailey away but it didn't work. She managed to forward the picture to the one of me, "You look great in that picture Taylor! Did Adam take that? Maybe he is in the wrong profession, or maybe, he just had an amazing teacher," she smiled up at her friend.

"No, he took it all on his own. Photography is great but the object of the photo, not the best," I stared at the picture of myself. I couldn't remember the last time I was in a picture and now I knew why... the scars on my face showed up even more in pictures.

"Taylor, you look great in this picture! Why are you so hard on yourself? What other pictures did you take?" She started pushing the arrow forward again, completely shocked on the next set of pictures. They were ones of Adam and I together, "You guys look great together, you seem to fit well with each other."

I thought back to my body being smashed up against his, his heated touch, the need that flowed through my body as his hands roamed over my body. I almost moaned out loud but caught myself.

"Couples pictures, wow! What a step in the relationship direction." Hailey stared at the final pictures trying to control the huge smile on her face, it was of the two of them kissing.

I stared at the picture on the screen, my blood began to boil again, my body started with the needing him feeling again. Damn, I was only looking at him kissing me and I was going all weird. "Hailey, I need to leave. It's time for me to go home."

Hailey was shocked. Leave now? That was the last thing she figured Taylor would be telling her that she wanted to do. After looking at them kissing on the screen she would have thought it would have been easier to convince Taylor to stay. "What do you mean you have to leave? Are you serious?" Hailey pointed a finger at the screen.

"That is why I am leaving. I can't let this go any further. I won't want to go home at all."

"So what? What is wrong with staying?"

"Hailey, it is not that easy. I have a life to get back to."

"Really? You have a life back in Napa to get back to? No offense Taylor, but working until you drop is not a life. You can do that anywhere you live. You never go out, you told me you have no friends back in Napa. Every time I talk to you on the phone you sound miserable. Answer me one question, what exactly are you running back home to or better yet, maybe I should ask what are you running from here?"

I didn't say anything for a moment. I had to calm myself first. I was beginning to get mad at Hailey. How dare she talk about things she had no idea about! Yet when I thought about it for a moment I realized what I was really becoming mad over was the fact that what Hailey said was completely true, I looked back at the computer, the picture of Adam and myself kissing, "Hailey I didn't come here to get involved in a relationship, especially one with your bother."

"What is so wrong with getting into a relationship with Adam?" She pointed at the picture on the screen, "looks to be a good match to me."

"I don't want to be in a relationship right now, good match or not. Why keep this going if I don't want it?" I decided I sounded like I was trying to convince myself more than Hailey.

Hailey pointed at the picture, "Yeah looks like you despise kissing him and I can see where you wouldn't want this relationship thing to move on." She was starting to get mad, she loved her friend but she didn't want to see Adam get hurt. If all Taylor was going to do was break his heart then maybe her leaving was not such a bad idea.

Staring at the picture for a moment, Hailey decided, it was best if Taylor left, "You know, why don't you go ahead and leave Taylor? It would probably be for the best anyway. I don't want Adam to get hurt any more than he already is going to be." She got up from the bed and headed for the door, stopping and turning, "you know Taylor, you are the first girl he has been interested in since our grandfather died, so do me a favor, if you aren't serious about him then do him a favor and go home," and she quickly left the room, shutting the door behind her. She had never been more disappointed in Taylor as she was now. Taylor had changed far more then she had thought.

I stared at my closed door shocked at what had just happened. Hailey had just told me to leave and could I blame her? Absolutely not. This was not fair to Adam. Why had I ever agreed to even trying a relationship out with him? I did it because deep down I was tired of being alone. I wanted a life like Hailey had. A loving husband and children. I wanted it more than anything but I was scared to go through all of this again. I knew Adam was nothing like Mike, a lot of men were very different than Mike, but it didn't change the fact that I was scared. I had just managed to get a little normal life back and now this relationship was kind of a threat to have major changes again. I wasn't sure I was ready for change yet. I looked back at the picture again, a tear rolling down my cheek, I would leave tonight.

I wiped the tears from my face. I had no times for tears, I needed to get packing. Tonight when everyone went to bed I would have a cab come and take me to the airport. I knew if Adam found out I was leaving then he would try and stop me. He always had a way to get me to bend in the way he wanted. I connected my small printer up to my computer and printed out a picture of the two of us and one of just me, I did promise he could have one before I deleted them. As they printed up I wrote a letter to Adam and then went about packing my stuff. My heart was breaking and if I didn't busy myself with something then I was going to change my mind before I could leave.

I was a little worried that Adam would come up after me when I didn't show up to dinner but I was pretty sure Hailey would make some excuse as to why I wasn't there. I hoped deep down it would keep Adam away for the night then by tomorrow I would be gone.

I looked around, everything was packed, now all I could do was sit here and wait for everyone to go to bed. By now dinner was over and somehow Hailey must have convinced her brother to give me some time alone. I walked over to the window and looked out at Adam's house. A light was on upstairs in a room I figured to be the bedroom. Adam had offered to take me in and show me the house a couple of times but I had decided it was safe to not put us alone in his house just yet since out in the open we could barely control ourselves. I watched as his shadow moved around the room again and the tears began to flow down my cheeks. How did my life end up so messed up? I had no one to blame but myself. No matter how many times I verbally blamed Mike, I really knew I was to blame for my own life. I could have walked away from my marriage before things had become so bad but I didn't want everyone to think I failed at my own marriage. I was afraid of failing again.

I knew I should be heading for home, but I was still scared. I had already arranged to be gone for another week so I decided that when I got to the airport I would just see where the flights were heading and decide then where I was going to go. It would be good to be alone for a little while, do some thinking about my life and maybe make some decisions on what to change. I walked away from the window and sat down in the chair, looking at the clock. I had arranged for the cab to arrive at eleven. I figured that was a safe time for everyone to be asleep.

Hailey made sure Bryson was all tucked into bed for the night and then headed for her own room where Ryan was getting ready for bed.

Ryan watched as Hailey entered their room and went straight to the chair, sat down and buried her face into her hands, "Babe, what's wrong?"

Hailey looked up at her husband who was now squatting down in front of her, she shook her head, "I told Taylor to go home today."

Ryan was shocked, "What? Why? What happened?"

She took a deep breath and slowly exhaled, "Honestly, I am not sure. One minute we were looking at the pictures that she took today then the next I was telling her to go home."

"Alright, now fill me in on the middle section of this conversation. What happened that made you tell her to go home?"

"She started talking about how she needed to leave before things got any more serious between herself and Adam," she began the story, "telling me she didn't come here to get involved in a relationship. She kept telling me she had a life to get back to in California, so on and so on. But Ryan, you should have seen the pictures of them kissing."

"Wait," Ryan interrupted, "there are pictures of them kissing?"

"Yes, they took a couple of them together while they were out today," she waved it off like it was not really the important part.

"Honey, Taylor is probably scared. Look at what is going on right now and what she is going through. We can easily wonder why she can't move on from a failed marriage and one that ended in violence at that. Why would she want to jump right back into something that can just cause her more pain? With Mike just getting out of jail it is probably opening up all those wounds. She may not be ready for a relationship with all of this going on right now."

"Ryan, Adam wouldn't hurt her and she knows that."

Ryan nodded his agreement, "We know that and Taylor knows that but she has only been here for a week or so and look at how fast everything between them is going. Then you are talking to her about picking up her life in California and moving back here. She is worried about what is going on with her ex being released and now Adam. She is going to be scared. She is probably a little overwhelmed."

Hailey's tears started to roll as she listened to her husband. He was right. She had no idea what Taylor was really going through. Here she was trying to talk her into all these changes when all Taylor wanted was something solid, "You are right. How could I be so pushy? I should be supporting her and I'm not. I need to go and talk to her."

She started to get up from the chair but Ryan stopped her, "Give her some time tonight to think honey. You can apologize in the morning. She probably needs some time alone."

Hailey sat back down in the chair, "You are right again. I will talk to her before breakfast and if she still wants to leave I will support her on that and take her to the airport."

Ryan gave his wife a kiss then stood up, holding out a hand to her to help her up out of the chair, "Come on. Get ready for bed. You have a long morning of apologizing ahead of you."

Chapter 6

"Taylor, are you awake? Breakfast is ready and afterwards I would like to talk to you," Hailey spoke to Taylor's bedroom door then waited a minute but Taylor didn't answer.

"Taylor, I'm sorry. Please, let's talk about this. I messed up and I want to apologize for it. Please open the door." Again she waited and still no answer.

Hailey opened the door, "Taylor?" She looked around. Taylor wasn't in her room, she must have gone outside and no one had seen her go out. She turned to leave and noticed the two pictures and a letter addressed to Adam lying on the bed. Hailey picked up the pictures, one of Taylor alone and one of her and Adam together. The letter was addressed to Adam so she didn't feel right opening it. She looked around again, "Oh no," she said out loud. Taylor's stuff was gone.

Hailey ran down stairs and into the dining room where everyone was waiting on her and Taylor to join them, "Where is Taylor, dear?" Grams asked?

"Well," Hailey walked over to Adam and handed him the pictures and the letter, "she left."

"What?" Adam grabbed the letter and pictures out of her hand. He didn't even glance at the photos, he went right to the letter:

Adam,

I want to apologize for leaving like this. Please find a way to forgive me. I know this sounds generic but it wasn't you, it was all me. I'm not ready for the whole relationship thing. Why get deeper involved if I will have to end it and go home? It's not fair for me to lead you on. Hailey was right to tell me to leave, she only thought of how I would hurt you when she told me to go so please don't be mad at her. Here are two pictures to remember me by but if you don't want them I will understand.

Taylor

Adam stared at the pictures for a moment then looked up at his sister, "You told her to leave?"

"Well, yes, I guess I did but that isn't the whole story Adam. She was talking about leaving anyway. I got mad, I wasn't thinking straight. Actually, I was thinking about you. I didn't want you to get hurt. I was going to apologize this morning but she wasn't there."

"I can take care of myself Hailey. I don't need you to interfere. So why didn't you apologize last night? Why wait until this morning?"

Her brother was mad and she didn't blame him. She shouldn't have interfered. How many times had Ryan told her that before all of this? Let them do this between the two of them, she should have listened. "Because it was late I figured let us both sleep and calm down then talk in the morning. I really had no idea she would leave in the middle of the night, Adam. I am really sorry. I will go now to the airport and just maybe she is still there."

Adam stood up with such force he knocked the chair over. "No, I will go, you have done enough. Maybe she will listen to me and if I do find her and convince her to come back you are to stay out of what is going on between us. Do I make myself clear?"

He didn't even wait for her to respond to the question actually it wasn't a question, it was an order, and she couldn't blame him. She screwed up and she would admit it.

I was trying not to fall asleep. I had been up all night and was physically and mentally drained and then with the fight with Hailey, and now being upset about leaving Adam, my eyes were fading fast. I hadn't realized that it would be so hard to leave him. Sitting here in the airport waiting on my flight, I realized my heart was tearing apart knowing I was actually leaving him. I hadn't realized I had such strong feelings for him already but I couldn't think about that right now. I had to leave. In two hours I was going to board a plane and go to Florida. I had decided that I wasn't ready to head back and face Mike and my mess of a life back in Napa, so Florida looked good. I could do a little thinking and figure out some sort of plan for my life. Maybe I should move away from everyone and everything, start over with no one knowing where I was or who I am?

I had two hours. I pulled my phone out of my pocket and set the alarm. A little sleep didn't sound like a bad idea. Maybe if I was sleeping I wouldn't be tempted to cancel my flight plans and run back to Adam. I laid my head back against the wall and closed my eyes.

Adam ran into the airport after breaking many speed limits to get there in record breaking time. Where to start, he didn't know. He looked up at all the flights to see which ones were leaving to California. This was useless. How would he know if the flight hadn't left during the night? He decided to just start looking around although his hopes were not high on finding her. So much time had gone by. He'd thought about calling her but something told him she wouldn't have answered it anyway. He walked quickly, scanning the area around him, and then stopped dead in his tracks. There she was. Sitting in a chair, head up against the wall. He released the breath he hadn't realized until now that he was holding. He walked up to her, she didn't move. She must have fallen asleep. He knelt down in front of her and stared at her for a moment. This was fate, he was sure of it. What were the chances that she would still be there after all this time? His heart had dropped back at the house when Hailey had told him she had left and had just replaced itself when he saw her sitting there. If this wasn't love he didn't know what was. He couldn't believe it, he was in love, and with his sister's best friend! Life was always making funny turns.

"Taylor, wake up." he watched as she stirred a little.

I was now dreaming of Adam's voice, this was crazy.

"Tay, Tay, come on. Wake up."

Wait a minute, how could I be dreaming and talking to myself at the same time? I opened my eyes to find Adam squatting in front of me, "Adam, what are you doing here?"

"Well, hello to you too. You didn't say goodbye," his hands took hers.

"Adam you are making this harder than it needs to be. You shouldn't have come."

"If I hadn't have come after you then you would never hear what I have to say."

I took a deep breath, something that was already hard to do was about to get a lot harder. It was a lot easier to say goodbye in a letter then looking into those blue eyes and saying it in person. "Adam, please don't. It's going to be easier for both of us if I go now. Why keep trying at a relationship if I'm going to leave soon anyway?"

"Tay, tell me you have no feeling for me. Tell me you can leave without wondering the "what ifs". If you can tell me that then I will leave and let you go wherever you were going."

I thought about telling him all of that. Lying to him just so that he would go and I could get on my plane and leave but again, those blue eyes were making it impossible for me to sit here and lie to him. "I can't tell you any of that Adam. What I can tell you is that you make me feel things that I don't think I've ever felt. You make me feel beautiful even though I think you must be blind. You are making me feel things I swore I would never feel again. Yet even with all that said, I am only here to visit. My home, my job, and my family are all in California. The longer I stay, the harder it will be to say goodbye when I have to go home."

Adam understood what she was saying. He had thought about all of that many times in the last week, but he was willing to risk the heart ache. "Why don't we let the future take care of itself and just live in the present? I'm not ready to say goodbye to you Tay. I want to take the risk. Please take that risk with me. I am not saying to move away from your home, I am saying just give us the chance you first agreed to give and see where it leads us. If you need to leave in a week then we will decide together how to deal with it. I understand I am asking you to suffer what may be more heart ache but take that chance with me please."

I couldn't answer, I was split. Part of me wanted to run and run fast. The other part wanted to throw myself into his arms. I had already given my heart to this man but I had to be honest with myself, I wasn't ready yet to pick my life up and move.

"Taylor, how long can you stay away from work?"

I shrugged, "Maybe until after the fourth, that would be pushing it but I could do that at the most." "Alright so give us the next two weeks. Take a chance with me please. I am willing to let down the walls I have built around me. Please do the same."

I couldn't answer him. Was I able to knock down those walls as easily as he was? Adam stood up a little in order to claim my lips. This was not fair. I never thought rationally when he kissed me and he knew it. I pulled away, "That's not fair."

Adam smiled, he almost looked like a little boy yet at the same time a devilish man, "What isn't fair?"

“You know what I am talking about. I can never say no when you kiss me like that,” my smile sobered, “Your sister asked me to leave.”

“Hailey was going to apologize this morning to you. She doesn’t want you to leave Taylor and you know it. Friends argue and fight, but you also makeup and move on,” Adam stood up and held his hand out to me, “So now that you have no more excuses, are you ready to go home?”

It sounded right to hear Adam say let’s go home. I looked at his out stretched hand. Was this a good idea? I really had no answer but I did realize when I looked up at him from his hand I wasn’t ready to say goodbye to him. I placed my hand into his, he pulled me up from the chair so fast that I slammed into his solid chest. His arms circling around my waist, his lips claiming mine. This time the kiss was tender, warm and full of promises.

Adam pulled away from her slightly a puzzled look on his face, “Where were you going anyway?”

“Florida.”

“What is in Florida?”

“Absolutely nothing, that is why I decided that would be a good place. I figured it was a good place to think things over. I needed to decide on a few things in my life and make some changes.”

Adam kissed the tip of her nose, “Well we have lots of open, no one around land around the ranch, so if you need time to yourself to think please do it there and promise me you will never leave without saying goodbye again.”

I smiled. I didn’t say anything because I couldn’t make promises I wasn’t a hundred percent sure I would keep, instead I brought myself up onto my tippy toes and claimed his lips with mine hoping that would be answer enough for him.

Adam had realized she hadn't answered him but he wasn't going to push her. He smiled down at her, "Are you ready to go home? Hailey is probably going crazy."

"Yes let's go."

The moment the truck pulled up in front of the house I saw the front door slam open and Hailey fly down the stairs. I didn't even have time to open the door, Hailey flung it open for me, "You actually found her and was able to stop her!"

I jumped down out of the truck to have Hailey's arms automatically around me in a bone crushing, stop breathing, kind of hug. "Taylor I am so sorry! Please, please forgive me. I said things out of anger that I should never have said. The last thing I want is for you to leave, please believe me."

Adam jumped out of the truck, came around, and grabbed Taylor's bags out of the back, "You are very lucky little sister, that is all I am going to say. Tay I am going to take your stuff back up to your room." Of course what he really wanted to do was take her stuff into his house so that way there would never be another chance for her to leave like this again, but he knew she would object and he did not want to push her.

"Thank you." I watched as Adam walked towards the house then back to her friend. "I am the one who should be apologizing. I know why you said what you did. I don't blame you at all for telling me to leave. You were right and that is why I left."

Again, Hailey threw her arms around Taylor in a bone crushing hug, "It is no excuse, it should never have been said. You are welcome to stay as long as you want and I promise to not pressure you into anything," she stepped back, "especially where you and Adam are concerned. If you guys make it in a relationship that is great but if not I'm alright with that as well. Sure I will be very disappointed because I think you are perfect for each other and I promise that is the last opinion on the subject I give. I will now only be here to listen like a friend should be.

I smiled at my friend. I knew Hailey wasn't done with inputting her opinion of the subject, I knew Hailey far better than that and I wouldn't have her any other way. Adam coming out of the house caught my attention. As I watched him walk towards us I couldn't help but to admit to myself I was glad I made the decision that I did to come back. Just looking at him brought a smile to my face and my heart started to beat faster. I was falling hard for this man and that scared the hell out of me but at the same time excited me.

I looked back at Hailey, "We are going to take it one day at a time. I have decided to stay until after the Fourth of July, I needed a vacation and a little time away from everything in Napa," I smiled back at Adam as he came to stand next to me and wrap a very protective arm around my waist, "at that time we will decide together and until then we will take it as it comes. I'm not exactly sure I'm ready for all of this but I am willing to try and see what happens."

Adam smiled down at her. He still couldn't believe she was still at the airport when he got there. Someone above was making decisions for them and he was glad for that. He hadn't realized how much she had come to mean to him until he found out this morning that she had left. He looked over to his sister, "I have told her she is to no longer listen to a word you say," he teased his sister.

"I agree," Hailey nodded.

"I have some work to do so you two go and do whatever you two do and I will see you later." He leaned down and claimed my lips in a gentle but very promising kiss then turned to his sister again, "you better remember to keep out of this,"

Hailey held up her hand, "I promise."

We both watched as Adam walked away, once he disappeared into the stables I turned back to Hailey. "I'm not going to promise anything, Hailey.

I will admit that I have feelings for Adam and that scares me to death. I don't really know what to do about the feelings I'm having or even if I want to do anything. All of this is moving a little fast for me. I do know that I'm not really ready to leave him and this thing between us, I realized that when I saw him at the airport. Although I'm not ready to say that I want to leave my life in Napa either. One thing I know for sure though is that I will need my best friend to talk to, to borrow a shoulder to cry on, and to share with."

"Taylor. Again, I am very sorry for what happened last night. Things were said that shouldn't have been said. I would love for you and Adam to get together, there is no secret there. I think you both deserve complete happiness and I think you two can find that together. However, I'm going to be here as your friend only from this point on and try to keep my opinions to myself on your relationship, unless you ask for it. I promise to be here as your best friend and lend my shoulders and ears whenever you need them," tears began to slide down Hailey's cheeks. No more was said. We hugged each other then went into the house.

Adam walked into the stable to find Ryan working in the tack room. "Hey I thought you had to work today?"

"Suppose to but Hailey was so upset about Taylor and knowing if you didn't find her then you were going to come back and murder her that I figured I better stay home to referee the situation," Ryan smiled, "I see that you found her. Everything alright?"

Adam nodded, "Well I got her to come home with me at least," he went and sat down on a stool grabbing a piece of leather that was sitting on the work bench

Ryan watched Adam as he bent the leather back and forth in his hands. He would have expected him to be a little happier about bringing her back. "So what is wrong? Is she mad that you went after her? Did she not come back on her own free will? Did you have to carry her out of the airport kicking and screaming?"

Adam laughed, "No she came on her own, of course, I can't say that I wouldn't have done that if she decided she didn't want to come back with me, no, I realized something else today," he looked back down at the leather in his hand. Ryan and he were close, but sharing feelings isn't something the two of them did on a regular day.

Ryan could see that Adam was struggling with something, "Adam I won't judge."

"I know that." Adam put the leather strap back onto the table. "Ryan, I think I have fallen in love with Taylor."

"You don't seem real happy about that."

Adam shrugged, "She says she can only stay until after the Fourth of July. That is what two weeks away. Maybe I should have let her go today. What is two weeks going to do except cause more problems when she does go home because our feelings are that much stronger. I don't want a long distance relationship. Everyone knows those never work." Once again he picked up the leather strap and then threw it across the room in frustration. "What the hell am I supposed to do?"

Ryan followed the flight of the leather strap as it hit the wall then fell to the floor. Adam hadn't had a serious relationship since he was in high school. He was always saying the ranch was all he needed and it needed all of his time so seeing him interested in a woman was good but hearing him confess that he was in love with her was something they had all pretty much given up on happening with Adam. "I can only suggest that for the next couple of weeks you work on getting her to want to stay. She loves this place, which is no secret, so that is definitely something on your side. She's just scared. She knows her job can travel wherever she does, she is just using Napa as an escape. Does she love you?"

Adam shrugged, "I have no idea. I mean, don't get me wrong, she has admitted to having feelings for me but she has never said she was in love with me."

"So you haven't told her you love her yet, right?"

"Um no, for one thing, I have just admitted to those feelings to myself. I think if I was to tell her then she would run again. She isn't ready to hear them yet, that I am sure of."

"Adam you have always said that you never have time for relationships. That the ranch needs too much of your time to get serious with anyone. Well buddy, you have exactly two weeks to convince the woman you love that she needs to stay here with you so, I suggest you take a little time away from the ranch and spend it convincing Taylor. She loves this place and this way of life, you couldn't ask for anything more perfect in a woman."

"Ryan, I just can't stop working the ranch for two weeks."

"I'm aware of that but you will need to take a little time away from it and spend it with Taylor. Go for rides, she wants to take more picture. Find the time for her. We will all help around here and I promise you everything will run smoothly."

Adam thought about what Ryan said, he was right he did always say he didn't have time for a relationship but he never felt like this either. Most of the woman interested in him wanted all of his time. They had no idea how a ranch ran and what kind of commitment it took to run one. Taylor though, on the other hand, loved this kind of life as much as he did. She wasn't after his money which every other woman he had met was. When she was around the ranch it all seemed complete. Ryan was right, he needed to make sure he took a little time for Taylor. "You up to going out tonight?"

Ryan slapped Adam on the back, this was a good start. "If Grams is alright with watching Bryson than I think going out tonight it a great idea."

“Ryan are you in here?” came Hailey’s voice from the front of the stables.

Ryan and Adam walked out of the tack room to find both women standing there, “Yeah babe what’s up?” He walked over to Taylor and gave her a hug, “Good to see you back.”

“Thank you,” I smiled up at him then walked over to Adam and wrapped my arm around his waist.
“Your brother in law here can be very convincing.”

“Well, Adam and I were just talking about taking you two beautiful women out dancing tonight.”

Adam smiled down at Taylor. She had walked over to him and wrapped her arm around his waist. This was the first time she had gone to him, definitely a step in the right direction. He vowed to himself that from this moment on he would do whatever it took to convince her to stay.

“Perfect we were just coming over to tell you guys we were going to go out shopping for a little while and grab some lunch. Now we have something to go shopping for.”

Ryan laughed, his wife was always looking for a reason to buy new clothes. “Are you leaving Bryson here with me?”

“No you guys have work to do. I’ll take him with us.”

Bryson came running into the stables, “Do I have to go shopping? I want to stay with daddy and Uncle Adam!” He ran up to his dad and wrapped his arms around him. “Please daddy can I stay with you?”

Ryan laughed and picked up his son, “I don’t blame you buddy,” he looked over at his wife, “he can stay with us. We’re going out to fix some fencing so he can come with us.”

“Thank you daddy,” the little boy wrapped his arms around his father’s neck.

Hailey walked over to her husband, "I am the luckiest woman in the world to have a husband like you," she kissed him.

"Ewww! Kissing, yuck!" Bryson wrinkled up his nose and closed his eyes, "I'm never going to kiss girls. That is gross."

Everyone laughed at the innocence of the child. Ryan rustled his son's hair, "I am going to remind you of that one of these days."

"Hailey, is it crazy to think that by staying for two more weeks, it is going to make things any easier when I do have to leave?" I pulled on the pair of jeans I brought into the dressing room to try on.

Hailey rolled her eyes, "I thought you were going to take it day by day, you haven't even made it through one day." She turned in the mirror looking at the outfit she had just put on. The jeans were a perfect fit she decided and then stepped out for Taylor to see. "Taylor that is the outfit for tonight! You look amazing!" She looked over the perfectly fitted jeans that hugged her friend's tiny waist, and then she picked the perfect color of green for a tank top with a white loose blouse that gathered at the waist. The green tank top made her eyes pop. She spun around for Taylor to see her whole outfit, "What do you think? I believe these jeans were made just for me!"

"You look phenomenal in everything Hailey. I have never seen you wear anything that doesn't look amazing on you. I watch Ryan when he looks at you, he is so proud to be next to you," I sat down on the bench that was between our dressing rooms, hating to have to admit to myself that I was a little jealous over my best friend's life. I watched as Hailey spun around and looked at her butt in the mirror, "You are right those jeans were made for you, your butt looks amazing," I laughed.

Hailey sat down next to me, "Taylor I see that look in Adam whenever he looks at you, he is crazy about you. You need to stop worrying about all of this leaving in two weeks and do exactly what you two had decided on. Take it day by day. If you don't start letting it go you will never know what will happen. Enjoy yourself for the next couple of weeks, you never know, you may decide to stay." Hailey knew she was treading in shallow waters with talking about Taylor staying but she didn't start this conversation, Taylor had, so technically she wasn't interfering.

"Hailey," I warned.

"Look, I am going to be honest with you. What do you have back home, Taylor? A lot can happen in a couple of weeks. Don't close your mind to all the possibilities."

"Hailey, my entire life is back in California, my job, my home and my family. It's not that easy to just up and move an entire life because of a couple week fling."

"Stop looking at the end of these two weeks and look at now. I know it's hard and you're scared but you used to be adventurous. You loved taking chances, not everything is going to work out in life perfectly just because you took those chances but at least at the end, even if it didn't work out, you know you had fun while finding out and there won't be any reason to look back and ask yourself "what if". If things between the two of you are supposed to work out then they will, if not, then at least you know."

I stared at the wall straight ahead for a moment thinking about what Hailey had just said, "Alright," was all I said then got up and walked back into the dressing room.

Hailey stared at the closed door of the room her friend had just gone back into. She hoped everything worked out between Adam and her. She didn't want to see her brother or her best friend's hearts broken. They both deserved happiness and she knew they could give that happiness to each other if Taylor would just let go a little and let things happen. She stood up and headed back into her dressing room, "We better start getting back. Grams will have dinner ready by the time we get home and then I am sure the guys will want to get ready to go."

Chapter 7

"This place is packed tonight," Hailey looked around, then back at me sitting across the table.

I leaned across to get a little closer to Hailey, "Is it just me or are eighty percent of the women in this place throwing me some very dirty looks."

Hailey looked around and began laughing, no Taylor was not imagining it. The single women of the place all seemed to have daggers shooting out of their eyes and directed at her, "What do you expect? You have just taken the most eligible bachelor off the market."

Adam and Ryan sat down handing each of us a beer, "This place is packed tonight. I am surprised you two found a table," Ryan commented as he looked around the room.

"Hi Adam," the voice came from behind me, I looked up over my shoulder.

"Taylor? Is that you?"

I focused on the girls face, "Lindsay?"

Lindsay smiled and adjusted her spot now placing herself behind Adam. She placed her hands on his shoulders and leaned into him, "Yep. It's been a long time since you've been back here."

I remembered Lindsay well, she was beautiful, always had been. She had been a cheerleader at school and one of the most popular girls. All the guys wanted her. Of course, I also remembered all the stories of Lindsay that went around the school so there was no wonder why all the guys wanted her. Now she had her hands on my guy. I looked at Adam who seemed to be leaning as far forward as the table would allow him and was staring down at his beer. I looked back up at Lindsay, "You look great, it's good to see you again."

Lindsay gave me a beaming smile. "Thanks you look mostly the same as well," that was a comment I wasn't sure how to take. "Of course if it weren't for those scars across you face you wouldn't have changed a bit." I tried not to but I know I flinched a little with that comment. I also noticed she smiled more when she saw that she struck a sensitive spot with me. What a bitch! She had never really liked Hailey and myself in school, which was no heart break for us, and I was pretty sure that wasn't going to change now. I watched as she brought her attention to Adam, "I came over to see if you would like to dance?" I fought the urge to hide my face but that action would only make Lindsay know that what she had said had struck me to the core.

Adam stood up. I had to keep from gasping out loud. I was both surprised and crushed, he was really going to dance with her. My temper started to boil up. I looked away so that Lindsay and Adam couldn't see the hurt in my eyes. I wouldn't allow her to see how hurt I was but if Adam thought after tonight I was going to be trying any kind of relationship with him he was going to be very wrong. How could he even entertain the idea, to even accept a dance offer from her after the comment she just made. I wanted to jump up, slap him in the face and leave but I wasn't giving either one of them the satisfaction of knowing how much they had hurt me. I will wait until the walked away and then I'll leave. The feeling of Adam's hand taking mine brought my eyes back to him. He pulled me up out of my chair placing his arm around my waist, "Sorry I'm here with Taylor, but thanks anyway. Come on, let's dance." Together we walked past Lindsay and out onto the dance floor.

Hailey and Ryan stood up, Hailey trying very hard not to laugh. Lindsay's facial expression was priceless. "Nice to see you again Lindsay," she politely commented then followed her husband out onto the dance floor.

Adam wrapped me into his arms and started dancing slowly to the beat of the song. “Alright, you can’t honestly tell me you believed I was going to dance with her?”

I tried to seem surprised, “What do you mean?”

Adam laughed, "The expression on your face when I stood up was saying it all sweetheart. It looked like you were ready to pounce on both of us.”

“Well, I have to admit, she is beautiful,” subconsciously a hand came up to my forehead and rubbed the scar.

Adam grabbed my hand and pulled it away from my face, then lightly kissed my scar, “Taylor everything about you is beautiful and I’m telling you right now, I am interested in no one except you, alright?”

I nodded but kept my face averted down until Adam placed a finger under my chin and pushed my face back up, our eyes locked, then our lips. I about melted down to the floor. What power this man’s lips had over me. His arm went back around my waist and pulled my body closer to his. Hips rubbing against hips, stomach against stomach, chest against chest and then there was his lips. The final spark setting my blood on fire was when his tongue pushed through my lips and into my mouth eagerly seeking mine, what was he doing to me? Driving me crazy, that was what he was doing to me. For a moment I forgot there were other people around us and knowing what I was feeling pressed up against my stomach was a reaction to him just kissing me. I almost didn’t care that there were people around us, I wanted Adam and I wanted him now.

“You two need to find a room,” the voice came from behind me and broke the magic between us, which was probably for the best right now. I looked around to find Hailey and Ryan dancing. I smiled at my friend and then looked back at Adam but something over his shoulder caught my eye. I looked up to find Lindsay dancing with a guy that I also recognized from school although I couldn’t remember his name. The daggers that

Lindsay was throwing at me with her eyes was telling me she wasn't very happy to be dancing with anyone but Adam, I would say I saw a little threat behind the look. I sent a look back informing Lindsay I wasn't intimidated by her one bit and to stay away from Adam. There were no words spoken between the two of us but the both of us knew that each understood the other.

Adam's voice brought my attention back to him, "Would you stay with me tonight Taylor?"

I was shocked then I had to admit a little scared and strangely at the same time turned on. I wasn't sure if I was ready for the sexual part of this relationship. Just a minute ago I had completely lost myself in his kiss and was admitting to myself that I wanted nothing more than to have him deep inside of me, but, no matter what my body was saying, my mind was screaming at me to slow down.

Adam could see the fear pop into her eyes and the shock all at the same time, "Just stay with me. I promise nothing more than you want, we can even just stay up and talk all night. I'll be honest, it kills me to say goodnight every night and leave to my own empty house. If at any time during the night you want to leave, no problem." He watched as expression after expression changed over Taylor's face. She was thinking about it that was better than saying no right away. The final expression was not a positive one. He could tell he had to convince her quickly, "Taylor, please trust me. I promise no more than you want."

I smiled up at him, "What are you afraid of? That I will leave in the middle of the night or something?"

Adam smiled. He had to be honest, that did play somewhere in the back of his mind, "No, I plan to convince you somehow someway that leaving isn't a good idea," he waited for a moment longer, "Taylor, please stay with me tonight."

"What would your sister say?"

Adam rolled his eyes, "Taylor please, I'm surprised Hailey hasn't suggested it herself or came over and dropped off all your stuff at my house. But, we are grown adults I don't really care what she or anyone thinks, but I honestly don't think she is going to be bothered by it."

I thought about it, he was right. I knew that. I was looking for an excuse and that one was a poor one. I noticed the song had ended only to be followed by another slow song. Adam never broke his hold on me, we just danced right into the next song. Our bodies were tightly meshed together and my body was screaming at me to tell him yes and to be honest, if it meant he would hold me all night like this then my brain was following with the same answer.

I looked up at Adam. He was watching me, waiting for me to answer him. He wasn't pushing me into anything. Of course I remembered the day we had rode out to see the herd by the stream. We had almost lost all control there. Would I be able to keep enough control to say no again? Did I want to say no to any of it?

I had to start breaking down some of my walls. I knew that if I was going to give us a fair chance then maybe starting with this one would be a good start. I nodded my head, "Alright I will stay with you tonight," I answered before I could talk myself out of it again.

Adam realized the first barrier had finally been broken down. He claimed her lips in a heated kiss, he could find no words. This kiss however, did all the talking for him.

The ride home seemed to go quicker than normal. My heart started beating faster and faster with every mile we passed, bringing us closer to the ranch. The closer they got to being home the more I realized I couldn't do this, I wasn't ready. Sure, Adam had said that nothing more than I wanted would happen tonight and I knew I could trust Adam to keep to that and not force me into anything, but even just staying with him seemed to be too much even if nothing happened. Who was I fooling? Did I honestly believe we could sleep in the same bed and not have anything happen? If I had to be honest with myself, I knew I didn't possess that kind of will power against him, the day out with the herd and tonight on the dance floor completely convinced me of that. That knowledge alone made me realize that staying the night with him was not a good idea. I wasn't ready for all of this. Just this morning I was ready to fly away from Adam and now I was talking about staying the night with him. What was I thinking? As soon as we were home and alone I would let him know I had changed my mind and hopefully he wouldn't be too mad at me.

The truck pulled up in front of the house. Adam jumped out quickly and opened the passenger door behind him where I was sitting. I didn't move at first, I just looked down at my hands, "Taylor come on please trust me!" Adam's plea brought my eyes up to his. I almost had to admit to him that it wasn't him I didn't trust, but myself. I took his hand and jumped down from the seat.

"Night you two. See you in the morning," Hailey said not looking back as her and Ryan went into the house leaving us outside alone. This was the time to tell him. We were alone and I was close to the house. I could tell him I had changed my mind then make a dash for the house before he could say something charming to change my mind.

I heard Adam's laugh. I felt him take my hand and then wait, yes that is what I thought, my feet were moving, I was walking with Adam to his house which was taking me further away from the other house. I had to stop this and now, but no matter how much I kept telling myself to speak up, no words were coming out of my mouth. My feet just kept moving in the opposite direction than where I wanted to go.

I followed him up the stairs to the porch. Run, yell, do something I kept telling myself. Why was no part of my body listening to me? We stopped right in front of the front door, finally my feet listened. I looked up at Adam expecting to find him frowning and wondering why I stopped but instead he was smiling down at me. Wait, did I stop us or did he? Adam leaned forward and kissed me tenderly on the forehead then he opened the front door, he stepped inside pulling me with him.

Once I stepped inside I looked around. His home was.... well, very surprising. It opened up right into a living room. One large brown sofa, a love seat that matched, and a recliner were placed in the middle of the large room all sitting on top of a hug area rug. Redwood floors stretched through the entire area. The large living room opened up right into a large size kitchen with all stainless steel appliances. To the other side was the dining area with a large pup table, the three rooms creating one large great room. Decorated all cowboy of course, that part not surprising to me at all. This ranch, the horses, this was Adam's life and he was surrounding himself with everything he loved in his life. To top off my surprise, it was clean! Not one thing out of place. I looked around the rooms and then noticed the stairway that lead to the upper floor which must be where the bedrooms were all located.

Adam watched as Taylor looked around. She seemed surprised and he told her that, finally breaking the silence. "Why do you look so surprised? Just because I live alone doesn't mean I don't know how to keep a place clean."

I looked up at him. He was smiling, that smile that melted me every time. "Sorry," I hated that he knew what I was thinking, "but yes I am surprised," I told him honestly. "Your home is beautiful."

He laughed and led me over to the couch. "Thank you. I am glad you approve," he pointed at the couch, "Have a seat and relax a little," he turned and headed for the kitchen.

I watched as he went to the frig and opened it pulling out a couple of beers holding them up to her, "Would you like one?"

Nodding, "Yes please." I watched as he closed the frig and came back to the couch and sat down next to me. He handed me the bottle and laughed, "Tay honey relax. I am not going to attack you, you look like a deer caught in headlights."

I took a long drink of my beer and then took a deep breath and sat back against the soft cushions of the couch.

Adam watched as her face seemed to relax a little after a couple drinks of her beer. He knew she was fighting the need to run out of the house and away from him. He could read everything in her face from the moment she jumped out of the truck. He was relieved however, she may have wanted to run away from him but she hadn't and he was going to make sure she didn't. He finally had her over at his house, they were alone and he had made up his mind that he was going to make her change her mind about wanting to go home in a couple of weeks no matter what he had to do. He loved her too much to let her go, "Are you alright?"

I looked up at him a little surprised of his question. Damn, he knew I was nervous, he knew I wasn't comfortable. I took a deep breath, one more drink, then forced myself to smile before I answered, "Yes I'm fine."

"You don't lie very well sweetheart," he laughed, leaned over, and claimed my lips in a very simple kiss. "You want to see the rest of the house?" His face was only inches from mine.

I looked towards the stairs. The only thing left that could be up those stairs were the bedrooms, "Ummm, I think I can wait just a little bit to see the rest. I'm not finished with my beer yet." I turned my attention back to him and found myself starring straight into those crystal blue eyes, my heart melted. I could lose myself in those eyes and forget everything that is running through my mind telling me to take things slow, I had to be careful of that. If he ever found out that little fact I knew for sure I would lose the battle between us.

Adam noticed the change in her. It was almost like her eyes cleared and she relaxed a little. Or was he just imagining that? "I'm going to kiss you then."

The announcement a little shocking, I thought to myself. He had just kissed me. Why was he telling me that he was going to kiss me again?

Adam realized that this may have been the wrong idea, having her come tonight, because now as they both sat on his couch, in his house, alone he realized this meant a lot more than he could imagine. He wanted her in every way there could be. He leaned forward slowly, he wasn't sure if he started this if he would be able to just turn it off if she said no. He was hoping that if she was going to say no to him that she would do it before he kissed her. So by taking it slow he was giving her the time.

I watched as Adam closed the space between us, each inch he moved closer the more smoked over those beautiful eyes became. My breathing started to feel shallow. Now I understood why he announced that he was going to kiss me. He was giving me a chance to stop him. My heart began to race, I needed to stop him, I wasn't ready for this so why wasn't I able to create and speak the words I needed to. It was just one simple word, this one word would stop him and I knew that. Adam would never hurt me or force me, my heart completely told me that, but all the same, that one little word was not coming out.

At the first touch of his lips I completely lost my breath, it was like it was sucked right out of my lungs by him. Oh god, my words were not going to be created. My body was going to completely ignore my mind even if it was screaming for me to say something. The only thing my lips were going to do were kiss him back. The feeling that exploded through my veins from this first small touch of his lips was something I realized I had never felt before, not even when I thought I was completely in love with my ex-husband. My body had never felt like this.

Taylor wasn't the only one not prepared to feel what she did. Adam's mind spun out of control the second their lips met, "Tay," he spoke against her lips, "if you want me to stop please tell me to stop now."

His breath as he spoke smelled of beer and Adam, an intoxicating scent, one she had never paid attention to before but now, it just added to the flame building inside of her. She needed to tell him to stop but once again the words weren't forming. She found herself claiming his lips with hers. All thoughts of leaving and going back to her room at the other house disappeared from her mind. All that mattered to her now was trying to figure out how to get her body closer to his.

Feeling her lips take his was the invitation that Adam needed from Taylor. She was not going to tell him no, or at least he hoped she wasn't going to change her mind now and say no. He wasn't sure if he could stop now even if she pleaded. Pleading, the only thing Taylor was pleading about was for him to claim her mouth and body. His arms wrapped around her smashing her chest against his. He could feel the racing of her heart, no wait that may be his own heart. He pulled her up so that she was sitting on his lap, his lips trailing the curve of her chin, and when her head fell back exposing her throat to him he trailed kisses slowly down her neck, to her chest, lightly kissing her chest just stopping where one breast began to form under the collar of her shirt and then worked his way back up to her lips. Her arms wrapped around his neck and she smashed her chest to his, her hands moving and tugging in his hair. The low growl he heard was from his own throat.

His lips felt like magic against the flesh of my neck. Each inch of skin that he kissed seemed to burn after he left it how could just his lips send this kind of feeling pulsing through my veins. I felt like my body was going to explode from the pleasure and he was only kissing me. When his lips took mine again I hung onto him like a life line and when I heard the low growl from his throat I knew I was affecting him just as much as he was affecting me. As he started to pull away from my lips once again I heard myself whimper. I wasn't ready to give up those lips but he continued with small kisses up to my ear and I felt his hot breath in my ear as he spoke, "Tay you need to stop me now if you don't want this because, I will be honest, past this point, I am not sure if I will be able to stop. I want you too bad," I could hear the control in his voice was barely there.

I turned my head to look into his eyes, eyes of crystal now were deep ice blue, speaking passion through them. Both of our hearts were beating erratically, my core was throbbing, I could feel the moisture between my legs and against my leg I felt the proof of his passion, his manhood was hard and straining against his jeans. I felt alive again! It's been a very long time since I've felt like this. Honestly now that I thought about it, I wasn't sure if I have ever felt like this.

I looked away and down at his hand that was at my waist. I took his hand into mine and brought it up to my lips where I kissed his knuckles. Looking back up into his eyes I gave, what I hoped, was a seductive smile, "I want you Adam," and then I placed his hand onto my breast.

I watched as he closed his eyes and took a deep breath. I felt his hand squeeze my breast gently, I even heard a very low groan escape from him, "Tay," was all he said as he opened his eyes then claimed my lips in a kiss that threw even more fire racing through me, settling in my deepest area almost sending me over the edge before things even really got started.

His tongue darted into my mouth, seeking and finding mine. His hand massaged my breast through my shirt. I wanted nothing between us. I wanted to feel his skin on mine. My hands worked from around his neck, down his chest to the waist of his pants where his shirt was tucked in. I pulled it free as my hands slid his shirt up his stomach to his chest, my hands contacted with his skin, it was on fire but so smooth.

Adam moaned when he felt her knuckles graze his skin as she pulled his shirt free of his pants. His kiss became more intense, deeper his tongue went into her mouth, all he wanted to do was tear her clothes off. He hated this barrier that stood between them. He wanted to feel her skin on his.

I raised his shirt, our lips separated for the slightest second it took for me to pull it up over his head. I dropped it onto the ground and placed both palms against his chest. My hands running over the well-developed muscles, proof of all the hard work and time he spends on the ranch. "I want to feel your skin against mine," I whispered against his lips not waiting for him to take the hint. I pulled away just far enough to pull my own shirt up and over my head letting it fall carelessly to the floor. I wrapped my arms around his neck, our skin touched, my breath hitched.

Adam was afraid for a moment to move, she was in complete control, surprising him. Here he was afraid she would turn him away when it was completely the opposite. She was like a tiger pouncing on its prey and he would love nothing more than to allow her to devour him. He needed to regain a little control of himself, but the way her tongue was savoring his mouth, there was no possibility of that. His hand slid up her side to her breast again, she hadn't taken off her bra, and he wanted everything off, no barriers at all. His hand cupped one breast, he heard her moan against his mouth. He slid his hand down to just under her breast, he planned to just slide the bra up over her head instead of messing with the hooks, this would be faster, but the feeling of her skin had changed, it was like it raised a little, this caught his attention, he pulled away from her to look at what it was.

Him pulling away from my lips brought me enough out of my trance to notice where his hand was and what had caused him to pull away, his words just confirmed it, "Taylor what is this?" he rubbed his finger over the raised skin. Before he could see what it was, I pulled my arms up between us, pushing his hand away and covering the spot.

"It's nothing. I think we better stop." I quickly stood up and turned away from him. Adam grabbed my arm and spun me around.

With her standing and him still sitting on the couch, his eyes were directly at the level of where his hand had previously been. His eyes grew round with shock. It was another scar, much deeper than the ones on her face. It began just under her right breast and ran down to end just above her belly button. He looked up at her, she was looking anywhere but at him, "Taylor, how did you get this scar?"

I could feel his eyes on my face but I couldn't look at him. I didn't want to see the disgust in his eyes at my deformity. I couldn't believe I had gotten so caught up with how Adam was making me feel that I had forgotten about the most distorted part of my body. My scars on my face I had come to accept and look at every day. This scar however was different. I still couldn't look in a full length mirror if I was naked. No one had known about this scar except my parents and myself, not even Hailey.

I quickly pulled away from Adam, taking him by surprise by such a quick movement that I was able to pull out of his grasp. I found my shirt and as fast as my shaking hands could manage, I pulled it back on.

Adam quickly stood up, grabbed my arm and pulled me around to look at him. I kept my eyes diverted down, "Taylor don't close me out again. Talk to me. How did you get that scar? Did Mike do that one as well?"

Hearing the disgust in his voice, I brought my eyes up to look at him. I tried to pull my arm free but he wasn't releasing it, "Let me go please?"

Was that fear in her eyes that he was seeing? Was she afraid of him? He almost released her then he decided against it. She had to start trusting him, "No! You are not going to run from me this time Tay. You need to talk to me. Did that bastard do that?" His eyes looked down at her stomach now covered by her shirt.

Again, I pulled at my arm. This time Adam released it. I took a couple steps back to put some distance between them. "It doesn't matter how I got the scar Adam."

Adam stood silent for a moment and he just stared at her. No more, he couldn't do this, he threw his hands up in the air in a surrender gesture and took a couple steps back creating more distance between them. "Fine! If you aren't going to talk to me, to trust me, then this thing we have between us is never going to work. To be honest, I don't think that even bothers you! You have fought this thing between us," he gestured with one hand waving between them, "since the beginning. I give up."

He waited for a moment for her to comment back, but she just stood there, arms crossed at her chest, tears filling her eyes but not spilling over yet. That was almost his undoing, he knew she was in pain, he knew her ex-husband had hurt badly but that scar was making him realize there was a lot more to that story then he knew, and if this relationship was going to work she was going to have to start opening up to him. Her silence at that moment told him she was not willing to do that and no matter how much he loved her, he was not going to be able to handle her shutting him out.

"You can run home or to Florida or where ever in the hell you want to go Taylor. I'm done with the games," he turned from her and headed for the stairs, "you know where the door is," he said as he climbed the stairs never looking back at her, she watched as he disappeared.

I stood there for a moment looking at the stairway. I wanted to run up the stairs and wrap my arms around him but I wasn't ready to answer the questions that he wanted answers to. Those tears finally began to roll down my cheek. He said he was done, told me I could leave and I wasn't going to beg. No, I was going to leave tomorrow.

Adam watched out his bedroom window as Taylor walked across the yard to the other house. A part of him wanted to run after her and beg her to forgive his words, but he knew if she couldn't open up to him than their relationship would never last. No matter how much he loved her he couldn't live with the fact that she didn't trust him. His hand came up to his still naked chest, it felt like it was being crushed. Feelings from years ago came rushing back, he now remembered why he swore to never get involved again. He was convinced he had been wrong to think like that with Taylor, but she had too many skeletons in her closet. This time though the pain was more intense, he loved Taylor. He no longer questioned it, but she just didn't love him back.

He turned from the window when she disappeared into the house. He walked over to his bed and laid down, an arm going over his eyes, one tear escaped down his cheek.

I was almost to my room when Hailey came out of Bryson's room. Her hair was a mess and she wore a robe, Hailey looked at me confused when she asked, "I thought you were staying with Adam tonight?"

I stopped one hand on the door knob of my room. I didn't look at my friend, "Plans changed and tomorrow I'm leaving. This thing between your brother and I isn't going to work," I opened my door and went inside, never looking at my friend and then shut the door behind me.

Hailey stood there staring at the now shut door of her friend's room. She was shocked! How did everything change so fast? She knew she had promised she wasn't going to get involved with her friend and her brother anymore, but something was very wrong and she had to know what happened.

She didn't bother to knock. She knew Taylor probably wouldn't answer the door if she had. She walked in to find Taylor standing at the window, her back to Hailey. "You want to tell me what happened?"

I knew Hailey wouldn't leave without knowing. I rubbed the scar on my stomach through my shirt, "my scars got in the way," was all I said, never turning around.

Hailey stood there for a moment. What was that supposed to mean? Her scars never bothered her brother and she had thought Taylor had gotten passed her fear of that. "Taylor, I am sorry but I don't understand. What do you mean your scars got in the way?"

Taylor said nothing, at first Hailey wasn't sure if Taylor was even listening to her, then surprised her when she quickly removed her shirt and spun around to face her best friend. Standing there in her jeans and bra Hailey's eyes went straight to the large scar on Taylor's stomach. Hailey's hand flew up to cover her mouth but not before a gasp escaped her lips. She took a couple of steps closer but stopped when she saw Taylor shy away.

My arms went around my stomach, trying to cover the scar, surprising myself that I reacted by showing my friend the way I did. Hailey however had already gotten a pretty good look at the scar. It was about two inches wide and started just above her belly button and disappeared under her bra at her right breast, "My god Taylor! Why did you never tell me? Mike did that to you, didn't he?"

I slowly nodded then turned away from my friend to look back out the window again. "Yes, he wanted to make sure I had no chance of having the baby. There was no chance of the baby living through this kind of injury, so he got what he wanted. Now I get to live with the constant reminder."

"So what does this have to do with you and Adam?" Hailey knew her brother wouldn't turn his back on her because of this. "You can't tell me he ended things between you because you told him about this."

I shook my head, "No, he ended it because I wouldn't tell him about the scar. He said I didn't trust him and that I didn't want this relationship so why fight it anymore." I started sobbing, my arms tightened around myself in a hug, "You didn't see the disgust in his eyes or hear it in his voice Hailey."

Hailey walked over to Taylor and turned her around, "Why would you think any of that was aimed at you? He was disgusted I am sure, I am too, but not at you. It's at Mike. How could any person do that to another? That man is insane."

"Hailey look at me!" I threw my arms out giving Hailey once again a full view of the scar, "Look at all the reminders of how weak and stupid I was. Your brother doesn't need someone like that, he needs a woman with strength to stand beside him. I couldn't handle seeing that look in his eyes every time he looked at me." Tears were streaming down my cheeks, my chest was very heavy, the pain all around was beginning to be too much.

Hailey wrapped her arms around Taylor. This was crushing her, all this pain her friend was going through, it made her want to fly out to California, find Mike and beat the hell out of him. Hailey also knew her brother well enough to know that was what he was thinking as well. She pulled back and looked at Taylor, "You need to go and tell Adam everything that happened that night with Mike, Taylor."

“He told me to leave Hailey. He even told me to go home, he was done, he is pretty mad at me. I could see it in his eyes.”

“If you looked deeper it was probably more like pain then anger. Adam cares for you, Taylor. You need to give him a chance to prove it though. You need to trust him fully, you need to go and talk to him.”

I pulled out of Hailey’s arms, “I will think about it. Maybe tomorrow.” I walked over to my bed and sat down.

“No, not tomorrow, you need to go tonight. Either you go over there and talk to him or I am going over there and bringing him back here, you decide, but you are talking tonight.” Hailey was waiting for Taylor to tell her to mind her own business, she knew she was pushing her friend but she knew that Taylor had read Adam wrong.

“What if he doesn’t want to talk to me?”

“Taylor, I seriously doubt that, but if some slim chance things don’t work out tonight then I will take you to the airport myself and I will never mention your relationship with each other again.”

I sat there for a moment contemplating what Hailey had offered. I pulled my shirt back on that I had been holding and took a deep breath. I was tired of Mike’s actions taking over my life. I knew deep down that Adam wasn’t disgusted at me or by the sight of me, he was mad at what he thought had caused the scars. I didn’t want to leave Adam but I knew Hailey was right, I did need to trust Adam enough to tell him everything that had happened that night and I needed to tell him tonight, “Alright, you’re right. I probably handled everything wrong and he deserves better than that. I will go over there and try to talk to him.” Without waiting for Hailey to say anything else I got up from the bed and left the room.

Hailey stood there for a moment. She couldn’t believe how much she didn’t know about that night between Taylor and Mike and she had spent how many days with her in the hospital? How was it that she never found out about all of it? She knew Taylor had been pregnant, she knew she had lost the baby, but she thought that was just because of the beating that Mike gave her. Picturing that scar again in her mind made her sick. That man had taken a knife to her. Hailey's heart broke, her friend would always have that constant reminder of that horrible night and everything that she had lost. Taylor had said she had been stupid and weak. Her friend had been anything but stupid and weak. To live through that kind of attack showed how strong and brave her friend had been. She was very proud of Taylor and she knew that once Taylor confided in Adam about that night, everything would change between her friend and her brother.

Chapter 8

I stood in front of Adam's door for what seemed like forever. I had no idea how to approach this. I didn't know if I should knock or just walk in. I brought my hand up to knock just as the door opened up. Adam stood there, still in just his jeans and no shirt, although he had removed his boots and now stood barefooted.

"I heard footsteps on the porch," he answered the question in my eyes.

"Can we talk please?"

Adam looked down and saw her twisting her own fingers within each other, she was nervous. "I don't think we have much to talk about, Taylor."

I had to admit, I didn't like it when he called me Taylor instead of Tay. It usually meant he was upset or frustrated with me. I took a deep breath and closed my eyes, "I want to tell you about the night Mike attacked me." I opened my eyes and a tear escaped down my cheek.

Adam fought back the urge to wrap his arms around her. That one single tear broke his heart but he knew if he took her into his arms now then she probably wouldn't tell him anything and he wanted her to talk to him. He moved aside so that she could enter the house. He didn't look at her as she walked passed him.

I entered the house and stood there in the living room. I turned and watched as Adam shut the door, still without looking at me he pointed to the couch, "Have a seat, do you want something to drink?"

I shook my head, "No thank you," I sat down on the couch and watched as Adam sat across from me in the recliner. I was disappointed that he didn't sit next to me. I needed to feel his strength next to me but he made it clear he wasn't going to make this very easy for me, and I didn't blame him. I closed my eyes for a moment finding my own strength. I don't talk about that day at all, but I knew it was time to with Adam. I took a deep breath and opened my eyes.

"The day started with my doctor's appointment. I hadn't been feeling well so I decided to go see someone and find out what was wrong. Well, I found out nothing was wrong, I was pregnant."

Adam saw the sparkle that entered Taylor's eyes when she spoke of being pregnant, yet he had to admit he felt a little jealous.

"I was so excited when I found out. I couldn't wait to get home and tell Mike. I had hoped when he found out we were going to have a baby he would change." Adam wanted to ask her about how she wanted him to change but he decided not to interrupt. "I got home and found Mike in the kitchen cleaning some camera equipment. I walked up and just told him. I was waiting for the excitement but instead I got his anger. He first accused me of cheating on him and how my bastard child was never going to be born."

I rubbed my stomach and closed my eyes and tears started streaming down my cheeks, "I will never forget the look in his eyes. I didn't even recognize him. He punched my face a couple of times I guess, honestly, I don't remember exactly. The whole thing is still a little blurry for me. I remember him shoving me back and I fell against the coffee table hitting my head and knocking me out. Next thing I remember I am waking up in the hospital. My mom told me that her and my father had found me. That is when I found out about losing the baby." I stopped speaking for a moment, I never opened my eyes though, but I knew Adam had come to sit next to me but he still didn't touch me and all I wanted to do was bury myself into his chest. I knew I would feel protected in his arms I always do but I had to do this without his arms and protection. I had to open up to him with my own strength.

"They told me it looked like he had taken a knife and sliced in one movement from beneath my breast to my belly button. I wasn't supposed to live through the night. Once the night passed they told my parents it would still be touchy for at least a week, but I made it." I took a deep breath to calm myself and finally opened my eyes. I wasn't facing Adam though, I was looking straight ahead. I wasn't ready to see his reaction, "I can honestly say for the first six months, especially during the physical healing part, I had wished I had died. No one knows that though. I always tried to be strong around my parents, but I looked at the scars every day. I was going through a divorce and I couldn't protect my child, I had seen myself as a failure in every way."

I looked down at my hands that were folded in my lap, "Hailey didn't even know about the scar on my stomach. To be honest I'm not sure why my mom never said anything to her and when I was awake and aware I had begged my parents not to say anything."

I took another deep breath and then finally turned my head to look at Adam. I was surprised to see anger in his eyes. "I am sorry Adam for everything I have put you through. You are the first guy I have even attempted to have a relationship with. Trust me, I didn't come here looking for a relationship either. Everyone was scared for me with Mike getting out of jail. I apologize for everything I have put you through. I don't blame you for being mad at me. I am very upset with myself. I am leaving tomorrow that way you can get back to your normal life without a half crazed person screwing up your life." I looked back down at my hands and rubbed them across my pant legs, "I thank you for giving me a chance to explain." I then stood up and started walking past him to leave. I was going to burst into tears again any minute and I didn't want to do that in front of him. That was the moment I realized leaving was the last thing I wanted to do but I knew I had already ruined things between us.

Adam grabbed my hand as I tried to leave. I looked down at him. His eyes had changed, there was no sign of anger anymore, but there was something there in his eyes, something I hadn't seen before. "Where are you going?"

Surprise flashed across my face, "Honestly, I am going to cry my eyes out and pack."

Adam pulled me down to sit on his lap, "No packing will be needed and you crying, well, you can use my shoulder for that."

Puzzled, I looked at him, "Earlier you told me you had enough. I understand that, trust me. It's not easy living with myself, I could only imagine what it is like for someone else to handle me."

Adam smiled at me, one of his heart stopping grins that I was falling in love with. "I only wanted you to trust me, Tay," he pushed a piece of hair away from my face, "I want nothing more than to show you how you deserve to be treated. You are amazing but you had to find it in yourself to allow me in. You coming back and telling me everything is all I wanted, for you to feel like you can talk to me, that I'm not judging you. I can now understand a little more when things you do or the reactions you have to certain situations."

"You looked so angry a minute ago when I was telling you what happened," I pointed out.

"Hell Tay, I'm not going to deny my anger. I would love to rip that man's head right of his shoulder for what he did to you but I could never be angry with you. Even earlier tonight I wasn't angry with you. I was hurt because you were pushing me away again. It was killing me that you were once again not trusting me."

As I listened a sense of relief wash over me knowing that Adam now knew everything about my past. Strangely I felt better, ready to move forward with him and this relationship and where ever it may lead us.

Adam watched her for a moment. She didn't say a word but he could almost sense her body relaxing. He placed a hand behind her head and claimed her lips in a very slow kiss. My mind began to twirl just from one touch of his lips. Everything from my past faded and the only thing I could focus on at the moment was the tantalizing play of his lips on mine. Although he wouldn't deepen the kiss, he just played with my lips with his and it was driving me crazy. My body ignited all over again, just from a small play of his lips. My body shuttered and I could feel the moisture between my thighs again. The little kisses weren't enough, I needed more. I wrapped my arms around Adam's neck, my fingers digging into his hair. I tilted my head slightly and demanded more of his lips, his mouth opening just enough for my tongue to dart inside seeking his. I heard his deep moan and almost giggled, he was just affected by me as I was by him. God how I wanted this man and I wanted all of him, I could freely admit that now, there were no more secrets to hide. Not saying I was comfortable with the scars that marred my body but at least I didn't have to hide them. Then it hit me like a ton of bricks. The realization that I loved Adam, it shocked me so much that I quickly ended the kiss and pulled away from him, to the point that I almost fell right off his lap. I just sat there staring wide eyed at him. I wasn't falling in love with my best friend's brother that I have known most of my life, I was completely in love with him.

Adam quickly tightened his arms around Taylor to keep her from falling to the floor when she quickly ended the kiss that she started. What the heck was that all about? One minute she kissing him like her life depended on his lips, the next basically throwing herself off his lap. He looked at her wide eyed expression but he couldn't read what she was thinking. He searched her eyes for a moment and just waited for her to say something, but she said nothing, she just stared at him. One thing he did notice was she wasn't pulling out of his arms, which had to be some kind of a good sign, "Tay what's wrong?"

"Make love to me." It wasn't a question it was more like a plea and Adam wasn't sure he heard her right. From the expression on her face he was pretty sure she was just as surprised at herself for saying it.

I wondered for a moment if I had actually said that out loud and by the expression on Adam's face I was pretty sure the answer to that was yes! I just told him to make love to me. I wasn't sorry that I had said it though, I wanted him, I loved and wanted all of him. I was completely sure of that now.

The look that transformed into her eyes shocked him even more than complete seduction, and that smile, he didn't understand how one smile could make him hard. Dear god, this woman was going to drive him mad! Her hands snaked back around his neck and back into his hair. She pulled him so close that this time when she spoke her lips brushed across his, "Make love to me, please." He searched her eyes for a moment, their lips still just grazing each other's, "Are you sure?"

I nodded. I was positive. I had never been surer of anything then I was about wanting him, "Yes very sure," Adam watched as her eyes dimmed a little, "I will leave if you don't want me."

"Hell no you aren't leaving," he shot up from the couch still holding her in his arms and walked over to the stairs. He stopped just before he started to climb them, "Tay if we go upstairs and make love, I am warning you now, I am going to do whatever it takes to make you stay here with me. You won't be moving back to California if I can help it."

Surprisingly, that didn't scare me anymore. I loved him and I was pretty sure there was no way I could leave him now that I had admitted these feelings to myself. I smiled, pulled his head down to mine and then right before claiming his lips, "Make love to me Adam."

That was all he needed to hear, he took the stairs possibly two at a time, he really wasn't paying attention. All that mattered to him at that moment was getting her into his room before he took her right there on the stairs. He never let go of her, not even when he placed her onto his bed. How he managed that without falling on top of her he wasn't sure, but he wasn't going to release her for nothing. He was too afraid this was some kind of dream and if he let her go, he would wake up and find his arms empty.

I however, felt the softness of the bed under me and realized we must be in his room in his bed. Curiosity started to kick in for a brief moment. What did his room look like? Was it as neat as the downstairs had been? Of course those questions only lasted seconds in my brain, I would have to wonder later about the room, right now his lips were tracing a path down my neck and my blood was beginning to boil. Dear god, I was going to melt. I knew there was no way my body could with stand the kind of heat that was being created, my breasts ached, and my very moist center was throbbing for him. His skin felt amazingly smooth under my hands, I could feel the muscles ripple along his back as my nails lightly traced up and down his spine.

Adam found the edge of her shirt and his lips only left her skin for the quick moment it took him to pull her shirt up over her head. He rolled her over just enough to unhook her bra and then discarded that onto the floor with her shirt. He waited briefly, they had been in this position a couple of times, each of those times she was completely driving him mad and then stopping him instantly. He wasn't sure if he could stop this time if she asked. She wasn't stopping him. He looked down at her, there was just enough light flowing in from the hallway for him to see her, "You are beautiful," he whispered before claiming one nipple with his mouth.

I gasped at the first contact of his tongue on my nipple, arching my back wanting so much more, needing so much more. I had never felt the molten heat that raced through my body before like I felt it now with Adam. He circled my nipple with his tongue, I moaned. He traced his tongue across one breast down the valley between both of my breast then back up the other breast finding what he searched for my other nipple making sure that one received attention as well.

Adam sucked gently on her left breast has his hand found her right. His finger once again came across the scar just below the breast, he lifted his head and brought his eyes down to her scar, he bent forward and lightly kissed the beginning of the scar.

I felt his lips just below my breast right where I knew the scar began, I sobered enough to put my hands on each side of his face and stop his kisses, "Please Adam don't ruin this by bringing attention to the ugly parts of my body, they were caused by ugliness and I am not proud of it."

Adam pulled his face away from her grasp, his eyes never leaving hers once again he gently kissed the raised flesh under her breast, "Everything about you is beautiful Tay," he laid a couple more kisses down the length of the scar, "this is proof of how much strength you have. You fought to live! That strength and your fight are two the reasons I have completely fallen head over heels in love with you. After tonight there will hopefully not be one inch of your body that I have not kissed." He continued as he kissed to the end of the scar then back up once again claiming one of her breast.

I looked at him in shock for a moment did he just say that he loved me? Not much time was given to that thought for I felt his lips sucking one breast into his mouth once again and gently sucking, my world began to spin once again. I could feel him hard against my thigh, the core in between my legs throbbed and threatened to explode if I didn't have this man soon.

I rolled us both over now, I straddled him. My hands slowly ran down his chest, my eyes never leaving his. I watched as he laid there crossing his arms behind his head as though he was watching a show. I traced my fingernails lightly around one flat nipple, then the other. I watched as Adam closed his eyes and took a deep breath, slowly letting it out. I smiled. Yes, I had the same effect on him that he had on me.

Adam knew if he didn't control himself a little he was going to attack her, just the feeling of her nails on his skin was driving him crazy. No one had had this amount of control over him before, and here was Taylor creating feelings inside of him that were almost scaring him. He felt her fingers trace a path down his stomach and stop at the waist band of his jeans, this brought his eyes back open. She was still watching him, her fingers began to unbutton his pants, first the top button then the next until they were all loose. She folded her fingers into the waist band of his boxer briefs and at the first touch of her knuckles touching his skin, Adam shot up so fast and had them both on their feet in front of the bed before she knew what happened. Once he made sure she had her balance he released her and quickly removed the rest of his clothing. He stood there for a moment as he watched her eyes look at him from head to toe.

My breath lodged in my throat. Here in front of me stood this man, perfectly chiseled from years of hard labor. A body that was not only muscle but you knew that would be amazing to be curled against, feeling nothing but protection. My hands moved to my own jeans, the only clothes that I still had on and the only barrier that would stop the touch of his entire naked body to be against mine. I unbuttoned my pants, and then followed with the zipper but before I was able to pull them down over my hips he stepped forward and pushed my hands away. He slowly pushed my pants and remaining garments down over my hips, past my knees, and then I stepped out of them his hands slowly running up my legs to my hips. He pushed me back slightly and drank in my body with his eyes.

I fought the urge to wrap my arms around my naked body. I hated looking at myself in a mirror, why should he enjoy looking at it? My hands started to come up but Adam grabbed them almost like he knew what I was thinking, "Beautiful, my god Tay, there are not words to describe how gorgeous you are." He wrapped his arms around my waist and pulled our bodies together. That first feel of skin against skin was almost the end of both of us. The bolt of electricity that shot between our bodies was so powerful it buckled my knees.

Adam caught her and picked her up laying her back down on the bed next to him. His lips found and devoured the taste of pure pleasure on her lips. Adam traced his tongue down her neck, across her chest and once again found home with one of her breast, sucking it into his mouth, while his hand began a journey at her knee up her thigh until he found the spot that was radiating heat, begging for his touch. His finger lightly brushed over her satiny folds of skin in between her legs. She was hot and wet. He sucked a little harder on her nipple, she raised her hips, spreading her legs wide inviting him into her. That move almost caused him to lose all control. He slide one finger deep inside of her. Taylor moaned and thrust her hips up pushing his finger deeper inside. Adam slid his finger out only to thrust back in over and over, "You are so wet, you have no idea how much I want to taste you but right now I only want to be deep inside of you."

His words moved me into action. There was nothing more that I wanted right now then him inside of me. My hand clawed its way down his back to his butt and then circled around and wrapped around his manhood. That first contact of my hand wrapped around his shaft surprised him so much that he bit my nipple. The bite shocked me but it didn't hurt I found it turned me on that much more. With every thrust of his fingers I matched it with stroking him. He quickened, I followed. We were driving each other crazy with need.

Adam's lips once again found hers. He removed his finger from her and moved himself out of her grip. He pulled away from her slightly, her lips were swollen from his kisses, her green eyes were like emeralds. He wanted to look into those eyes when he entered her for the first time. He pushed himself and her up, she was straddling him, they were eye to eye this way, "Don't look away from me Tay, I want to see what you are feeling when I enter you for the first time." Then with ease he lifted her up just enough to position himself between her very wet folds.

I gasped and fought the urge to close my eyes when I first felt him enter me. His crystal blue eyes were almost pure white it seemed and I watched them fill with passion as my body wrapped him inside of me. I wrapped my legs around his waist and squeezed him into me as far as I could, I couldn't seem to get enough of the feeling of him inside of me. I felt full, I felt complete, but honestly, I was feeling greedy. I wanted more of him in me. I felt his hand upon my hips, he slightly pushed me away and with just that little movement I felt the loss of him inside of me, but then he pulled me back into him again. His manhood diving deeper in me. I could feel him slide out then slam back in, each time I tightened my legs around his waist hoping he would be deeper in then the last time. I couldn't believe the feeling boiling up in me, all of him sliding in and out faster and faster, the friction against my inner walls causing a need he could only fill. I needed to feel myself pulse around him. I knew that would pull him into me more, I needed more of him. My head fell back, his mouth sucked onto one of my nipples that was it, that was my undoing. Both sensations were too much! I was going to burst. His tongue began to twirl around my nipple and my world began to explode. Wave after wave pulsed through me.

Adam wasn't sure how much longer he was going to be able to hold onto his own release but he wanted to make sure her release came first. The feel of her silky body wrapped around him in every way was driving him mad. He could feel her legs tighten around his waist every time he thrust into her bringing him deeper and deeper into her. He heard her tiny whimpers at first, and when he began twirling his tongue around her nipple they grew louder, her arms tightening around him forcing her breast more into his mouth. Her release began, he felt her body pulse around him pulling him deeper and deeper into her core.

I thought I was going to go mad! My body bucked, tightened, squeezed all at once. I heard myself call out his name. I felt myself tighten up around his thickness, felt my body pull him in more and more, the feeling was explosive. I then felt Adam's body begin to shake and I heard my name on his lips. He thrust harder and deeper if that was even possible and then it happened both of us found release together. His seed poured into me and nothing had ever felt better than feeling his life poor into her.

I didn't want to move. I was wrapped tightly around him, my legs and my arms my whole body. His voice brought my head up to look at him from its resting spot on his shoulder, "Are you alright?"

I lightly kissed him and smiled, "I am perfect, and you?"

He didn't answer, he somehow managed to move me onto my back, him over top of me but never removing himself from me. His answer was tiny little kisses and then those tiny kisses became more demanding and soon I found I was starting to lose myself once again. He began to rock against me again, slowly at first. I giggled, "Round two?"

"Hope you are up to it. I haven't gotten enough of you yet, not sure if I ever will."

I laughed again, the vibration of my laughter going through my body straight to his manhood causing him to thrust harder and faster. I wrapped my legs around his waist, "Ride me cowboy."

This was an angel sent from heaven special ordered just for him. He had no control with this woman, he quickly thrust into her until he once again felt the contracting of her body around him and again he released his seed into her.

Later laying entwined in his arms I listened to his even breathing. I had never felt like I did at the moment. I had never experienced love making like that before. My body was still pulsing inside which I had to suppress the giggle I wanted to release because it almost tickled. I did have to admit laying wrapped up in someone's arms felt amazing. Mike never held me. I pulled back but Adam held onto me as if I was going to disappear if he let go but I didn't mind that, I felt protected.

"Are you sleeping?" He asked me when I would have sworn he was a sleep.

"No, I am awake."

"What are you thinking about," Adam whispered into my ear and then trailed tiny kisses along my neck.

I closed my eyes for a moment and enjoyed his lips, I inhaled and slowly exhaled, "Just how nice it is to lay here with you. I feel like nothing can harm me as long as your arms are wrapped around me."

He answered that by tightening his arms around her even more, "You know this means I'm not going to want to let you go back to the other house now. I've had you now and I'm not going to be able to sleep in this bed without you again."

I rotated my body around so that I was face to face with him. I thought back to earlier, had he really said he had fallen in love with me? How did I even ask him about it? I didn't want to ask and find out he didn't say it, I would look and feel like a fool.

Adam watched the play of emotion run across her face, she was wondering about something, that much he could tell, when her eyebrows drew in together like she wasn't sure of something, "Would you stay with me again after tonight," he asked?

I smiled, "I don't know. I would have to think about it, although I am pretty sure you could figure out a couple of ways to persuade me to say yes," I playfully poked a finger at his chest.

Adam caught the finger that was poking him, "What is there to think about?"

What the heck I thought to myself? I had to know if I heard him right earlier and there was only one way to find out, I had to ask him. I dropped my eyes down to look at his chest this way he couldn't see the embarrassment I was feeling at that moment, "Umm Adam, earlier you.... I mean, I though you said.....well."

Adam smiled, he could take a pretty good guess at what she was trying to ask about. He placed a finger under her chin and lifted her face so that way she was looking at him again, "Yes Taylor, I said that I have fallen in love with you."

My eyes went wide. He loved me! I had heard him right the first time. I loved him and he loved me, this made what they just shared that much more understandable. Only two people in love could experience that kind of love making. The only problem was he could tell me he loved me but I wasn't sure if I was ready to voice my feelings. Last time I fell in love things didn't work out to well. Of course comparing Adam to Mike was completely wrong. There was no comparison, they were two completely different men. Yet I wondered what this meant for my future. How could I now go back to California knowing he was in love with me and I was in love with him? Although voicing the fact that I loved him or not wasn't going to make anything any easier.

Adam watched the play of emotions across Taylor's face, "I am not expecting you to say it back, Tay. I had to tell you though. I think I fell in love with you that first time we went out dancing. I can't explain it I haven't even been a little interested in anyone for a very long time. All I cared about was this ranch. I knew that if I got involved with anyone it would just take my time away from this place. Then you show up, and I seemed to have no choice. I couldn't help myself and ,trust me, I tried to talk myself out of it I mean come on, I have known you since you were a little girl. You are my sister's best friend. Then I remembered my grandfather once told me that when you find the right girl there will be nothing you can do to ignore the feelings your heart has. You walked into my life, his words came tumbling back into my head, he was right. Knowing everything about what happened with you and your ex-husband I completely understand if you are scared to make any kind of commitment to anyone, but I'm not going to deny my feeling for you. I will do what it takes to convince you we belong together and that I'm worth the risk for you to take. Tay, you deserve to know what it is like to be loved by a real man, someone who will cherish you and I am going to be that man."

A tear slid down my cheek, how could I not be completely in love with him, he was one of a kind.

Adam wiped the tear that ran down my cheek away with his finger, "I love you Taylor," he bent forward and gently kissed me. I wrapped my arms around him and crushed him to me instantly, deepening the kiss and igniting that flame between us once again. This time their love making was slow, almost like they were trying to memorize each other's body completely. It was both of them speaking of their love for each other through their bodies, their hands, and their lips.

Later I once again found myself laying, my back to him, his arms securing me in their safety, I took a deep breath, "I love you Adam," I whispered. I wasn't sure if he heard me, I barely heard myself, but when I felt his arms tighten around me I knew he had heard me.

Chapter 9

Swinging slightly back and forth, I rested my head on the back of the porch swing and closed my eyes. It had been a week since that first night with Adam, we hadn't spent a night part from each other since then. I had even moved all of my stuff over to his house. I felt at home, it felt right and I was about to the point of admitting to myself that I knew I wasn't going back to California any time in the near future. I wouldn't be able to leave Adam, just him being somewhere on the ranch and out of my sight made me miss him terribly. How was I expecting to move thousands of miles away and not go crazy? The calls for photography and photo shoots would find me anywhere. I started my business once I can do it again. Sure I had great clients back home but like Hailey pointed out before, I could just use the excuse to go visit my family back home and book appointments while I was there.

"My brother keeping you up all night or what?" Hailey joined me on the porch swing.

I smiled and sat up on the swing, "No, I was just thinking."

"Wow, this is the first time you and I have been alone in a while. Bryson is taking a nap and Grams is knitting something," she looked towards the house where you could hear Grams soft humming, she always hummed the same tune when she was knitting, "So I can finally be nosy, how are things going with you and Adam?"

"Good," was my answer and I knew that was going to drive my friend crazy. We haven't had much time with just the two of us lately and now that I wasn't staying in the main house where we would usually talk after Bryson was put to bed, we never really got a chance to talk, I felt a little guilty about that. Adam and I usually leave shortly after dinner to go back to his house.

Hailey rolled her eyes, "Really that is the only answer you are going to give me, come on Taylor really? I know things must be going good, you moving your stuff over there kind of gave us all that answer."

I laughed, "What, you want all the romantic details? Normally, I wouldn't have a problem telling my best friend everything and anything if she wanted to know it, but, since he is your brother I figured you wouldn't want to hear all the details."

"Well some details you are right about, you can keep those limited, but you still have to give me a little more than just good."

I looked out at the land surrounding them, the horses grazing. It felt right to be here, the peacefulness of it all, "Things are amazing right now. We haven't had any kind of fights in what, a week?" I joked around and Hailey laughed, I looked back my friend, "I will be honest though, it still feels a little strange at times. I would never have thought Adam and I would be a couple much less me basically living with him."

"So the fourth is next week, what are you planning to do?" Hailey knew Adam had talked to Ryan about his concerns on next week but she and Taylor hadn't had a chance to talk about anything.

I shrugged, "I will say I have been thinking about little else. Right now I can't imagine not being with Adam, even for a second, let alone being thousands of miles away from him. How do you make such a large decision on a relationship that is only a couple of weeks old? If you really look at it, it's only been strong for the last week or so."

"Taylor, it's not like you two just met at the bar. You two have known each other most of your lives. You know just as much about my brother as I probably do. Well alright, now that things have moved to a romantic level I may have to say you know him better than I do. Is moving really about Adam or about your photography?"

I shrugged. I had to stop using my photography as an escape for this topic plus Hailey always had an answer to whatever problem I came up with, "Yes a little is that but honestly, not a lot. My business is able to be moved. I started it once I can again like you have said, I can take phone calls and travel no matter where I live but relocating because a relationship of three weeks is doing well doesn't make a whole lot of sense."

"You are right," Hailey agreed, "But you and Adam are not in a normal relationship."

I laughed, "Do you mind explaining that one to me? What kind of relationship are we in if it isn't normal?"

"You know what I mean."

"Actually, no I don't. Please explain."

"What I meant was, like I said earlier, you guys have known each other for years so it wasn't like you just met, had to get to know each other, that kind of stuff, plus come on, you guys are perfect for each other."

I laughed, Hailey was set on this and I knew even if I did decide to not stay Hailey would probably lock me up just so that I couldn't leave. "Hailey there was and probably still is many things Adam and I don't know about each other even though we have known each other for years. Being in a relationship with him has been a little different than just seeing him when I came over to visit you."

Nodding again Hailey agreed, "Alright then how do you answer this question? Do you love him?"

"Yes I love him, you know that."

"What better reason do you need then? He adores you he doesn't even have to tell me he loves you I see it in his eyes every time he looks at you. I have never seen that look in his eyes before."

My head dropped back against the seat again and I took a deep breath. Why couldn't one thing be easy in life, "I don't know Hailey, my heart says yes my head isn't so convinced. I hate rushing into things that is how I ended up in the other mess."

Hailey hated when Taylor compared Adam and Mike, or the two relationships with each other,
"Taylor you know Adam is nothing like Mike."

My head snapped back up when I heard the edge in Hailey's voice with her last comment, "I was not comparing the two men Hailey. There is no comparison and I completely know that. I was merely saying I jumped into things with Mike real fast."

"I am not saying you have to marry Adam right now."

"Good lord Hailey it's not about the marriage part I am talking about either," I was beginning to get a little short with my friend now. When it came to this relationship with Adam, Hailey always seemed like it was all or nothing, "So what happens if I move out here and let's say six or so months down the road the newness of the relationship wears off and we find we are not really made for each other. Adam would be in fine shape, he didn't have to relocate his entire life but, what happens to me? Now I wouldn't have a home here or in California. I am much too old to have to move back in with my parents."

Hailey understood where her friend was coming from on that, she was making the larger life changer but she knew deep down that Adam and Taylor belonged together, it was all about taking the chance, "I guess that is a chance you take and we worry about it if it is ever to happen."

Really? That was the answer and the advice her friend was going to give her? Wow, what help she was. Hailey had a lot more confidence in this relationship then I did. I would love to just see the happily ever after, it would make things a whole lot easier. Yet I knew life didn't work that way and there were always bumps in the road.

"Taylor, Grams always says if decisions are hard to make then always lean to the direction the heart is leading you, you can never go wrong."

"Trust me, my heart has been screaming to move back from the moment I got here, being with Adam just added to it. I have told you a number of times I missed Nolansville. This is home and I will always think of it that way, but moving back is still a large decision."

"Hailey, Bryson is awake and calling for you up stairs," Grams called from inside of the house.

Hailey stood up but turned to me before she entered the house, "Tay, trust me, I understand what you are saying. I know this must be very scary for you but you need to listen to yourself when you talk, everything you say would be leading you into staying. I understand you had a rough patch with Mike, you made it through that and trust me that was huge compared to what a break up would be if that was to happen with Adam. I am not just saying that I think you two will make it because you are my best friend and he is my brother. I honestly feel that you two were meant to end up together. Some time we need to just jump in life and here I know my brother will be there to catch you. He loves you and you love him, sometimes we have to just let our hearts lead the path and trust them that they are leading us the right way."

I stared at the door for a moment after my friend disappeared through it. This would be a lot easier if I just let my heart lead me, the answer would be very clear but my head keeps getting in the way. My mom always said I think too much on things, sometimes I just needed to sit back and let things happen. Wait, my mom, that was it! I knew my mom would help me with this decision. I hadn't even told my parents what was going on yet. I pulled my phone out of my back pocket and dialed, one ring, two rings, "Come on mom pick up your phone," three rings then finally, "Hello."

Just hearing my mother's voice made me smile, I missed my family, "Hi mom."

"Taylor, sweetheart! How is everything going?"

"Actually things are going good, really good that's why I am calling you. I need some advice and I know you can help." Mom and I talked all the time, my mom was the only person who knew everything, there weren't any secrets between us at all, "Mom, since I have been here, well, Adam, Hailey's brother and I have been kind of in a relationship."

Sandy smiled to herself, her daughter hadn't been out with anyone, even her friends, since everything had happened. Taylor had told her a number of times that she was never getting involved with anyone ever again and that always broke her heart. Her daughter had a lot of love to offer to the right guy, "Honey that's great! I remember Adam he was a good kid, I am sure he is the same hard working man as he was when he was a kid. Is this a serious thing?"

"Honestly, yes it is! I am completely in love with him which is the problem."

"Alright a little confused on that statement. How is that a problem?"

I knew my mom would be excited, she was always telling me that I needed to get out and meet people. She said she always understood why I was scared but that I couldn't live my life under a rock. I had to learn to trust men again. Of course I never thought that was ever going to be a possibility but then Adam came into my life, "Mom, I am thinking about moving back here."

Sandy's breath caught in her chest. Did she hear her daughter right? Of course she wanted her daughter to find love, move on with her life, even get married again but this all seemed a little sudden. "Taylor, are you serious? I mean don't get me wrong, Adam I am sure is a great guy, but you honestly think that moving in with him is something you should do after just three weeks of a relationship?" Her daughter hadn't so much as gone out with anyone since the whole thing with Mike and here she meets someone and she is rushing it.

“Mom, trust me, I know what you are saying, but we love each other. Who cares how long we have been together?” Strange, Taylor thought to herself, she was starting to sound like Hailey when they were arguing about this subject. She was defending their relationship almost upset at her mom for questioning her reasons or her love for Adam.

“Taylor I am not meaning to upset you sweetheart,” Sandy could hear the edge in Taylor’s voice. Although she had to admit this sounded like her old Taylor. The one with a passion for what she believed in, the one who stood by her decisions. Her daughter always thought long and hard on what choices she made, well, except for the one she made about Mike. Of course, Mike had everyone fooled at the beginning. The difference between Adam and Mike was the family knew Adam. There were no guessing games. He was a good guy, he was a family man and a very hard worker. Taylor had found a good man this time, maybe she shouldn’t try and fight her daughter’s decision this time. “I was just asking if you have thought this through, that’s all.”

“Honestly, mom, all I have thought about is this move. Ever since I got back here I have realized how much I miss this place. We have gone on rides, I didn’t realize how much I had missed being on a horse until I took that first ride. I miss the smell in the air, the small town surroundings. The Fourth of July is next week and watching this town get ready for that I have realized how much I miss it. Falling in love with Adam has just added more to the reasons why I want to move back.” Taylor took a deep breath and when her mom didn’t say anything she continued, “Mom it’s strange, the way I love Adam. What I mean is, I thought I knew what love was when I fell in love with Mike, but, I honestly don’t think that was love. I think that was more like infatuation. There is not one similarity between the two guys and being with Adam has opened my eyes up to that. Mike was all city boy, Adam is all cowboy.”

Yes, her daughter was returning to her old self and Sandy was pretty sure Adam had a lot to do with that. She had to remember to thank him the next time she saw him. “Taylor I don’t think you need me to help you with this decision, honey. I think from what you have told me that you have made up your mind on your own. Your father and I will support whatever choice you make."

"Mom, you really haven't helped me here," Taylor realized she had called her mom hoping her mom would give her a yes or no answer.

"Taylor the way you are defending this relationship when you thought I was attacking it should be the answer you are looking for. This isn't something anyone can decide for you, you have to make this choice on your own. Adam is a good guy. Your father and I wouldn't be against you two being together, you have to be the one to make the decision though," Sandy explained. She had to admit she would miss her daughter terribly if she moved back to Tennessee but she would feel a lot better about the fact that she was nowhere near the town that Mike was in. They hadn't heard anything from or about Mike since he had been released but there was still a feeling in her heart that it wasn't going to stay that way.

"So you don't think I am crazy for making a change like this?"

"Honey, the heart is very powerful. If you feel this strong about Adam then I don't think it matters if it has been a month or years, sometimes it is just meant to be."

"Mom, what if I think it is meant to be, then a few months down the road we find out that it really wasn't?"

Sandy knew that Taylor was calling, looking for her mom to tell her what to do, but she knew it really wouldn't make a difference, "Taylor trust me, everyone wishes that there was a way to see the future, but we can't and there is no way to tell what will happen in time, but what you need to decide is if it's worth taking the chance on. You know though, I will say this; my opinion of this just from listening to you at the beginning of this conversation is that you want to take the chance but your head is fighting with your heart, let that wall down honey."

I blinked away the tears that threatened to escape. My mom was right, if I decided to stay with Adam that last wall would crumble. Walls I had spent the last few years making sure no one would break down, and here Adam has knocked down every single one of them.

"Let me say this though, Adam is a very nice choice honey, he is one good looking cowboy."

I laughed, "Glad you approve mom." A movement from the stables caught my eye, I looked over to see Adam walking towards me. All strength, all man, but those arms were so tender when we were making love, "Yes he is pretty amazing. I will call you as soon as I decide."

"Alright we love you, tell everyone there hi for me."

"Love you too. tell dad and Mathew hi and I love and miss them. Talk to you later," I quickly hung up the phone and slid my phone back into my pocket just as Adam stepped up onto the porch. I watched as he walked up to me, leaned down and claimed my lips. My heart flip-flopped in my chest, my blood began to boil and moisture formed between my thighs, just his kiss was driving me crazy. He pulled away from me and I took a deep breath, trying to calm myself. One minute more of that I would have been attacking him right there on the porch.

He sat down next to me on the swing, "Why are you sitting out here all by yourself, everything alright?"

I nodded, "Everything is fine. Hailey was out here a few minutes ago but Bryson just woke up so she went in to take care of him, I just got off the phone with my mom."

Concern was etched in Adam's facial expression, "Is everything alright? Any issues going on?"

I hadn't even thought to ask my mom anything about Mike. Of course, she had never mentioned anything about him either. "Mike's name never came up. I um.. called for some advice."

"What kind of advice?"

I looked down at my hands, the conversation of me moving back had been brought up but he had never asked her to move in with him. Of course, Hailey had invited her to move into her house, "Well I wanted her advice about moving back here. Hailey and I have had the conversation a couple of times. Every day I am here, the harder it is to imagine leaving again."

"What did she say when you mentioned it to her?" Adam was trying to desperately hide his smile, she was thinking about staying. She was calling her family about it that had to be a good sign.

"She said that she couldn't make that decision for me but that she would support whatever decision I make, she knows I have always missed being here."

"So have you decided?"

I shook my head and looked up at him, "No, I still have to think about my business and most of all where I am going to live," I didn't want him to think I just assumed I would move in with him.

Adam frowned, "What is wrong with where you are living now?"

"Nothing," I shrugged my shoulders and looked back down at my hands, "But I am not moving in with your sister and her family. I have to have a place to go if I decide to move back."

"Taylor look at me," he waited until I looked up at him, "I wasn't talking about you moving into this house. I am asking about my house, you would move in with me not my sister."

I felt my body relax, he did want me to move in with him and he wanted me to stay not with his sister or in town, but with him.

"Taylor why would you even think you had to move in with my sister? You practically live with me now, why would I ask you to stay if I weren't figuring you would be staying with me?"

"Adam, I don't want you thinking I just assumed I would live with you. Sure it's been mentioned between us about me moving back, your sister and I have talked about it a couple of times, but you and I haven't actually sat down and talked about me moving in with you."

Adam patted the swing with his hand, "Well we are sitting now so let's talk about it."

I didn't know where to start now that he was putting me on the spot, I didn't want to say something to offend him or make him think I was second guessing my feelings for him.

"Tay I love you, you know that right?"

I smiled-yes I knew that. His voice and the first time he told me that he loved me runs through my mind all the time. "I love you too, but Adam we haven't been together for very long. What happens if we find out in six months or so that we just aren't going to work out?"

Hearing her have doubts about their relationship started to make Adam mad, but then he thought about it. It was her past rearing up, could he really blame her for doubting things after everything she had been through? He would just have to convince her, "Tay I haven't met anyone before that I have said I love you to. I know my feelings for you but everything we do is by chance. We cannot run our lives on what might happen, you have to decide if something or someone is worth taking the risk for."

"I understand all of that, but Adam I am giving up everything. I have to move my entire life that is a huge decision to make and then have it not work out."

Adam stared at me for a moment. I couldn't read the expression in his eyes, but I was sure what I just said may have come out wrong. I watched as he got up from the swing and walked over to the banister, keeping his back to me, "I'm sorry you feel like you are giving up everything. I am sorry that I can't move an entire ranch to California."

I heard the sarcasm in his voice, he was upset and that wasn't what I had wanted to do. I got up and walked up behind him, I wrapped my arms around his waist and settled my chin against his back, "Please don't be mad at me Adam, it came out the wrong way. Can you please turn around and look at me?" I felt him take a deep breath and then he twisted in my arms to face me, but his arms didn't wrap around me he kept his hands on the banister behind him. "All I meant was that I have rushed into things before but I will admit every time I think about not being around you my heart breaks."

Adam looked away from her for a moment, he took another deep breath. He knew he may be taking things a little too personal. She was right, this was a big step for her. She was the one having to make the move, her job, her home, her whole life. He needed to be a little more understanding. But every time he thought about the possibility of her not staying.. Damn, he needed to remember that this was a big step. Adam was a bit surprised that it wasn't scaring him more, but that was why he knew that she was the one. "Tay all I can promise is to love you and give you all of me. I cannot tell you what will happen in the future but I am willing to find out where the future takes us."

I rose up onto my tippy toes to claim his lips, I felt his arms wrap around my waist finally and pull me tight against him. My whole body came alive; at that moment I knew I couldn't live without him, I knew my days would feel completely empty if I couldn't hold onto him and kiss him, wake up to blue eyes admiring me. I didn't have one doubt that Adam loved me and I knew I loved him with all of my heart. I couldn't let him go and I wasn't going to be able to leave him.

Adam ended the kiss and looked down at me, "Taylor, I know I am asking a lot from you and if for any reason I felt a doubt about you and I, then I wouldn't even consider asking you to stay. But I don't have any doubts. I love you and if I could leave this ranch and go with you, I would. If you do go back to California, I very well may find a way to follow you there. All I know for sure is that I want to be with you. I don't want to live without you next to me, waking up next to me, loving me."

I felt a tear escape and slide down my cheek. Knowing he would leave the ranch for me was all I needed to hear, I would never allow him to leave this place. He loved the ranch and so did I. I smiled up at him, "You ready for a roommate?"

Adam crushed his lips into mine, he took me up into his arms and started for his place. No, wait, he started for their place.

I felt my feet leave the ground, my arms tightened around his neck. I had no idea where we were going and I didn't care as long as it was somewhere private because I was going to tear all of his clothes off.

Adam practically ran to the house and up the stairs and to the room. My feet touched the ground and I went straight to undressing, pulling my shirt up over my head. Our eyes never left each other's as we discarded our clothing. Adam stepped out of his boots and pants, then his arms went right around me again, smashing our bodies together. At the first contact of skin against skin I sighed deeply and laid my head against his naked chest, and tightened my arms around his neck. Adam lifted me up and laid me back down in the middle of the large bed, him hovering over me.

He began his kisses along each of my scars on my face like he usually did. He told me once when I asked why; it was him cherishing the signs of me fighting for life, because if I hadn't been as strong as these scars had shown evidence to, then I would not be here for him to love. I realized that it didn't bother me like it used to after he said those words to me. To have him pay so much attention to what I always considered my weakness, I always believed those scars created people to stare at me in pity but Adam made me feel beautiful no matter what marks I had. I felt his lips run down along my neck and then finally they captured one peeked breast. I moaned, my nails raked across his back. Adam lightly nibbled on one sensitive bud of a nipple, then twirled his tongue around it, then once again devoured the full breast into his mouth.

Adam felt the edge of her scar against his lips, he ran his tongue the length of the scar all the way to her belly button, passing over her stomach. Just before he reached the most sensitive core of her, she stopped him with her hands on both sides of his face and pulled him back up, "It's my turn today," she pushed him over onto his back and straddled him.

"Do you think I can handle and ride this cowboy?" His grin dared me to try.

My smile was wicked, I had hoped. I leaned forward and passionately kissed his lips. My tongue swirled around his tongue. My hips rotated against his hard manhood and my breasts rubbed up and down his chest. I traced a path with my tongue down his neck, I looked up at him as I did. His eyes were closed, his head bent back to give me full access. He smelt of sweat from a hard day of work, oddly a smell that turned me on. I traced each hardened nipple with my tongue then ran down the middle of his strong stomach.

Adam's eyes flew open at the first touch of her tongue on the tip of his hardened dick, "Good God Taylor stop," he tried to wiggle free but was stilled when she wrapped her lips around his manhood, stroking him with her mouth and tongue.

I looked up when I had him fully in my mouth, he became harder and thicker as I ran my tongue on the underside of him. His eyes were closed tight and his hands were in my hair, pulling enough to hurt a little. The pain only drove me to suck him harder and faster. I felt his hips thrust up towards me, his breathing was harder and I knew he was close. I swirled my tongue over the tip of him and then in one swift motion sucked him in as far as I could.

The moment I sucked him in completely, Adam knew he wasn't going to last much longer. He didn't want to come in her amazing mouth. He wanted to come inside of her, feeling her body convulse around him and pull him in deeper and deeper as he filled her with his seed.

Adam's movement was so quick that I quickly found myself straddling his lap and my legs wrapped around his waist and him completely inside of me. We were eye to eye now, but I wanted the control, I wanted to drive him crazy. I placed my hands on his chest and pushed him to lay back, "Let me ride you cowboy," I smiled down at him, his hands were at my waist moving me in rhythm with him. The thrusts were slow at first, but each one building to a faster speed, and each one driving him further and further inside of me. My head fell back and my back arched which pushed him in that much deeper. I felt the sweat on his chest, my fingernails dug into his pecks "Please Adam, please."

Adam heard her plea combined with her breasts bouncing in front of his face, her long hair swaying against his legs. He felt his own release just holding onto the edge, but he wanted her release first. He pulled himself back up into a sitting position and found one of her nipples with his mouth, a couple more thrust and he felt her body begin to convulse around him, pulling him deeper and deeper into her. With every wave of release her body had, still he never slowed the pace. Couple more thrusts and his body rocked with his own release spilling his seed into her core.

I sat straddling Adam, my head tucked into his neck. He was still fully extended inside of me, I needed to catch my breath. Adam's lips brushed lightly over my shoulder. The core of me began to heat up again, how just his kiss could ignite this kind of fire in me, I didn't know but I had to have him again. I slowly began rotating my hips against him again. I looked up into his eyes, my forehead against his forehead, "I love you," I said before I claimed his lips.

"I am supposed to be getting some work done you know," he said against her lips although he knew nothing was needing more of his attention on this ranch than the woman in his arms.

I smiled down at him, "Then get working on these." I pulled his head to one of my breasts, my head falling back at the first touch of his lips on my nipple. My hands went behind me and rested on his thighs, which arched my back so that he had all access to my breasts, my hips began to thrust harder and faster, driving him further into me.

Adam wrapped his arms around my back after giving some of his attention to each nipple. Thrusting in front of him, he pulled me up and I wrapped my arms around his neck again. "Open your eyes Tay, look at me as we come together." Crystal blue eyes bore into heavenly green eyes as our bodies rocked together and released together for the second time.

I glanced over at the clock on the night stand next to the bed, "It is almost five, we should probably get up and get ready for dinner. Grams will be calling for us shortly."

Adam tightened his arms around me, "I'm not hungry. At least not for dinner. I have an idea, why don't we skip dinner, stay right here and later when I get hungry I will snack on you?" he began to nibble on my shoulder.

I took in a deep breath trying to calm my body and the blood that was beginning to boil again, "You don't think they will come looking for us?"

"I can run downstairs and lock the door and then we can just ignore the knocks."

I felt Adam move away from me and get up from the bed, I quickly grabbed his hand to stop him, "No we can't do that. Grams works hard when she cooks for us, we can at least go to dinner.
Besides, you will have me all to yourself every night."

Adam watched me get up from bed and begin gathering me clothes, he slid into his jeans then sat down on the edge of the bed watching me as I dressed, "You're sure about all of this right? I don't want you to regret your decision."

I pulled my pants on then my bra. I walked over to where he sat and stood in front of him, "Are you trying to talk me out of it?"

Adam wrapped his arms around my waist and looked up at me, "I'm not trying to talk you out of anything. Trust me, I am thrilled that you decided to move, but I want to make sure you are going to be happy with your choice. I want you to be happy here."

I bent down and kissed him tenderly, "Am I scared? Very scared, I won't lie about that. But when I think about being away from you, my heart feels so heavy. I swore to myself that I would never get myself involved in another relationship, I didn't want that pain again. After what I went through with Mike I felt like I couldn't trust my judgment in men. Adam, you are the first guy I have even dated let alone anything else since Mike attacked me. When I arrived here and saw you, my heart flipped in my chest. I tried to fight it trust me, I didn't want to fall for you but you were persistent." I smiled down at him, "You made me want to start allowing myself to care again to feel something again, you started crumbling down my walls that I built up around my heart. I know I can trust you, I know you will never hurt me in a physical way like Mike did. I know that I love you more than I thought I could ever love another person. I could never ask you to move away from this place, not knowing how much you care for it, but I love it here as well. My photography can be picked up anywhere, I have even thought about stopping all the traveling and just focus on shoots around here. I miss this place and I would miss you even more if I left and went back to California, so to answer your question, yes I am sure about staying with you here."

Adam smiled up at her, "Whatever you decide to do about your photography I will support you on. If you decide to keep traveling I will stand by you with it, I will miss you like crazy but as long as I know you are coming home to me I am happy. I do love you Taylor I promise to give you all of my heart but you do understand I do have to work around here? I can't always have you kidnapping me for a day full of love making," he teased her.

"Yes, next time I have the feeling to sweep you off your feet and carry you to bed I will think twice about it."

Adam laughed, "I really wish you knew how much I love you."

"I think I know," I leaned down and kissed him one more time. I pulled away and picked his shirt up off the floor tossing it at him, "Finish getting dressed," I then grabbed my shirt and pulled it on, then sat down on the chair to pull on my boots.

"Come on Grams, if we don't get going we are going to be late, "Ryan yelled from the front door.

"Alright, alright I am coming. Did you guys grab my pies for the contest?"

"Everything and everyone is ready to go but you. Adam and Taylor have your pies in the truck with them. You are driving over with Hailey and myself, so come on," Ryan led her out the front door and to the truck where everyone was waiting.

"Young man, you better not ruin my pies," Grams told Adam as she passed by him. I was waiting in the truck.

"Lady, you better get in that truck! My truck is smelling pretty good right now and I am hungry," Adam teased with his grandmother.

"Young man, you touch one of those pies I will break your fingers."

"Big talk Grams, then let's go," Adam yelled at her from the window laughing.

"You are terrible," I shook my head.

"Yes, but you love me," he leaned across the seat and gave me a quick kiss then started up the truck.

I looked around at all the festivities going on for the Fourth of July around the small town. I loved this festival. When I was living here and if I hadn't already made up my mind to move back this would have made my mind up for me.

Ryan and Adam had entered the pie eating contest and they both lost to a thirteen year old girl. I had eaten so much food through the day I thought I was going to explode. Grams won first place on one of her pies, which was no surprise to anyone, her pies were the best in the county and now she had one more ribbon to add to her collection that she proudly displayed at the house.

The day had been perfect, now the sun had gone down and the dancing had begun. A local country band was playing and lines of people were dancing a line dance to the song. Nothing could bring me down, my cheeks hurt from smiling and laughing so much through the day, I had even reunited with some friends from school.

"Alright we are going to slow things down for all those couples out there," the lead singer announced.

Before I could think I was pulled out onto the dance floor and Adam's arms were tightly wrapped around me, "Having fun?"

I nodded, "This day has been great. I missed all of this. I have to admit it is good to be home."

Adam smiled and claimed my lips, "I am glad to hear it."

Fireworks blazed up into the sky above us one after another. It was a perfect ending to a perfect day.

Chapter 10

It was nearing the end of August and finally a breakthrough, Mike thought to himself. He had finally gotten an answer from someone as to where Taylor was living. Yet as he sat there in his brother's car, on the side of the road across from her house, his anger returned. When he pulled up he spotted the moving trucks and movers in the driveway, packing up her house. Everyone had been saying that she was out of town on a photo shoot and even though a shoot that lasted longer than a month was not common it wasn't like it couldn't happen. Now he realized she wasn't out working, she was somewhere hiding from him.

He got out of his car and walked up to the truck were two men were loading boxes, "Excuse me," he said as he waited for the guys to acknowledge him. One of the men stopped on the ramp, "Yes, can we help you?"

"I am sorry to bother you but yes, I am hoping you can help me. The girl who lives here, I was hoping to surprise her with a visit, we're old friends from school. Can you tell me where she moved to so I can stop by there and catch up with her by chance?"

"Sorry buddy, but we are moving this stuff to a place in Tennessee some small town outside of Nashville," the guy shrugged his shoulders and then went back to his work.

"Thank you for the information, I appreciate it," Mike then turned and walked back to his car leaving the men to their work.

He sat in the car for a moment and just watched as the crew carried boxes and furniture out of the house. So, she was leaving the state, little town out of Nashville, that was probably that town she used to live in. She still had a friend there is he remembered right. He should have thought about that before now. Well, it looked like he was going to be taking a little road trip. He started up the car and pulled away from the curb. He was going to get his wife back for the hell he went through in prison.

When he returned to his brother's place, he walked right in and past his brother without saying a word. Kevin watched his brother walk by him, he knew that look in his eyes and it meant trouble. He got up and quickly followed him into his room, stopping in the doorway to the room, he crossed his arms at his chest and leaned a shoulder up against the door jam. He watched as Mike grabbed a suitcase and started filling it with clothes, "So where are you going?"

"I am taking a little road trip. I need to borrow the car too," Mike proceeded to put his clothes in the case.

"I don't know if you remember this or not but you are on parole brother. You can't leave the state."

"What makes you think I am leaving the state?"

"Because Taylor's whereabouts were a big secret, well, someone I know saw the moving vans and asked a couple of questions. News travels fast around here. I thought you were going to leave this alone?"

Mike glared at his brother for a minute, how long had he known and not said anything to him? It didn't really matter, he knew now, "She caused me to lose eight years of my life Kevin."

"Mike, you almost killed her! I am still trying to figure out how your lawyer got you off with only ten years and how you managed to get out just after eight," Kevin pointed out.

Mike's glare turned black when he looked at his brother, "the bitch was cheating on me! She was pregnant by another guy."

"Mike, if you leave the state they will throw you back in jail for good this time. Is she worth that risk?"

Mike closed the suitcase and started out of the room, "I'm taking the car."

It wasn't a question, it was a statement. Kevin had never stood up to his brother but he wasn't going to have any part of this, "No you aren't. You want to go, you find your own way. Leave me out of it!" Kevin left the room and quickly grabbed his keys running out the door and quickly to his car.

Mike stood there for a moment in a little bit of shock. Kevin leaving with the car was a surprise. His little brother never stood up to him. The shock turned into anger, he would deal with his brother after he dealt with his cheating wife.

Taylor woke up again to Adam gone. I usually heard him get up and leave for the day but the last week or so I hadn't heard a sound. I sat up in bed and the room began to spin. Was I getting sick? My answer came when my stomach began to turn. I flew out of bed, threw open the door to the bathroom and reached the toilet just in time for everything in my stomach from dinner the night before to come back up.

I hadn't heard anyone come into the house so I was surprised to hear Adam at the doorway of the bathroom, "Tay, are you alright?"

I put my hand up to stop him at the doorway, "Don't come in please, you don't need to see me like this. I will be fine," I didn't want Adam to see me like this but before I could really see if he had left the bathroom my stomach turned again and I heaved into the toilet once more.

Adam was right behind me holding my hair back with one hand and with the other reaching for a wash cloth that was on the counter, wetting it down for me, he handed it to me when I started to bring my head up from the toilet, "Hon, are you alright?"

I wiped my mouth and flushed the toilet, setting the lid back down, I was pretty sure my stomach was settled for the moment at least, "Besides being completely embarrassed, yes, I think I'm fine. Something I ate last night must not have agreed with me."

"Why are you embarrassed?" He helped me up from the floor and slowly led me back into the bedroom and into the bed.

"You shouldn't see me like this. I thought you had already left."

"I had forgotten my keys on the dresser. Ryan and I are heading out to fix fences today but now that you are sick I'm going to go down an tell Ryan it will have to wait."

"Adam go. I am fine, really. Like I said, I probably just ate something that didn't agree with me. You have been talking about needing to fix those fences for a week or so. Ryan is finally here to help you so go. I am fine, really. I think I will just lie back down for a while, it will pass."

I could tell he was fighting with himself on if he should go or not, "Fine but I have my phone with me. If you get any worse call me, you promise?"

I nodded and laid down. Adam pulled the covers up over my shoulders then leaned down and kissed my forehead, "Love you."

"Love you too," Adam left not feeling good about leaving but she promised she would call and before he left he would go tell Hailey she wasn't feeling well, he knew his sister would keep an eye her.

I was almost back to sleep when I heard the front door open and close, then steps coming up the stairs, "Taylor, are you awake?" Hailey's voice came from the hallway before she appeared in the doorway of the room.

"Yeah I am awake."

"Adam says you aren't feeling well."

I sat up and my stomach rolled once more, I flew out of bed and back to the bathroom. Hailey followed grabbing my hair back into a ponytail while my face went into the bowl. People getting sick had never bothered her, "How long have you been like this?"

I wiped my mouth with the washcloth again then headed back to bed, and laid back down, "The last couple of mornings I have been sleeping in more but this morning was the first time I actually threw up. It is probably something I ate or a bug of some kind. I'm fine really."

"Or..." Hailey said laughing letting the word hang for a moment.

"Or what," I asked when my dear friend didn't continue on?

"Seriously Taylor, it has to have crossed your mind?"

I looked around for a moment as though I was looking for the answer somewhere in the room, "What are you saying Hailey?"

"Fine, I will get personal. Are you or Adam using any kind of protection at all?"

Hailey watched as Taylor thought about the question. Hailey would put money on why she was sick, she almost started laughing when Taylor finally realized what she was talking about.

"Hailey, there is no way!" Of course there was a way but it was a slim chance, that's what the doctors had told me so I had never thought about using protection and I knew Adam wasn't using any either.

"Taylor, if neither of you are using anything to stop it then why do you think there is no chance of it happening?"

I covered my face with my hands. No, I just had the flu, bad food, something, but not pregnancy. I started to cry.

Hailey couldn't figure out why Taylor was so upset, "Taylor, this isn't a bad thing. I figured you would be thrilled, I know Adam will be."

I shook my head, "No, what if he thinks I planned this to trap him? He probably figured I was taking care of the protection."

Hailey grabbed me by the shoulders and shook me, "Why are you talking crazy? Adam won't feel trapped, heck, I think the only reason he hasn't proposed is because he didn't want to rush you. I figured you would be excited to be pregnant, you've always wanted to be a mom."

"Hailey, the doctors told me that I probably wouldn't be able to have children because of the damage done by the knife."

Hailey covered her mouth, "Oh god Taylor, why didn't you say something earlier? You must have been devastated when you heard that. All you have ever wanted was children."

I nodded, I would never forget that day. All at once I had found out that I had lost the child I had been carrying and then the bomb really dropped when the doctor followed that news up with the fact that they didn't believe I would ever be able to get pregnant again. "Because I never wanted to believe there was no chance or maybe it was that I didn't want to accept the fact. I also knew that if I told Adam I may not be able to give him a child that it may change his feelings for me."

"You know Taylor, you have to start giving Adam a little more credit than you do. He loves you that would never have been something that would change his feelings for you. Look, now you know you can have more children."

I didn't dare hope that I really was pregnant. The chances the doctors had given me were something like close to nothing. I probably only had the flu or something, I wouldn't even start to get my hopes up on it meaning anything else, "Hailey, me throwing up doesn't prove anything. The doctors gave me next to no chance of pregnancy. I am sure it's a bug or something."

"Well there is only one way to find out, "Hailey knew why Taylor wasn't getting her hopes up on the pregnancy fact but she wasn't giving up on it until they knew for sure. "I'm going to the store and I will be right back."

Before I could say another word or even stop her she was up and gone from the room. I thought about it for a moment. Could I really be pregnant? I couldn't allow myself to get my hopes up. The chances were slim to none according to doctors that was just another pleasure in life that Mike had taken away from me. I had always wanted a house full of children but I had finally accepted the fact that I would never have my own. Hailey seemed very sure though. Of course she would believe anything that she thought would bring Adam and me closer to the marriage status. I'm going to take the test for Hailey. It's going to break my heart even though I'm ready for the negative sign to appear on the stick. It's just going to be a reminder that the doctors were right and I would never be able to have children, then I'm going to have to sit down and have the conversation with Adam about the fact that the two of us will never become parents naturally.

"Come on Taylor, you have to go check. Go on, go see what the little stick says. "Hailey sat with me on the bed. She had been holding my hand for the last five minutes while we waited for the results of the pregnancy test. My hands were cold and shaky. This could be a life changing result no matter which why the test came out.

"No, I can't. What if it comes out that I am pregnant?"

Hailey smiled at me, "We get excited, I can't wait to be an aunt."

"What if I am not pregnant? What if I only have some kind of bug? What if I can't have children?"

Hailey felt for Taylor. She knew how badly Taylor wanted to be a mother, "Taylor, we need to find out but I promise you this, Adam will love you no matter which way this goes. Now, go check the stick." I looked over at the bathroom where the results that can change everything were waiting for someone to go check on, "No, I can't go. You go for me please Hailey."

Hailey looked at Taylor. She looked terrified, "Alright, I will go check." She got up and I watched as she disappeared into the bathroom.

My eyes never left the doorway into the bathroom. Why was Hailey taking so long how long did it take to see if there was a plus or minus sign on a stick? Then all too quickly Hailey was standing in the doorway of the bathroom holding the test in her hand. She wasn't smiling, all she was doing was staring at the damn stick. Oh god, I wasn't pregnant. If I was Hailey would be screaming right now.

"I knew it! He destroyed everything for me," I started to lay back down. I wanted to be alone to cry because even though I had prepared myself for the negative sign to be there I had a small spark of hope that the doctors were wrong.

Hailey looked up at me, she held the test out for me to take, "Here."

"I don't want it."

"Taylor, look," Hailey said a huge smile spread across her face.

I closed my eyes and held out my hand for the stick. Hailey placed the test in my hand, "Taylor open your eyes."

I opened my eyes, the tears started flowing.

"Taylor, you are going to be a mother. He didn't destroy your life! He made you stronger and now you get to bring a child into this world to two loving parents who love each other very much."

I looked over at her and nodded. I was pregnant with Adam's child! The doctors had been wrong, I was going to be a mother. The tears flowed down my cheeks.

Adam tightened the last section of barbed wire that they had to fix. He wanted to be done so he could get home and check on Taylor. He hated having to work and not be able to be there taking care of her. He had been beating himself up with the fact that he shouldn't have left her, the fences could have waited another day or so.

"Hey Ryan, the rest that needs fixed, I can come out and cut tomorrow. I want to go and check on Taylor if you don't mind calling it a day."

"Sure, not a problem. Honestly, I am surprised you made it this long," Ryan picked up a couple of the tools and placed them in the back truck.

When Adam pulled up to the house he saw Taylor down at the arena, she must be feeling better. He walked up behind her and wrapped his arms around her waist, "Glad to see you are feeling better."

I turned in his arms so that I was facing him. I had tried to plan out what I was going to say and how I was going to tell him but nothing I came up with sounded right so I decided I was just going to say it. "Yes I am feeling better. I figured out what was wrong, well actually, your sister figured out what was wrong."

"What is it then," he asked?

I looked up into those crystal clear blue eyes, I hoped our baby get their daddy's eyes. I took a deep breath, "Adam, I'm pregnant."

Adam couldn't believe what he just heard, "What?"

The last time I told someone I was pregnant I ended up in a hospital. I knew Adam wasn't going to hurt me and Hailey was sure he would be very excited but I wasn't so sure of it myself. He didn't look very excited, "I said, I'm pregnant. We are going to have a baby. Are you mad?"

Mad? Why would he be mad? Shocked, now yes, he was very shocked. He was just told he was going to be a father. "Taylor, why would you think I would be mad? No, I'm not mad but are you sure?"

I nodded, "Yes, actually, your sister was the one who figured it out, like I said before. She went and bought the test. I took three of them to be sure. They all came up positive."

"You don't seem too happy about all of this," Adam noticed and it was killing him to think she wasn't happy about it.

"Adam, I was told after the attack that I probably wouldn't be able to have more children. They weren't sure exactly how much damage the knife did. That is why I wasn't using protection. I figured I wouldn't be able to have children. I am not upset that I'm pregnant, I'm scared that you would be upset. I didn't want you to think I did this on purpose."

"Tay, I could never be mad about finding out that our love created another life. I didn't take any precautions either so I couldn't have blamed just you anyway. I am excited! I want to have children and you are going to make a beautiful mother."

Tears poured down my cheeks, "I love you so much."

Adam's lips claimed hers, "I love you too. I think we need to go out and celebrate. You feel up to that?"

I nodded, "I'm fine, at least until probably tomorrow morning."

"Come on! Let's go tell everyone, well at least Grams, that is if my sister hasn't already told her," Adam pulled me close to him wrapping his arm around my waist and together we walked to the main house.

They walked into the house, "Grams, Hailey, Ryan can you guys come into the living room for a minute please."

Hailey came running into the living room and through her arms around her brother's neck.

"Congratulations my brother! I'm so excited I'm going to be an aunt and you are going to be a father finally!"

Grams came down the hallway mumbling all the way into the living room, "What is all the commotion? I need to get dinner started."

Ryan followed Grams with Bryson on his heels, once he saw Taylor in the room he smiled. “Glad to see that you are feeling better. This guy drove me nuts all day worrying about you and beating himself up for leaving you alone sick.”

I looked up at Adam, he was beaming. My heart flipped in my chest, he looked so proud.

“Grams, don’t worry about cooking tonight we are all going out to celebrate,” Adam announced.

“Yeaaa, we are going out for dinner!” Bryson yelled, “where are we going, Uncle Adam?”

“Better question is what are we celebrating?” Ryan asked.

“Wow sis! I am very surprised you haven’t said anything. I am very proud of you.” Adam turned shocked eyes over to his sister.

“Let me tell you, it hasn’t been easy, especially around Grams. Ryan just got home but it is killing me so tell them before I explode please,” Hailey hugged her arms around her husband’s waist standing beside him and beaming at her brother and friend.

“Come on out with it! Don’t keep us waiting. What is the big news?” Grams asked.

Adam looked around at his family then rested beaming proud eyes onto Taylor at his side, “Taylor is pregnant.”

“Oh my, Oh my,” Grams repeated, “This is so exciting! I’ve been hoping I would see a grand baby from you. I am so excited for the both of you,” Grams hugged them both, tears rolling down her cheeks. “Congrats buddy,” Ryan slapped Adam on the back, “I have to hug the beautiful mommy to be.”

“So we are all going out to celebrate on me of course so everyone go and get ready. We will leave in about an hour,” Adam turned still holding onto Taylor and started out the door.

“Adam, can I speak to you for a moment.”

“Sure Grams,” he looked down at me. I could see the confusion in his eyes.

“I will head over and start getting ready,” I smiled up at him. I hoped everything was alright.

“I will be over in a minute. I have to take a shower before we go,” Adam watched as Taylor walked out the door then turned to his grandmother, “Is something wrong?”

“Heavens no! I am thrilled! I am so excited you have finally found someone to share your life with but come with me for a moment will you?” Grams turned and led the way down the hall and to her room. She walked inside her room, moved aside for him to enter, and then shut the door behind them. “When Ryan asked us to marry Hailey I gave him your mother’s ring and he put your mother’s diamond from her ring into the ring he had found for Hailey,” Grams slid her diamond ring off her finger leaving only her wedding band. “Your grandfather and I decided together your sister got your mother’s ring and you would get mine. Taylor being pregnant, your grandfather would tell you that you will propose and do right by her. So take this ring,” she placed her ring into Adam’s hand, “take the diamond and go create a beautiful engagement ring for that beautiful woman you have.”

Adam held the ring back out to his grandmother, “Grams, keep your ring. I will get Taylor a ring. I don’t want you to give this up, I had already planned on proposing, trust me.”

Grams shook her head, “Your grandfather and I talked about this before he passed and I would be honored to give it to you. I would rather be alive and see Taylor’s face when she gets it than wait to be dead.

Please, take it for me and your grandfather," a tear slide down her cheek, "he would be so proud of you Adam. I know I am."

Adam squeezed the ring into his hand and wrapped his arms around his grandmother in a hug, "Thank you Grams, I love you."

"I love my boy too, now, go get ready so we can go and celebrate."

I walked into our house and went and sat down on the couch. Grams looked concerned. It hurt me to think Grams could be disappointed in us. I buried my face in my hands and cried. I couldn't handle being a disappointment to Grams.

Adam ran back to his house coming through the door and found Taylor not upstairs getting ready for tonight but instead her sitting on the couch crying. He rushed over to her and knelt down in front of her, "Tay, honey, what's wrong?"

I looked up, tears streaming down my face. "I can't handle it if Grams is disappointed in us Adam."

"What would make you think that Grams was mad at us honey?" He wiped a tear that was running down my face.

"I saw the look on her face Adam when she asked to talk to you."

Adam wanted to tell her what had been said but that would ruin everything, "Honey, she isn't upset, she is over joyed, I promise you that. She wanted to tell me something my grandfather wanted me to know. I promise to tell you about it soon but trust me for now please. She is in no way mad at us she can't wait to have another great grandchild and she loves you to death so please, calm yourself down." He brought himself to sit next to me on the couch and pulled me onto his lap, "I love you."

"I love you too," I placed my hand on the side of his face and smiled, "Just for the record, I am very excited to be having your baby." I then claimed his lips in a kiss that spoke louder than any words I could have spoken.

Adam wanted nothing more than to strip her of her clothes and make sweet love to her but they had people that were going to be waiting on them. “I need to take a shower and if I don’t do it now then I am going to tear yours clothes off and have my way with you right here.”

I smiled, “Well you did say we have an hour. How about I join you in that shower and help wash your back?”

Adam stood up with me in his arms and headed for the stairs, “How did I manage to get so lucky and find you, my love?”

“I do believe I am the lucky one cowboy, now come on, let’s go get ready.”

Chapter 11

Mike opened the door and entered the dance/eating place in this small town. It was a Friday night and for such a small town the place was pretty busy. He stood there for a moment and looked around, it should be pretty easy to find out where Taylor was, small towns were always the easiest to get information about people, he just had to find the right person to ask.

He walked around for a while and decided to just hang back for a while and check out his surroundings. One thing he had to remember as well was that in a small town, you being a new comer and starting by shooting out a lot of questions about someone, can start people wondering as well. He had to find that perfect person. He looked around a couple of times, his eyes always locking with this one woman at the bar.

She was leaning against the bar, mid-twenties, brunette, and a very pretty woman, the kind of woman who liked an adventure or just a quick roll in the hay as the people around this place would probably say. She was perfect, as long as she knew who he was looking for then the rest would be a piece of cake.

Mike never had a problem talking to woman, or getting woman to do what he asked, he had a charm about himself that woman just fell for. He walked straight up to her at the bar, stopping about two feet from her, "Can I buy you a beer?"

She looked him up and down and then smiled, "Sure."

He signaled for two beers at the bartender then brought his attention back to the woman standing in front of him, "I'm Mike."

She smiled a sly seductive smile, "I'm Lindsay."

Lindsay could tell this man wasn't from around here, people usually didn't walk into this place dressed in khaki pants and a button up shirt. He looked like he belonged in an upscale restaurant in the city not a country ba,r but all the same, she never refused when a good looking man offered to buy her a beer.

He handed her the bottle neck beer and smiled, "So, are you from around here?"

Lindsay took a drink but her eyes never left his, "All of my life."

"Well perfect I just got into town and am looking for someone to show me around."

Lindsay once again looked him up and down. His blonde hair and amazingly clear green eyes were almost hypnotizing. "Well I do believe you have found your tour guide."

Mike gave his dazzling smile. He knew he was good looking, women easily feel at his feet and this woman was no different. Her eyes were telling him everything she wanted from him and why not while he was here take in a little fun time as well. This woman was more than willing, he could tell by the way that every time she went to take a drink of her beer she ran her tongue lightly over the tip of the beer.

"So, what brings you to town?"

"Well, I will be honest with you since I don't play games, I go after what I want," he moved a couple of inches closer to her, "I am here looking for my wife," he saw the disappointment cross her face. "No, you don't understand, I am here for a little revenge and I think you could help me with that. You see, I went away on business and when I got home I found her and my stuff gone. The bitch took everything. Well I found out she came here, possibly with another man, and well I would love a little pay back of my own, get some of my stuff back, destroy the relationship she is possibly in and then divorce her. However in the meantime," he ran a light finger down her arm, "I would like to get to know you a little better."

Lindsay was a little shocked at first, this guy wasn't hiding or holding anything back. He knew what he wanted, and what did she care if he was married or not? She wasn't looking for any long term relationship. He was the type that knew he was good looking and she would bet all the money she had that he wasn't the type to stay loyal to just one woman. She didn't care, she wasn't looking for a commitment from him, but she could only imagine what kind of bed partner he was and that she would love to find out. It worked out better for her if he wasn't looking for anything else but a one night stand, "So, who is this woman you are looking for?"

Mike smiled, "Her name is Taylor Kennedy. I am pretty sure she is going by her maiden name." Lindsay's eyes widened slightly, you had to be kidding. Taylor was married to this man? This was going to be way too easy. She could help this man find her, break her apart from Adam, then once again he would be available for her to go after.

Mike smiled, she knew Taylor. He could tell from the spark that lit up her eyes. "So I am guessing you know my wife?"

Lindsay nodded, "Most of my life. We went to school together. You are correct, she is back in town."

"So, you have seen her then?"

"Yes and I just heard recently that she had decided to move back to town."

Mike smiled, this was going to be easy, "So do you know where I can find her?"

"Yes but what is in it for me to tell you where to find her?"

Mike leaned close to her and placed his hands on the bar on both sides of her, bringing his face within inches of her. His lips brushed her lips as he spoke, "How about you and I enjoy a little time together, you show me what that tongue you keep using on that bottle can do to a man."

Lindsay smiled this man was completely conceited, much like herself. Mike claimed her lips in a fierce almost punishing kiss, he would be a little rough. She liked her love making a little rough, her blood started to boil he would be a fun lover.

She broke from his kiss and smiled, "How about tonight you and I learn a little more about each other and tomorrow I show you where your wife can be found."

Mike grinded up against her this was all a little too easy. He wanted nothing more than to find out where Taylor was, make her sorry for what she had put him through, and then leave this place but, he hadn't had a woman in a long time and this beautiful one was completely willing to give him sex and information. Finding Taylor could wait until tomorrow, tonight he had to have this woman."My hotel sound alright to you?"

Lindsay smiled wickedly. Perfect, she never took guys to her place, "Sounds perfect," she kissed him once more and then lead the way out of the bar. She didn't have to look back, she knew he was following.

Chapter 12

"We are going to have to get you an appointment for a doctor soon. We also need to decide what room we want to use for the baby's room.... actually, now that I think about it we have a lot to do." Adam laid there holding Taylor after a night of celebrating.

I smiled, "I do believe we have some time to get everything done."

Adam agreed but it would go by fast, here he lay on his side, Taylor's back up against him, his arms wrapped around her, his hand lightly stroking her belly. He kissed the back of my head, I turned my head only to look at him, I smiled. God how he loved this woman and now she carried his child. His hand rubbed a little more on her stomach. The two of them through their love making had created this little person and faster than he knew it, this little one will be in his arms. Man, how fast life can change. "Tomorrow I need to run into town to take care of some ranch business."

"Did you want me to go with you?" I asked hoping tomorrow morning was better than this morning.

"No, I just wanted you to know I would be up early and gone. How about when I get back we take a ride?"

I turned myself over to lie on my back, "Don't you have work around here you have to do?" I knew that since I arrived here Adam had probably taken more time off then he ever had.

"I have spent every day since my grandfather's death at the ranch. I have never taken a vacation, never just said today I am taking a day off. I had no reason to, until now, so I believe if I want to take a day off to be with the woman I love and the mother of my child then I deserve to by now."

"Adam, I just don't want you thinking that I'll get upset if you weren't spending time with me. I know what ranch life requires I'm not one of those woman who cries and throws a fit when her man isn't giving her all of his attention," I smiled up at him.

He leaned to me and kissed me lightly, "I have no idea what I did to deserve you in my life. Honestly, I figured I would die an old man, no kids, no wife because my life was this ranch. This ranch will always be very important to me but now I have two reason's to put it on the back burner every once in a while."

"You're sure you don't want me to go with you in the morning?"

Adam smiled down at her, "I'll be leaving early and there's no reason for you to be up that early if you aren't feeling well again. I won't be that long, I promise. Before I get back help Grams put a lunch together for us."

"Alright, I'll allow you to steal me away this once, but after this time no more taking breaks, it's back to work," I teased with him.

"Man you're harder to deal with than Grams. I'll have to remember this for the future, get some sleep we have a full day of riding in front of us before you get to big to ride," Adam teased me hand rubbing my stomach and then kissed me tenderly.

"This is the place," Lindsay pointed out to Mike as he walked up beside her car. He had followed her from town to the ranch. "That large house is the main one and I will put money that your wife is staying in the other house off to the left with Adam. They seemed pretty close the last time I saw them."

They had spent the entire evening having sex. She would have almost believed that he had been trying to make up for lost time or something. He never stopped and she would have to say it was probably the best she had ever had. Although she was correct last night when she figured he would be a rough bed partner, but she didn't mind a little pain, it actually turned her on just that much more.

"You can go now," he said and then walked around the front of her car and stood on her passenger side his eyes glaring down the very long driveway. In the distance and behind all the massive trees he could make out the two buildings that would be the house. Taylor was in his reach now, she wouldn't be able to hide any longer.

Lindsay rolled down her passenger window, talking to his back, "Will I see you tonight?"

Mike never turned around to look at her. Last night had been alright for him but he wouldn't say the best. She had been able to give him what he hadn't had in a very long time and it wouldn't bother him to have her again, but he would have to see how things went today. "We'll see. I know where to find you tonight."

Lindsay pouted a little but that did her no good, he wasn't even looking at her. "Yes, you know where to find me," she rolled her windows back up and then decided it would be best to leave. She didn't want to chance Adam or one of the other family members seeing her.

After Lindsay pulled away Mike stood there for a few more minutes, then he decided to walk down a little ways and see if he could get a better view of things, it was still pretty early in the morning hopefully no one would be up and about yet.

Just as he reached about half way down the driveway a truck appeared in front of him. Trying to figure out what he was going to say, he stopped walking and waited because there was absolutely nowhere to hide. He just hoped it wasn't the best friend, he was sure that would be the only person here besides Taylor who would recognize him. As the truck came closer he realized it was a man driving. He pulled up alongside of him, stopped and rolled down the window, "Hello," was all Mike said.

"Can I help you?" Adam asked. It was very early in the morning, actually a little too early for someone to be walking up the driveway. He looked harder at the man. He looked familiar but he couldn't figure out where he had seen him before.

"Do you live here?" Mike asked, hands in his pocket and as calm as could be, acting like it was a completely normal thing for him to be walking down the driveway at this time of the morning.

"Yes," was all Adam answered. There was something about this man that he didn't like.

"Well then, I'm very sorry to bother you, it seems that I have the wrong location," Mike played it off.

"What place are you looking for, maybe I could point you in the right direction?"

"You know I was hoping to surprise someone so I'll figure it out. Again, I am sorry to bother you. Have a nice morning," Mike then turned, hands still in his pockets, he began to walk back towards the road.

Adam sat there in the driveway and watched as the stranger walked back down the road and turned the corner. He could swear that he knew this guy from somewhere but he couldn't for the life of him figure out where. He then watched as a silver four door car drove past the guy at the wheel. Why had he been walking down the driveway if he had a car with him? He sat there for a few more moments then decided he didn't have time to worry about it now, the guy was just looking in the wrong spot that's all, right now he had more important things to do, and he had an appointment he didn't want to be late for.

“So how are you feeling today?” Hailey asked Taylor as they were sitting down for breakfast.

I pushed the food around on my plate, “Alright I guess, I mean, I didn’t have to run to the bathroom this morning so that was better but my stomach isn’t settled right now.” She looked back down at her plate, “Sorry Grams, I didn’t mean to waste your breakfast.”

“Don’t be silly Taylor. Believe it or not, I still remember what those first few months of mornings felt like. Honey, if you aren’t hungry then don’t eat, you can always have something in a couple of hours if you are feeling better.”

“How long should I expect to be feeling like this?” I pushed my plate away from me and settled with just drinking my orange juice.

“It all depends. I was pretty lucky when I was pregnant with Bryson, I really never had any sickness, but I have known women who have had it for just a couple of days, up to all the way through their pregnancy,” Hailey explained.

“Oh god, please allow me only to reach the couple of days mark.” I looked up at the ceiling as I said my plea.

“Why are you sick?” Bryson asked with a mouth full of pancakes.

“Bryson, you know better than to talk with your mouth full of food,” Hailey scolded him.

Bryson swallowed his food and smiled up at his mom, “I’m sorry mommy.”

I smiled at the little boy sitting across from me. “I’m not sick like you think I am buddy. I am going to have a baby,” I explained then realized how strange it was to say that, it was definitely going to take some getting used to.

“Oh,” was all Bryson said but from the look on his face he was completely confused by the answer that he got.

Hailey laughed and placed an arm around her son bringing him into her for a hug, "I will explain it to you later little man."

"Who is the daddy?" he asked.

Hailey sometimes thought her son was a little too smart for his age but with always hanging out with adults what did she expect? "Uncle Adam is the daddy."

Bryson shook his head, "Nooo he is Uncle Adam, not a daddy."

The three women at the table laughed, now that was the innocence of a five year old. "You are right, he is your Uncle Adam but now he gets to be a daddy too and you will finally have a little cousin to play with," Hailey explained.

"Hope he likes playing with cars because that is all I like to play with." Bryson said then shoveled another fork full of pancake into his mouth.

"Well the baby may be a girl," Grams spoke up from the end of the table.

"No, only boys are aloud. I better tell Uncle Adam no girls," he answered Grams with a very serious look on his face, and then went back to eating his breakfast.

The women broke into laughter, Bryson looked around at them, "What's so funny?"

I wiped a tear away from my eyes that escaped from my laughter, "Little man we'll do our best to have a boy alright?"

"Where is my dear brother this morning?" Hailey turned the conversation around.

"He had an appointment in town this morning about the ranch. When he gets back we are taking a ride," I answered hoping that by the time he got back my stomach had settled or I wouldn't be going anywhere.

"What kind of appointment?" Hailey was confused, her brother never went into town on business, it was usually brought to the ranch.

I shrugged, "I didn't ask details."

Grams smiled, she knew what the appointment he had was about and she was very proud of him. Her husband and her had often talked about how worried they were that Adam would put too much of himself and his time in the ranch and never find someone to have a family with. To her surprise the angel just appeared and she was so happy, "I'm sure he will be home soon." Grams stood up from the table and started collecting dishes.

"Grams, do you know where Adam went?" Hailey was a little bothered with the fact that her brother would tell Grams about ranch business and not her and if Ryan knew anything then he hadn't said anything to her either.

Grams didn't say a word, she just started humming as she disappeared into the kitchen.

Hailey looked at Taylor. She didn't seem that bothered with the fact that she didn't know why Adam went into town. Taylor shrugged her shoulders, got up and started gathering the remaining dishes on the table then headed into the kitchen after Grams.

It was around twelve and I had packed a lunch and was ready for the ride with Adam this afternoon, I even had my camera ready to go. Even better my stomach had settled for the day, I hoped. I was actually looking forward to the food that had been packed for our lunch, the only thing missing now was Adam, he was still in town.

I decided to go out and sit on the porch swing and wait for him. It was a beautiful day outside. I sat down just as Hailey and Bryson came out of their house.

"Go get your bike, buddy, and ride here in front so that I can watch you. I'm going to sit with Aunt Taylor and talk."

"Ok mommy," Bryson ran towards the barn to get his bike.

Hailey walked over to her brother's house and up the stairs to the porch, sitting down next to her friend, "Adam still isn't home?"

I shook my head. "No he isn't even answering his phone. If he is in a meeting then I wouldn't think he would answer the phone anyway."

Hailey studied her friend for a moment, the last couple of days she hadn't been acting the same. "Taylor what's wrong?"

Taylor looked over at Hailey puzzled, "What do you mean? Why do you think something is wrong?"

"Because we have known each other for a very long time and in that time I've learned to read you like a book, that is what best friends do, they pay attention to their friends and realize when something isn't right. You haven't been yourself the last couple of days. Something is bothering you and I think you need to tell me what it is."

I knew I could never hide anything from Hailey, she always knew when something had been bothering me. "I can't really say anything is wrong it's just that the last couple of months have been crazy and things have changed so fast. I went from doing nothing but working all the time and ignoring people and friends that I use to hang out with all the time before Mike and I got together, to starting a relationship, falling in love, hardly working, moving and now pregnancy. It's a lot to swallow in such a short time."

"I will agree you have had quite the changes in your life in the last couple of months, but it's all good right? I mean, I know you must miss working, but other than that?"

“Strange thing is, I really don’t miss the working part so much. I mean, don’t get me wrong, I love taking pictures. I guess now that I have slowed down a little I kind of realize that was all I was doing, working. As soon as things settle down here a little and I get the first doctor’s appointment out of the way and get my stuff moved in then I will start advertising again.”

Hailey watched her friend for a moment. She watched the way she stared off and her fingers ran lightly over her stomach, “Taylor, aren’t you happy about the baby? You are going to be a mother, I thought you would be a little more excited.”

I looked down at my still very flat stomach, then back up at my friend, “I’m scared Hailey. I’m afraid it will somehow all be taken away from me.”

Hailey grabbed my hand, “Taylor, you can’t think that way! You will only drive yourself crazy, plus being worried like that all of the time will only cause you to stress and that isn’t good for the baby. Nothing is going to happen. You are going to have a beautiful little baby.”

“I know, I just need to straighten out my mind is all, like I said, just a lot to take in.” I knew that my life right now was completely different from my life eight years ago, my relationship with Adam was completely different, our baby would be fine. Wow, mine and Adam’s baby, now that I thought about it I got the giggles.

Hailey looked over at me puzzled when she heard me laughing, now that was a fast turnaround of moods, “What is so funny?”

“What would you have said back in high school if someone would have told you that I would one day be pregnant with your brother’s baby? I must say in all those years I would never have seen this coming.”

Hailey began to laugh with me, “You know, Ryan and I were just talking about that last night when we got home from dinner. It’s funny how life ends up. I am so excited that it was you who my brother finally fell in love with. I couldn’t think of two people who were more perfect for each other than you guys, well except Ryan and myself of course.”

The sound of a truck coming down the driveway caught both of our attention, "Well look who has finally made it home." Hailey leaned over and gave me a hug, "Listen to me, everything will be fin,e I promise. You two go out and enjoy your ride and time together, I will see you later this evening."

Hailey stood up and started down the stairs. "Thanks Hailey," I called after her and watched as she walked away.

Adam jumped out of the truck as his sister passed him. "It's about time you made it home."

Adam ignored his sister, he had expected to be home a couple of hours ago, but things weren't quite ready when he arrived to his appointment. He ran up the stairs and over to the porch swing where Taylor was sitting, "Tay, I am so sorry. I really didn't expect it to take this long. Are you still up for our ride?" he asked hoping she was. He had been looking forward to this ride all day.

I held my hand out to him, he took it and pulled me up right into his arms, "Of course I'm still wanting to go. It's only a little past twelve plus I'm starving! Grams made us a great lunch and I didn't eat much for breakfast."

"Not feeling too well this morning again?" he asked.

"Actually, it was better this morning than yesterday morning but my appetite wasn't really there, but now I'm starving."

Adam smiled down at me, "Well than go get the stuff. I will go and saddle the horses and we will be on our way." He gave me a kiss then pushed me towards the house as he ran back down the stairs and went to the stables.

"So let's see it," Grams came up behind Adam as he cinched down one of the saddles.

"See what?" Adam smiled to himself not turning to look at his grandmother. He knew what she was talking about, he should have figured she would be searching him out see the finished product.

"Don't try and play stupid with me young man. I know where you went this morning," Grams patted the neck of the horse. "Adam, come on let me see it."

Adam stopped what he was doing and turned to look at his grandmother. She wasn't going to leave until he showed her so he decided he better move quick before Taylor walked in. He looked around to make sure no one was around then quickly dug into the front pocket of his jeans. Pulling out his hand and opening it in front of Grams.

"I had the guy design it last week, he had already started on it for me. I know we have only been together for a few months but my heart tells me she is the one. I have never felt like this about a woman. When she agreed to move out here I decided I was going to ask her. Of course I wasn't sure when I was going to ask, it may have been a couple of months from now," Grams took the ring from his hand, "Yesterday when she told me she was pregnant I decided not to wait. I want us married before the baby is born. When you gave me your diamond I called the guy right away asked if it could be done if I brought it into him today. I went in this morning and it took a little longer than we both thought but I think he did an amazing job."

Grams couldn't believe the stunning piece of jewelry in her hand. There gleaming up at her was the diamond that her dear husband had given to her so many years ago. It was surrounded by six smaller diamonds looking as though they were dancing around the grand one in the middle. All of them held together by white gold. She remembered how proud her husband was of that ring when he asked for her hand. He had worked so hard and saved so much to give her a ring that he said he wanted her to be proud to wear for many many years. Of course she would have proudly stood by that man's side in marriage even if there had been no ring. Adam was a lot like his grandfather, he took care of whatever he loved.

She handed the ring back to Adam and watched as he quickly slid it back into his pocket, "It's beautiful," wrapping her arms tightly around her grandson, "I am so proud of you Adam. You both deserve to be happy and now with what I'm sure to be an absolutely beautiful child on the way you will have a family of your own. Your grandfather is smiling down at you my son that I am absolutely positive of."

Adam hugged his grandmother tightly. She was the world to him, "Thank you grams."

Adam and Grams never heard anyone enter the stables until Taylor spoke, "Is everything alright?"

Grams quickly wiped the tear from her cheek before turning around to Taylor, "Of course, why wouldn't everything be great? I just came out to make sure we got everything that Adam had wanted for your picnic today."

I had noticed the tears in Grams eyes, she wasn't asking about the picnic. I was still worried that Grams was disappointed in us. Adam had reassured me that Grams was excited for us but I'm starting to wonder now what Adam wasn't telling me.

Grams gave me a hug, "You two have a great afternoon, we will see you later this evening," and then she left the two of us alone.

I watched as Grams left. Once she was out of sight I turned back to Adam, "What is going on? Why is Grams crying? There is something you are not telling me Adam."

Adam quickly took the bags out of my hands and gave me a quick kiss, "Everything is fine, I promise," then went about tying the bags to the saddle.

We rode to the spot that Adam always took me to. It was usually the best spot to see the horses that were running free on the property.

Although today there were no horses, which I found myself feeling a little disappointed about. Watching all the horses in the open always made me feel at peace.

We settled in under the large oak tree that stood right next to the stream and right away went into having lunch. I was starving now since I hadn't been able to eat anything at breakfast. If I ate like this through this whole pregnancy then I was going to be as big as cow. Conversation was sparse while we ate, which was making me think that something was definitely up with him, "So, did everything go alright in town today with your meeting?"

"Everything went great. Sorry it took me longer today. I really didn't expect to be there that long, some of the decisions took longer than I thought they would."

I picked up my plate and put a hand out to Adam, "Are you finished?" Adam nodded and handed his plate to me. I turned my back to him but could feel his eyes watching me as I put everything away.

The moment that she turned her back to him he quickly dug into the front pocket of his jeans and pulled out the ring. He balled his fist tightly around it, leaned back against the giant tree and waited for her to turn back to him.

I finished packing everything away and turned back around. Adam was casually leaning back against the tree, holding a hand out to me, "Come sit with me."

I crawled across the blanket and settled myself between his legs, my back resting up against his chest. I laid my head back against his shoulder and took a deep breath and let it out slowly. Adam's arm came around and his hand settled on my stomach, this was something he did now since finding out I was pregnant. I smiled to myself and brought my hand up to rest on top of his, under both their hands was the life they had created together.

Adam kissed the top of her head, he tighten the fist that he made around the ring he was holding, his nerves started to shake a little, "So, I know you must miss your job. Have you decided on when you think you may want to start it all back up again?" He needed to calm down a little.

I nodded, "Actually, I was just talking to Hailey about all of that before you got home. I am missing it but I am thinking about waiting until after the doctor's appointment, ask a few questions I have then start advertising after that. I actually did have a couple who called me about a week ago and asked if I could do their wedding, I shot her sister's wedding a couple years ago in Napa. She loved their pictures and called me for her wedding. Difference is this wedding is in Southern California, I told her I was honored that they thought of me and that they liked my work but that I couldn't."

"Tay, if you want to go you can."

My fingers played with Adam's and I closed my eyes. At first it had been hard to turn the work down but now I was alright with staying close to home, "I know but strangely I am alright with turning them down. Don't get me wrong I hated that I told her no. It's hard for a bride to trust someone with the photos that will capture the biggest day of their lives, but I'm ok with my decision" I rubbed my hand over his.

Adam's arm tightened around her just a little more. He was happy to hear she was alright with her life right now, knowing that should help with his nerves a little. He knew that he wanted to marry Taylor, have a family together, but she had mentioned a couple of times how much her life was changing and how fast it was happening. Hearing her admit to being good with turning down a job and starting to plan for starting her business up here was something he needed to hear from her. "I just want you to know I will support you with whatever you decide to do."

"I know you are and I love you that much more for supporting me," Something was wrong with Adam, I could hear it in his voice. I sat up and turned around to look at him, he smiled at me, "Are you alright?"

"Of course I'm alright." No, he was pretty sure his heart was going to beat right out of his chest at any moment, the ring in his palm seemed to be burning him.

I looked at him for a moment longer. No, something was definitely going on with him, I could read it in his eyes. I looked down at the hand that rested on his knee that hand had never relaxed. Actually, now that I looked again his knuckles were white, he was squeezing his fist so hard. I slid my hand down his arm and rested it on top of his fisted one, "Adam what is going on?"

His eyes never left mine but he did turn his hand over, my hand now cradling his in my palm and I felt his hand open as if showing me something but I couldn't tear my eyes away from his. They were almost pleading with me. I blinked then looked down at his now open hand.

Adam heard her sharp intake of breath the moment she opened her eyes and saw what he was holding. He felt her hand beginning to shake under his, his heart hammered in his chest. He found himself holding his breath waiting for her to say something. He watched as the first tear escaped from her eyes and slid down her cheek.

I couldn't speak, I could only stare at the most amazingly beautiful ring I had ever seen. It gleamed as the sun caught the diamonds, it seemed to be dancing around for me. Then I noticed it, this is why Grams had been talking with Adam, why she had been crying earlier, "That's Grams diamond!"

Adam's eyes never left her face. He wanted to see her complete reaction but she surprised him when she said it was Grams, "How do you know that?"

I couldn't remove my eyes from the ring, "I have admired it on her hand many times. It's an emerald cut diamond, those have always been my favorite."

"Taylor," when she didn't look at him he took his other hand placed it on her cheek and turned her face to his. His breath caught in his chest, she was so beautiful. "Last week I had asked a jeweler to start this ring for me. After you announced that you were pregnant Grams gave me her ring and told me that before my grandfather died they had decided Hailey would get mom's ring and I would get hers if I was ever to marry. This morning I took it to the guy and asked if he could replace the diamond I had picked out for Grams, so now all I need to know is will you allow me the privilege of waking up to you every morning and falling asleep with you every night? Will you honor me with standing next to me as we watch our children grow up, will you marry me?"

Two weeks ago, maybe even last week, if Adam had asked me that question I knew I would have told him no. I had made one promise to myself and that was if I was ever to get into another relationship I would take it slow. Date for a year or so, plan a wedding for a year or so, make sure I knew the man and had absolutely no doubts. I may have only been dating Adam for a couple of months but I had known him all of my life and now I was pregnant with his child and that child was created through our love for each other. Well so much for taking things slow, "Can we have a large wedding?"

Adam wasn't sure if he had heard her right, out of everything he had prepared himself for her to say that was not one of them, "What?"

"Well, every little girl plans their big wedding. My last wedding was in front of a judge. I want my dad to walk me down the aisle. Hailey to be standing by my side. I want to walk down the aisle in front of family and friends and look down to see my soon to be husband looking dashing and proud. I want the cake cutting, first dance, garter toss and picture taking until our mouths feel like they are going to break from smiling too much."

Adam laughed, "Honey, if you say yes you can have whatever kind of wedding that you would like."

I held out my left hand, "Then would you please let me see how amazing that ring is going to look on my hand."

Adam smiled at me and started to place the ring onto my finger, stopping just before sliding it all the way on. "Once this ring is completely on your finger I am never letting you go, it will be until death do us part."

I smiled tears streaming down my cheeks. I slightly pushed my hand forward, the ring slid perfectly onto my finger, "Until death do us part."

Adam swallowed me up into his arms and claimed my lips for a kiss that sealed us together.

The ride back all I could do was stare at the diamonds dancing around and showing off in the sun light. Wow, first a baby and now a wedding. A couple of months ago if you would have told me this is where my life would be and to top it off this is who my life would be with, Adam, my best friends brother, I would have laughed hysterically. Oddly, I only felt happiness, not terrified like I thought I would have with all the changes that had occurred in my life in a matter of three days. Yet this did just prove never say never and no matter what plans you made for yourself and your life it doesn't mean that is how things were going to work out, no matter how much you fought it.

I placed my hand on my stomach and tears formed in my eyes. I was being given a second chance at being a mom, the last couple of days I almost didn't want to get my hopes up. I felt like at any moment all of my happiness was going to be taken away. I had to admit, at first, when Grams had ask to talk to Adam alone the day we announced we were going to have a baby and then today finding them in the stables alone and Grams crying I was scared that Grams was disappointed in us, upset because we were rushing things. Now however, I realized what Grams and Adam were up to and the first thing I was going to do when we got back to the house was find Grams and grab her up in the biggest hug I could.

Adam watched Taylor for a while as they rode back, she had stared at that ring most of the ride and now she was crying and her hand was on her stomach. He knew she wasn't hurting though, that smile on her face spoke more than any words could. How life had changed, he thought to himself. He would have sworn that he was going to grow old, single, and the only thing he was ever going to love besides his family was his ranch. Then Taylor walked into his world and turned it upside down. Who would have ever thought his sister's best friend would be the one he was going to marry and have children with? He looked up at the blue sky silently thanking his grandfather and god for bringing Taylor into his life.

He looked back over at Taylor and caught her looking at him, "Tay, I know I am sounding slightly old fashion here but I want us married before our little one arrives."

I shook my head, "That is great, fine, and dandy but I refuse to get married when I am hugely pregnant. Part of the wedding I imagined is in a beautiful wedding gown and looking amazing in it thank you."

"Honey, you will look amazing no matter how pregnant you are but if you want to not have a baby bump then I think we better do this soon. You have what, maybe two, three months tops before you start showing," Adam was laughing.

I tried imagining planning my dream wedding in two months, "Really? You think this is funny? Why can't we just wait until after the baby is born? Old fashion is a little out the door right now don't you think?"

Adam pulled on the reins to his horse bringing him to a stop, Taylor followed. He grabbed Taylors reins and pulled the horses in together where his legs were up against Taylor's, "Tay I understand what you are saying but even though we are kind of putting the cart before the horse per say with already having the baby on the way I would really like to be able to call you my wife before our baby comes and we are calling you mommy. You and Hailey can pull this off."

I agreed it would be nice to be a wife first. I smiled at him, grabbed the front of his shirt, and pulled him over to me "You better hold on tight cowboy, it's going to be one fast ride to the altar," then I claimed his lips.

The kiss was intended to just be a small kiss but once his lips touched mine I was instantly on fire, I wanted him and I wanted him now.

I knew Adam still had a hold of my reins and I was feeling very frisky. I didn't know if that was because of the amazing day we were having or baby hormones but I wanted him. Without breaking the kiss I kicked his foot out of his stirrup with my booted foot then slid my foot in, placed my hand on his shoulder and lifted myself out of my saddle and swung over onto his lap straddling him.

Adam wasn't sure exactly how she managed but he didn't have time either to think about it, having her straddle him instantly hardened him. If he could make love to her right here on his horse he would but he knew that was going to be a little difficult. He looked around as she was trailing kisses down his neck and spotted a huge oak tree. "Hold on," he kicked his horse and moved them all over to the tree area. Hardest thing he has ever had to do he was pull himself away from her roaming lips. He lifted her up and help her slide to the ground, then jumped down after her.

I looked around grabbed the blanket we had brought and while he tied the horses up I spread out the blanket under the large tree. Adam came up behind me and wrapped his arms around my waist, his lips going to the side of my neck. I pulled away grabbed his arms and pulled him around in front of me. "Have a seat," I said and watched as he placed himself on the ground up against the tree looking up at me.

I held one booted foot up to him, "Can you help me out of these please?" I smiled down at him as he slid the first one off then I held up my second boot. "Thank you."

Adam watched as, after he removed her boots he expected her to come down and join him on the blanket but no, that wasn't the case. Instead he watched as she untucked her t-shirt from her pants and ever so slowly pulled it up over her head and then let it fall to the ground, her bra following. She trailed her left hand slowly down the valley between her breast, down her stomach and to the button of her jeans. She unbuttoned them and the zipper followed and then very slowly she slide them down her legs.

I stood there for a moment, the sun at my back, it felt great on my naked skin. I watched as his eyes traveled the length of my body and when his eyes met back with mine I smiled, "You better look as much as you can now because in a couple of months I am going to get a little rounder."

Adam swore an angel stood before him the way the sun beamed at her back, her blond hair hanging loose shining in the sun against her naked body. God, how did he get so lucky? He got to his knees in front of her and placed his hands on her hips, he looked up at her and smiled, "I personally cannot wait to see you round with our child." Then he leaned forward and kissed her belly.

I leaned forward and I pulled his t-shirt form his pants and lifted it up over his head and let it fall to the ground with my clothing. I knelt down in front of him but pushed him back to where he was once again sitting and leaning back against the tree. I quickly removed boots and socks. I slowly crawled up the length of his legs, my body beginning to straddle him. I ran my hand up his jean clad leg and my fingers brushed his now very hard erection. I smiled up at him, his erection was straining against his pants begging to be released and placed at home deep inside of me. My fingers worked up to the button fly and quickly unbuttoned each of them. As I pulled them down I felt Adam lift his hips, I pulled them off and my eyes worshiped his body and his erection that was standing straight up against his stomach begging to be touched.

I slowly started crawling up his length again my tongue traveling up his leg, once I made it up to the swollen tip of his erection my tongue circled him very lightly, I heard Adam take a deep breath, I looked up at him and smiled then watched him as I took him fully into my mouth.

Adam's head fell back against the tree, his hands dug into her hair as she stroked him with her mouth and tongue. He was losing his mind very quickly and didn't know how much more he could take. He wanted to be in her. He sat up quickly, he felt her mouth leave him and he placed hands on each side of her waist lifted her up and when he brought her down to straddle him as he slide himself into her velvet wetness.

I wrapped my legs around his waist and when I felt him enter me I moaned, when I felt his tongue on my nipple I almost screamed out. My hands in his hair I pressed his head to my chest begging him to take my breast fully into his mouth. His hands at my hips he guided me out then pulled me in slowly I felt every inch of him slid against my inner walls and hit that spot deep inside, I needed him deeper though and faster especially with every thrust we made he sucked just a little harder on my breast. Between the two actions I thought I was going to burst, "Adam please, please now," my body started to quake inside, I pushed my hips harder into him causing him to go deeper. The sensation of his urgent suckling and the thrusting between us was causing the flames in my veins to feel as though they were going to burst at any moment. Deeper and deeper my body began to convulse around Adam's erection.

Adam's body no longer able to hold back rocked with hers, together they came. Adam wrapped his arms tightly around her burying his face in the valley between her breast enjoying the feel of each of her convulsion around him pulling him deeper and deeper within her milking out every last drop he had inside of her.

Arms tightly holding onto each other, Adam still fully extended inside of me neither spoke nor moved while we tried to catch our breath. We could each feel the other's heart beating against their chest, they beat as one. I was the first to pull a little back, I kept my legs tightly wound around him loving the feel of him deep inside of me. I didn't care if we sat like this all day long. I claimed his lips intending on just a small tender kiss but instead my hips began to rock just slightly, "Tay if you don't stop then I am going to have to have you again," Adam warned his hands on each side of my hips trying to still them before I sent him over the edge.

I looked at him and smiled. I could still feel him hard inside of me. He wasn't done yet either, "I don't believe my ride is over yet," then claimed his lips once again and began to speed up tightening my legs even tighter around his waist and pulling him deeper inside of me.

Adam moaned and then took over the rhythm with his hands once again leading us both into heaven.

Chapter 13

Mike had made his way back to the ranch sometime around five. He had been laying low getting a little agitated that nothing much had been going on and he had not yet seen any signs of Taylor. He was starting to wonder if she was even really at this house. He was about to leave when he heard an older voice yell from the larger house that supper was ready. Movement caught his attention from the second house as two people came out the screen door. That's when he saw her, for the first time since that night and now here she was with another man. He watched as the two of them headed for the larger house hand and hand. They got to the stairs but before stepping up he could tell they were talking but, he was way too far away to hear what they were saying. The man was the one who he had run into that morning. Mike's blood began to boil as he watched the guy kiss Taylor then they both proceeded to go into the house. It took everything in him not to rush the man right there but he had been patient this long, he would get his chance. She was his wife and no one else was going to have her. As for his wife, she would regret cheating on him. The first time he messed up, this time there would be no messing up.

He sat for a moment after they disappeared into the house to make sure they were not coming back out, once he realized it was safe to move he went straight for the house that Taylor had just come out of. The screen door was unlocked and the front door was open wide. He walked in and looked around for a moment. Spotting the stairs he headed straight for them taking them two at a time. Reaching the top he stopped by each door until he found the master bedroom. Once inside he notice right off, the picture sitting on the night stand. It was Taylor and that guy. His temper rose and it took everything in him not to smash the picture against something but that would only give it away that someone was in the house and that was one thing he didn't want Taylor to know yet. He walked over to the closet, opened it up, and there he saw the proof of how deep this relationship was. All of her clothes were hanging there next to the man's, she was living here with him. He shut the door and turned towards the bathroom, upon entering the room he looked onto the counter immediately noticing the white stick. He picked it up and saw the pink plus sign. So, once again the bitch was pregnant with another bastard child. Well he would make sure this one wasn't born as well only this time, he would make sure the mom didn't live either. He placed the stick on the counter and walked back out to the room. Standing in the middle he glared at the portrait on the night stand. How easy would it be to just sit there in the chair and surprise them when they got back. It wasn't the plan though, it wasn't the right time. He really didn't have a time but he knew this wasn't it. He quickly scanned the rest of the upstairs memorizing the home then decided it was time to be on his way before he was caught.

Once downstairs he stood in the middle of the living room for a moment looking around. He had done everything for her. She was just a little nothing when she met him. He was the one who got her career going, making her the photographer that she was, and what had she really done for him? Nothing, she cheated on him, got pregnant not with him, put him in prison, divorced him, then took everything of his, found a different man and is repeating everything all over.

He walked outside and to the steps of the other house on the property. He could hear the talking and laughter coming from inside through the screen door. How easy it would be to walk right through the front door right now, no one inside would be ready. He took a deep breath, "Calm yourself Mike," he spoke out loud to himself, "It's not the right time, and you will get your chance of revenge." He stood there for a moment longer then turned and started back down the long dirt driveway. He needed a distraction and he knew just who to go see about that.

Adam and I walked into the main house hand in hand, Adam's fingers played with the ring on my finger, a symbol that I was his and would be his for the rest of our lives. When we entered the dining room everyone else was already seated at the table.

Grams face was beaming, Taylor had said yes, the proof was sitting on her finger. She wanted to get up and hug them both but she contained herself, she wanted them to announce it first. Her eyes met her grandson's, they spoke without words to each other. She hadn't seen Adam smile like that for years. He was happy and she was happy for him.

"About time you two decided to grace us with you presence, the food was starting to get cold," Hailey grabbed a bowl which had the rolls in it, she took one out for herself, placed one on her son's plate, then handed the bowl over to Taylor.

I accepted the bowl using my left hand, a huge smile on my face. Let's see how long it takes Hailey to notice. The bowl was knocked right out of my hand, a loud screech from Hailey and then a loud crash of the bowl hitting the table just missing the bowl of green beans, rolls went everywhere on the table indicated that Hailey noticed and I was pulled out of my chair to my feet being stretched across the table. Hailey wasn't letting go of my hand. "Is this an engagement ring? When did this happen? How come you didn't tell me?" She looked between Adam and myself for the answers to her exploding questions.

I laughed, "Easy Hailey, that arm is still attached!" I braced myself with my other hand on the table and at any moment I swore she was going to have my face in the mashed potatoes if she didn't release my hand.

Hailey was not releasing me. "Are you two engaged?" she asked once again.

I nodded my head yes, Hailey screech again even louder this time but my arm was finally released, almost too quickly though for I almost fell back into my chair but instead was caught by Adam's arm around me, "Easy little sister, she is pregnant, don't forget."

Before I knew it Hailey was around the table and engulfing me into a huge hug, "I am so excited for you guys I knew you were meant for each other." She pulled away from me and hugged her brother.

I glanced over at Grams, she had a heartwarming smile on her face and tears in her eyes which in turn caused tears to well up in my eyes. I walked over to Grams, she pushed herself away from the table and stood up wrapping me into a hug that could only come from a grandmother. "Thank you so much Grams! I love it and it means so much more knowing it was yours."

Grams kissed me on the check, "I am so happy for the both of you."

I started back to my seat but not before Ryan stood up and wrapped me into a big bear hug, "Welcome to the family."

"Thanks!" I made it back to my seat and sat down then leaned over to Adam and kissed him.

"So, have we decided on when we will be having this wedding?" Grams asked as she pointed to Hailey to clean up the rolls.

"We haven't decided on the exact date yet but I want to be married before the baby is born and Taylor says only if she isn't round with pregnancy," Adam answered.

Hailey put the last roll back in the bowl and handed it back to Taylor, "That would mean in the next couple of months."

"Are you wanting a large wedding or a small one," Grams asked?

"I want our friends and family for sure. I want my father to walk me down the aisle, I have always dreamed about that. Friends standing with us, garters being tossed and the cake being smashed in each other's faces. It doesn't have to be huge but traditional." I looked around the table as I explained my perfect wedding hoping no one would ask what my last wedding was like. I still felt like such a fool every time I thought back to how Mike had fooled me.

"Well then we better get started on planning this wedding. I am sure between Grams, you, and myself we can make this your perfect wedding. Have you told your parents yet?" Hailey asked.

I shook my head, "No, not yet. I am going to call them tomorrow and tell them everything. It should be an interesting conversation. I know they won't be upset or anything but I will count on them being completely shocked."

"Well, you guys can have the wedding here. Hailey and Ryan had their wedding here and it was beautiful," Grams suggested.

I remembered Hailey's wedding, it was beautiful, of course this place was amazing.

"I think having it here is a great idea!" Adam turned to me with a hopeful look on his face.

I couldn't agree more, plus, I would have never been able to tell him no after seeing the look on his face. He wanted it here on the ranch. "Of course that would be perfect."

"Great, one thing down. This may be pretty easy," Hailey shrugged her shoulders, "Now tomorrow after you talk to your parents we can run into town and get started on planning the rest of your wedding. Let's see, we have the invitations, which of course you will have to pick a date quickly so that we can get those ordered. We need the most important part, your dress. You need to pick out your colors, we need to find a DJ..."

"Hailey, breath," Adam interrupted his sister and stopped her. "We will talk to her parents in the morning and then decide on a date. First, I want to ask if Ryan would honor me by being my best- man."

"I would be honored to stand next to you when you tie yourself down for the rest of your life, hook on the old ball and chain," Ryan teased his best friend but he was honored that Adam asked him.

"Thanks man," Adam shook his head at his best friend.

I loved watching the family like this, all playful. I turned to Hailey, "And Hailey I would like to know if you would honor me with being my matron of honor?"

Hailey beamed, "Of course I would love to stand by you and watch you as you place that old ball and chain on my brother."

"Hey! What about me? I want to help put the ball and chain on Uncle Adam!" Bryson spoke up looking around the table like he couldn't believe they had forgotten to include him in on the game.

Everyone broke out into laughter. Kids, you had to love the things they come up with. "How would you like to be the ring bearer, little man?" Adam suggested.

"What's that?" Bryson asked back.

"Well it is the most important job of the wedding. You get to carry and keep the rings safe making sure nothing happens to them. Do you think you are up for that special of a job? It requires someone pretty grown up to handle it," I explained to him.

Bryson looked around the table, "I know I can do that! Can I please have that job? Mommy tells me all the time I am her big boy now."

Once again the table erupted into laughter, "Sure buddy, I think you are perfect for the job," Adam smiled over at his nephew then over at me, he took my hand I turned my attention to him and he quickly stole a kiss from me then whispered, "I love you."

"I love you too," I answered back.

"Alright you two, enough for now," Hailey commented shoving her chair back, she got up and left the room only to return quickly carrying a notepad and pen, sitting back down she starting writing a list. "Alright, so I will make a list of stuff we need to get done tomorrow, dress being the first, of course, then invitations."

"You need to make an appointment for the baby as well. Might as well do that when you are in town too," Adam suggested.

I took a deep breath, everything all of a sudden seemed to be closing in on me. There was a lot to be done and it all had to be done fast. How was I going to manage everything?

"Are you alright?" Adam asked, concern in his eyes.

I smiled the best reassuring smile that I could, "Sure, just a lot to get done all of a sudden. At one moment I am complaining I'm bored, the next I have a wedding to plan and doctor appointments to make, just a little over whelming."

"I will keep Bryson home with me tomorrow," Grams offered. "Ryan works tomorrow and he will be bored dress shopping, he will only drive you crazy."

"But Grams, don't you want to go with us?" Hailey asked knowing that asking Grams to stay at home and not be included in all of this was not fair. "Bryson will just have to come with us."

"Dress shopping? Yuck, that's for girls! I don't want to go," Bryson started complaining.

"Really dear it's no big deal, he is already complaining so how do you think he will be tomorrow?" Grams pointed out.

"Grams, you go with the ladies. You need a day away as well. Bryson can stay with me tomorrow. I was just going to go out and check on some fences and check on the herd and probably clean stalls. He can help me do all that, right buddy?" Adam offered knowing that Grams needed to get out a little too and he wanted her to be a part of all this as well, just not the live in babysitter that she so likes to put herself as.

"Mommy, please can I stay with Uncle Adam, please?" Bryson begged.

"That's fine, now finish your dinner," Hailey pointed at his plate.

Mike slammed into Lindsay hard. Lindsay liked sex to be a little physical, even a little pain turned her on but Mike was pushing the limits. Something was bothering him tonight, she could tell from the moment she saw him walk into the bar. He quickly drank down two beers, never really saying too much, then turned to her, "Come on let's get out of here," was all he said then he grabbed her hand and basically pulled her through the bar.

They had barely made it into his hotel room before he started grabbing at her. Once inside he slammed the door shut with his foot and slammed her up against the wall grinding his mouth into hers.

"Take your clothes off before I rip the damn things off," he demanded.

Her breasts were very sore, he didn't nibble, he flat out bit her nipples. There wasn't much foreplay and before she knew what happened she was on the floor on her hands and knees and he was taking her from behind which brought them to this moment. With each thrust he would go deeper and deeper, harder and harder. His hands were squeezing her breast with a punishing grip.

"Mike, you are hurting me," she finally found her voice.

"Shut up bitch! You like it rough, you told me that." As he spoke each word was hissed between his teeth and with each word he would slam into her even harder.

Lindsay didn't know how much more she could take. He wasn't going to stop and she had to get him out of her before she ripped apart. He went to pull out to slam into her again and she quickly pushed forward and flat onto her stomach, she heard his angry voice behind her, "What the hell are you doing?"

She quickly turned and got to her knees, the look on his face was murderous and it scared the living hell out of her. He was a mad man right now. Maybe Taylor had her reasons for leaving this man if this is how his temper was all the time. She had to calm him down that she knew for sure or this was going to turn bad for her. She quickly turned on her seductive smile, "It's my turn," was all she said, then with a hand on his chest pushed him back so that he was laying down, hoping and praying that this would work. She went straight down on him and took his dick into her mouth. The last time they were together he had pushed her down onto her knees and pushed himself into her mouth so she was hoping now this would give her the time to calm him down a little. It was a good thing that she didn't have a gag reflex and could handle this kind of thing.

She stroked him with her mouth quickly, she figured the faster she went the quicker he would be done and she could leave. His hands were on both sides of her head pushing her even harder as she stroked him. Lindsay was relieved when he finally released himself, hopefully this would satisfy him.

She wanted nothing more than to quickly jump up, collect her clothes, and run for the door but she knew that wasn't a good idea at all. She had to act casual. She didn't want him thinking that she had a problem or there would be no telling what he might do. All of her senses were telling her to be smart, to act calm.

Mike laid there and watched her get dressed. She was no comparison to Taylor when it came to looks. Of course there weren't many women in his mind that were. Although, her naked was not bad to look at and she knew how to use her body. She had managed to clear his mind a little, some of his stress seemed to have disappeared. "I will see you again tomorrow, same place same time."

Lindsay finished sliding on her boots, she grabbed her purse then looked down at him. He wasn't asking her if she would meet him he was telling her that he expected her to be there. She wanted to shout at him there was no way in hell that was going to happen but she knew that had to stay in her head. She smiled, nodded and then headed for the door, she didn't trust her voice right now to actually say something back.

Before she could make it outside he was up and his hand wrapped around her arm, squeezing, "Don't even think about not showing up either. I will find you, that I promise," he threatened.

Lindsay turned to look at him, he stood in the doorway completely naked not a care in the world who may see him. She had to admit he was beautiful to look at. His body perfect but as she looked up into his eyes she would swear she saw the devil. "Until later," was all she said leaving her answer very open and hoping that would convince him she was agreeing to the arrangement. She pulled her arm from his grip and turned away from him, leaving him standing there naked in the doorway. She wanted to run to her car but she kept her composure and walked causally to her car. She didn't dare turn around, she could feel his eyes watching her walk away.

Once at her car she opened her door then looked up at him in the doorway, forcing a smile, she waved then got in and started the car, leaving the driveway.

Mike watched as Lindsay left out of the hotel parking lot. He closed the door and walked over to the bed sitting down. He needed to be a little more careful around Lindsay. He will have to keep his temper in check around her or she could ruin everything for him.

Chapter 14

"So how should we go about this? Do we say that you are pregnant then proceed to tell them we are getting married? Do I ask your fathers permission first then announce the baby?"

I laughed. I was nervous too about this call to my parents but seeing Adam all jumbled up was cute and kind of funny. He was always so composed and always seemed to be relaxed with everything he did, even when he proposed he didn't seem this nervous. "Adam it's alright, no need to be so nervous. I will call them, we will be on speaker phone together, and we will wing it. Things never go as rehearsed anyway. Although I do believe we should have you somehow ask their permission. I mean, they really aren't all that old fashion but I think my dad would respect it."

"I should have called them before I proposed but things kind of happened a little fast and I wasn't really thinking of anything except getting you to agree to marry me." He smiled down at her. From the moment he found out she was pregnant his mind only wrapped around making sure he got her to accept his proposal.

"I really don't think it's going to be a big deal babe. I know we will give baby news first, my mother is dying to become a grandmother. Then we will mention the whole "wedding is right around the corner" news." Quickly I dialed the number to my parent's house and then set my phone on speaker and placed it on the coffee table in front of me.

I listened to the phone ring and watched Adam pace the floor before me. I stretched out my hand to him. "Adam, stop pacing it will all be fine! Come sit down with me, please."

Adam stared at my outstretched hand for a brief moment, took a deep breath and then went around the coffee table to join me on the couch. He sat down just as my father answered the phone, "Hello."

"Hi dad."

"Taylor, honey, how are you doing?"

"Good dad, everything is going great actually!" I grabbed Adam's hand and smiled at him. "Is mom around by chance?"

"Yes, she is out back in the garden, I will go and get her for you."

"Actually dad, I need to speak to both of you."

"Is everything alright hon?"

I could hear the sudden concern in my father's voice. "Everything is fine, just need to talk to you guys about something and it's easier if you are both on the phone."

"Alright then give me a second to call her in." I could hear my father walk through the kitchen from the living room where I figured he was sitting in his chair reading the morning paper and then I heard the back screen door open up.

"Sandy, Taylor is on the phone. Come on inside, she says she needs to talk to us both."

"Alright, I will be right there." I could hear my mom's response in the back ground.

As we waited I took a deep breath, my nerves were now starting to jump a little more. Adam squeezed my hand. I looked over at him and smiled, everything was going to be fine, my parents would accept this.

A click from another phone being picked up was heard over the line, "Hi honey! How is everything going?"

“Hi mom! Everything is good. How about there? Everything going good for you?”

“Just been working in my garden. My flowers this year are beautiful and my vegetables have made some fantastic salads.” I smiled, my mother always had pride in her voice when she would talk about her garden.

“So pumpkin, you had something you needed to talk to us about. What is on your mind? You have me wondering?” My dad interrupted knowing that if you got Sandy started on talking about her garden it would be an hour long conversation about each flower and vegetable.

I looked over at Adam, I knew my parents wouldn’t be upset about the baby, but I wasn’t sure how they were going to react about the very fast upcoming wedding. The last conversation with my mother was just about moving and she kept telling me not to rush things. Now I was going to talk to them about marriage.

“Taylor, honey, are you still there?” Sandy finally asked after a few moments of silence.

“Yes, sorry, I’m here and so is Adam. We are on speaker phone together.”

“Hello Mr. and Mrs. Kennedy,” Adam greeted both of them.

“Mom, Dad, we wanted to call and give you some news.” I squeezed Adam’s hand once again and took a deep breath, there was only one way to really say this and that was to just come straight out and say it, “Adam and I are going to have a baby, I am pregnant.”

“Before you say anything Mr. and Mrs. Kennedy,” Adam included quickly while he had some nerve left, “I want you both to know your daughter means everything to me and I love her very much. I never believed before she arrived that I would ever find someone to spend my life with and have a family with. My life was this ranch. I never figured I’d find a woman who would understand or have those feelings for this place like I do. Then Taylor showed up and turned my world completely upside down, she grabbed my heart. I will love her and our child for the rest of my life unconditionally and will treat her like the jewel I think she is so, now, I am asking you for your blessing to marry her?" Adam took a deep breath, everything was out and in the open. I was right, they couldn't have rehearsed that, it just flowed out of his mouth.

Silence stretched out for a little too long, I look at Adam concern etched in my forehead, I looked back down at the phone. "Mom dad are you still there?"

"I am going to be a grandmother?"

I smiled, I could tell my mother was crying but they were tears of joy. I knew my mother would be excited about the baby. A tear slipped down my cheek, "Yes mom and you are going to have a new son in law as well, just in case you didn't catch anything past the, I am pregnant part. I love Adam and I want to marry him, have this family with him. We are hoping for both of your blessing."

My dad spoke up for the first time, "Honey if you are sure this is what you want and you are going to be happy, I know Adam is a good man. Adam, I appreciate you asking for our permission even though I believe my daughter has already accepted your proposal. We give our permission as well, we would love to have you in our family and I know you will take good care of our baby."

Adam looked over at Taylor, tears were streaming down her cheeks, "Thank you sir," he wiped the tears away with his thumb.

"I am going to be a grandmother," her mother's voice came over the phone again.

I laughed, I wasn't even sure that my mother had heard anything besides the baby part, "Yes mom, you are going to be a grandmother but first, before baby, we need to plan a wedding. I want to walk down the aisle in a beautiful wedding gown on my dad's arm before the baby belly begins to show."

"Taylor, that would mean we would have to have the wedding in the next couple of months honey," Sandy seemed to awaken out of her grandma trance with the newest bit of news.

"Yes mom that is what it means. We have already decided to have the wedding here at the ranch. It's beautiful and would make a great setting, now, all we have to do is figure out a date but we wanted to talk to you guys first before we figured that out."

"Well, actually, I just put in for my vacation at work for the second and third week of September. Your mother and I were going to take a trip somewhere so I guess we will be going to Tennessee, if you think that could work for a date for you guys?" Robert spoke up.

Adam pulled out his phone from his pocket and pulled up the calendar he pointed at the date and I nodded my approval, "Well then how would the tenth of September work out for you?" he asked.

"It looks like we will be having a wedding in five weeks! Your mom and I will get there the Monday before that way if you need help with any final plans she is there to lend a hand." Robert finalized the plans.

"Thank you dad. I can't wait to see you guys, I miss you all tons. Listen, I hate to have to get off the phone so quickly, I know we have a lot to talk about but we had planned to go into town and get the invitations ordered. I will call you later today and talk more," I explained to my mom and dad figuring if we had some of the stuff done then some of the questions my mom was going to pile on me would be easier to answer, "I love you both very much."

"We love you too honey. We will talk soon, bye," Sandy finalized the conversation for everyone and the lines were all hung up.

"Should we have told her about Mike's disappearance?" Robert asked his wife once both of them had hung up the phones.

Sandy played with the cordless phone in her hands. A couple of days ago they had heard that Mike had left town and no one had any idea where he was heading too. "I don't think we need to worry her about anything yet. Between the baby and planning the wedding, she is going to have plenty to think about right now."

"I don't know Sandy, maybe we should at least tell Adam," Robert suggested.

"Let's just wait a little while longer. I don't know how he would have figured out where she went, no one knew besides the two of us and her brother and none of us have said a word to anyone. I think she will be fine," Sandy hoped she was right. Right now Adam and Taylor had plenty to do without the worry of Mike.

I hung up my phone, took a deep breath, and leaned back on the couch closing my eyes. Wow, it was done and over. Everything was out in the open and I felt very relaxed at the moment. Well, that is the key word, at the moment, because the hard part is over. Everyone knew about the baby and the upcoming wedding but now, the planning started. I have five weeks to plan a wedding when most people had months.

Adam watched Taylor for a moment as she lounged back on the couch, eyes closed, "Are you alright honey?"

I opened my eyes and smiled, "Yep, all the news is out, everyone knows everything now and the dates are set, now let the race against time begin."

"Tay, until you see a doctor and talk to them about what has happened I want you to take it easy. Please don't overdo anything."

I rubbed my hand across my belly, I felt the scar. "They said they weren't sure if I would ever be able to get pregnant. Nothing was said about me having a problem carrying the child if I did become pregnant."

Adam placed his hand over hers on her belly, "Tay, please, all I am asking is you don't overdo it until you talk to the doctor that's all."

Smiling up at him and nodded, "I promise."

Adam leaned over to me and claimed my lips in a very sweet and soft kiss, "In about five weeks you will be all mine."

"I am all yours now," I smiled and then claimed his lips in another kiss. My kiss wasn't soft like his had been, my kiss was more demanding.

"Don't start something we cannot finish right now. You need to get going and I have a little boy to go and fetch and fences that need finished being fixed."

"Are you sure we have no time for a little fun first?" My hand that was resting on his thigh moved up his leg and brushed the side of his erection.

Adam grabbed my hand, "What am I going to do with you? It's not me and my time I am worried about, it is yours. You have to get to work woman."

"Man you're denying me already? I may have to rethink this marriage thing. I'm pregnant and very horny," I started to stand but was caught around the waist and pulled down onto his lap.

"Woman don't try and threaten me. You said yes and you are stuck with me."

I rubbed my behind up against the crouch of his jeans, "Sir, I do believe you are." I moved side to side on his lap, "hard... to say no to?" I then twisted so that I was facing him and claimed his lips again.

"You are going to be the end of me." He kissed her once more then stood up with her in his arms but placed her feet to the ground quickly, "I love you," then he turned her towards the front door and with both of his hands on her shoulders pushed her towards it. "Hailey already told me she was sending little man over here so you and your pregnancy hormones will have to wait until tonight. It will be my absolute pleasure to make sure your pregnancy hormones are completely satisfied. Now go get Hailey and Grams and get going before everyone walks in on a show." He smacked her playfully on the behind to get her moving.

"Well as long as you promise! Love you," she said over her shoulder and picked up her stuff and left.

Chapter 15

"Alright invitations are ordered. Flower shop and cake are done and ordered as well. We have the company for catering but of course we still need to get the final head count for the food. Wow I would say we are making a pretty good dent in the wedding plans list," Hailey ran through all they had accomplished as she started pulling out of the driveway of the flower shop.

I sat in the back seat of the truck looking out the window, "Well it helps that you knew all these people from your wedding."

"We even made Taylor's doctor appointment," Grams added from the passenger seat, "Adam will be happy about that. So where to now? I would say we have just enough time for one last stop and then on the way home we will need to pick something up for dinner."

"Already thinking ahead of you Grams," Hailey said as she pulled into another driveway, "I am thinking the dress. This is where I got my dress for my wedding. The ladies were very nice and extremely helpful."

We walked inside the little shop and I looked around. Dresses of all sizes, design, and color filled the shop. "Welcome ladies, my name is Kathy, how may I help you?" The lady that greeted them had to be in her early fifties I would guess.

"Kathy, my name is Hailey. I don't know if you remember me, it has been about 10 years, but I bought my dress from you guys and today we are looking for a gown for my best friend here, Taylor," Hailey pointed to me as she spoke.

"Hailey, I would honestly say I wouldn't have remembered your name, I am sorry, but I can say that I do remember you! It is great to see you again. I'm glad to know that you came back, we love being referred," Kathy turned her attention to me, "Congratulations on your wedding! When is the day?"

"Thank you. Our wedding is in five weeks actually," Taylor answered.

"Not a problem at all. We'll find you your perfect dress I'm sure. What kind of style were you thinking?"

"I'll be honest, I have no idea." I looked around the store, it was a little overwhelming. I never thought about what my perfect dress would look like because I never figured I would need one. I just wore a plain dress when I married Mike and after that I swore I would never marry again.

Kathy studied Taylor for a moment, the poor thing looked terrified and a little lost and she would swear she saw tears in Taylor's eyes.

"Taylor, sweetie, are you all right?" Grams asked as she watched Taylor. Something was bothering her.

I turned around to face Grams tears rolling down my face, "Tay, why are you crying? What's wrong?" Hailey asked now noticing the tears.

I wiped the tears away with the back of my hand. "I'm sorry, I guess I'm just a little overwhelmed right now. What girl doesn't have her perfect dress etched out in her mind? I never really expected to get married again so I've never dreamed about my perfect day and my perfect dress. I was disappointed that when I married Mike I didn't get my ideal wedding but I got over that I thought and never thought about it again. Now here I stand in this shop, beautiful dresses all around me, and I have no idea what I am looking for."

Hailey wrapped her friend up in her arms. "Taylor come on, stop crying, that is why you have Grams and I here with you. I promise we will find the perfect dress." Hailey stepped back and wiped my tears away from my face and smiled at me.

Kathy stood and watched as Hailey comforted Taylor, she studied the scars on the young girls face. This woman had a story behind her and she would gather it had caused her a lot of pain, her heart went out to her. "Sweetie, you are not the first girl to walk through our doors and not have a certain style of dress in mind." She took her by the hand and started leading her through the store. "Come on, what would I be getting paid for if I didn't help a bride pick out the perfect dress?"

An hour had passed and I was starting to get very frustrated. Dress after dress I had tried on and even though they were all beautiful none of them stood out and said yes I am the dress you want. "I am sorry none of these are me." I ran my hand down the row of tried on dresses, "Maybe we should just give up for today and come back later."

At that moment Kathy came around the corner holding yet another dress in her arms. "How about one more?"

I backed away like the woman was carrying a snake in her arms. "I don't know. I just don't think I am going to be happy with anything right now."

"Come on Tay, just one more. I promise if you don't care for this one we will leave," Hailey tried coaxing me into the dress Kathy had found.

I glared over at Hailey. I didn't want to try on another dress this, was becoming very depressing. I looked over at the rack with all the tried on dresses hanging from it. How could I possibly not find a dress amongst those dresses? My mind just wasn't into this.

"Sweetie, I promise, last one," Kathy held the dress out to Taylor, "This one just kind of jumped out at me. It's the only one of this style we have in the store and it just happened to be your size. I think that's a sign, I have a feeling this is the dress."

Fine. One more to make everyone happy, I thought to myself as I took the dress from Kathy and went into the dressing room to try it on. Once I stepped into it, I came out and had Kathy button up the long row of pearls that lined the back of the gown. I then walked over to the raised rounded platform and stepped up.

Hailey squealed and clapped her hands, "Tay, that's the dress! It's perfect!"

I stared at myself in the three mirrors in front of me. I was amazed, the dress was beautiful. Wait, maybe I was just tired and thought the dress was perfect so that way I wouldn't have to try any more on. I turned away from the mirrors towards Hailey and Grams, both of them had tears in their eyes and were shaking their heads. I turned to the mirrors once again and the sight took my own breath away. The dress was off white, off the shoulder with a slight heart shape to the bodice area of the dress, pushing my breast up slightly. It hugged my waist down into a V shape then flared out into a princess style at the bottom the train ran about two feet behind me. No sequence, no floral print. The top of the gown just had a simple crisscross design to it. Once again tears formed in my eyes. I smiled at the three women behind me through the mirror, "It's perfect."

Kathy said nothing, she just took a deep breath and slowly let it out, smiling the whole time. Grams got up and walked over to me. "You are a stunning sight sweetheart."

"Thank you Grams."

"You are going to take Adam's breath away Tay! You look amazing in that gown," Hailey complimented me and quickly dashed the tears away.

I smiled and then looked over at Kathy, "Thank you for being so patient with me, I will take this one."

Kathy returned Taylor smile, "Dear, it has been a pleasure! I have the perfect veil and shoes for that gown."

Forty five minutes later the three of us ladies were finally heading out of the parking lot of the dress shop. The shoes and veil Kathy picked out were perfect and they would be back next week to pick up the dress after it had been cleaned.

"Let's just grab a couple of pizzas on the way home for dinner," Hailey suggested as they drove down the street.

I had to admit, finding my dress did make me feel better but I was exhausted all the same, it had been one crazy day. First the call to my parents and then there was the catering place, the flowers, and the cake and then finally the most emotional part of her day the dress. Pizza sounded good but my bed and a pillow sounded even better.

"I think we made a lot of progress today. We got a lot done, main thing is to go pick up the invitations in a couple days and get those out. We will need a head count as soon as possible for the caterers. Next we will have to go and figure out tables...." Hailey kept on talking.

Grams looked behind her at Taylor, "Hailey dear, Taylor isn't taking notes."

Hailey looked over at Grams confused, then to the back seat where Taylor was fast asleep, "The poor thing is exhausted, she has had a very productive day," Grams smiled.

"We did amazing getting everything set up though, at this rate we will have everything ready to go by the end of next week. We should get some kind of award for the fastest wedding planned. No matter what, I am going to make sure this day is perfect for her and Adam. They both deserve it."

"Hailey you will make it perfect I have no doubt about that," Grams smiled at her granddaughter.

“Tay, are you almost ready to go?” Adam looked at the clock sitting on the bedside table. He rolled his eyes and leaned up against the wall next to the closed bathroom door. It never takes her this long to get ready and today for some reason she was dragging her feet.

The door finally opened to the bathroom and Taylor walked out, “Calm down, we have plenty of time. Why get there early only to have to sit there longer because the doctor is never on time?”

I started to walk past him but he grabbed my arm and pulled me into his arms. Something was bothering her, he could tell her mood all morning had been very touchy. “Honey, what is wrong?”

Shrugging I tried to pull away from him but Adam just tightened his hold on me. I took a deep breath but I never made eye contact with him. “I’m fine, come on let’s go, we are going to be late remember? You have been howling at me for the last twenty minutes to hurry up, now you want to talk?”

That confirmed it, she wasn’t telling him something. Yes, Hailey told him sometimes pregnant women have major mood swings, but this was no mood swing, something was on her mind. “Not until you tell me what’s bothering you,” he smiled down at her, “we have plenty of time, doctors never run on time.” He threw her own words back at her.

I tried to not look at him but I did and that smile is something I couldn’t ignore. I began to smile but only a little, “Fine, I am not looking forward to having to tell the doctor all about my dark past. This should be a happy time and I have to bring in all the dark things about my life.”

“Tay, come on, really? All of this again? Three weeks ago we told the doctor everything and he said he was going to call and get your records from California. He has probably already gone through them. He may have a couple questions but like you said, the hard part was getting pregnant and well we have already fix that. This is a happy time, the doctor said we should get to hear the baby’s heart beat this visit.” Adam remembered his disappointment at the last appointment they had, a couple of weeks ago. He thought they would get more information then but no, they only took a pee test, asked a couple of questions, confirmed she was pregnant and then said they would have to make an appointment.

"I am sorry. I know you are right, I guess I am just nervous is all. I just want everything to be okay with the baby and me carrying the baby. I do need to leave my past behind me and I am trying, trust me. The last three weeks with planning this wedding really hasn't allowed me to think about too much else. Instead of my past I should be looking at my very bright future. In about two weeks I am marrying an amazing man and shortly after welcoming the new addition to our family."

Adam gave her a puzzled look, "Wait shortly after the wedding? Aren't you pregnant for nine months? We should have at least seven months to go right?"

I laughed, "Yes and those seven months will fly by."

"Well let's start with getting to this doctor's appointment," he bent forward and claimed her lips, happy to see that her mood had changed and she seemed a little more relaxed. He knew she wouldn't completely relax until the doctor told her everything with the baby was good and honestly neither would he.

I kissed him back and that feeling that only Adam's kisses could start in the pit of my stomach was starting and I knew if I didn't pull away we weren't going to make the appointment, we weren't even going to make it out of this room. Regretfully, I pulled away from him. "If you don't stop kissing me like that we aren't going anywhere sir."

Adam laughed. "Are you saying my kisses affect you that easily? I am going to have to keep that in mind for the future. Any other time I would love to find out exactly how they affect you but this is one appointment I really don't think we need to miss so come on, let's go." He grabbed her hand and led her out of their room.

I sat dressed in a hospital gown on the exam table and Adam stood next to me holding my hand. We both watched as the doctor read over the chart in his hand. No one said a word and silence was starting to drive me a little crazy. The doctor would look up for a moment and stare at me as though he was looking for some answer, then look back down at the chart again. My stomach was in knots. What if she could get pregnant but not carry the baby? My other doctor in Napa and I had never talked about that. No, I told myself, everything seemed to be fine with the baby so far. Of course how would I know if everything was fine? I wasn't far enough along to feel the baby. Once again the doctor looked up, I could tell he was eyeing my scars along my face. His eyes went down to the level of my stomach almost like he could actually see through my gown and the scar there. Then once again he looked back down to the chart. I wanted to scream, didn't he look over my chart before today? Wait, maybe he was trying to figure out a way to tell us the bad news. Oh god, what would Adam say if the news was bad? He is so excited about the baby. I willed the doctor to say something good or bad just stop with the silence and staring.

"Alright," finally the doctor looked up and shut the folder in his hands, "Young lady you have been through quite a trial in your life. I can't tell you how many times I have looked over this medical file and am amazed that you lived through it," he looked between the two of them.

I felt Adam's hand squeeze mine when the doctor mentioned that I shouldn't have lived. I was used to doctors telling me how surprised they were, I heard it all the time. I looked over at Adam and tried to give him a reassuring smile.

"Not only did you live through it but you did the one thing that the doctors said you couldn't do and that was get pregnant," he continued on.

"Wait," I interrupted him, "He told me he wasn't sure that I would be able to get pregnant not that I wouldn't be able to for sure."

The doctor opened the file once again, then pointed to a spot on the page, "Well right here he wrote from internal damage pregnancy would not be possible." He closed the file once again and looked at me, "but here you are, pregnant. We confirmed that a couple of weeks ago."

"Yes, she is pregnant but will any of that damage cause her to have any problems with carrying the baby," Adam asked?

I closed my eyes and my hand tightened around Adam's. If the doctor said any bad news I wasn't sure if I'd be able to handle it, not only for myself, but for Adam.

"Well my opinion is, she got pregnant the rest should be fine. Of course we are going to check her today. I am going to do an internal ultra sound but honestly, that doctor figured the knife did damage to the ovaries and that would make it impossible for the eggs to make it to and, well, the egg made it to the right location or we wouldn't be here having this conversation," the doctor smiled at both of us.

The doctor waited a moment for the news to sink in, "Alright why don't you go ahead lie down and put your feet up here in the stir ups and we will check out your little one."

I laid back and closed my eyes. Our baby was going to be alright. I felt Adam's lips on my forehead, "Are you alright?"

I opened my eyes to find myself staring straight into his crystal blue ones. I nodded, "I'm fine. I'm sorry that I'm putting you through all of this."

Puzzled Adam asked, "Through what?"

"All of this unknown stuff with the baby."

"Tay everything is going to be alright. You aren't putting me through anything except pure joy. Our baby is going to be fine." A strange sound in the room brought both of our attention back to the doctor, "What is that sound?" Adam asked looking around the room as if something would show the answer.

“That is your baby’s heartbeat, see?” the doctor pointed at the little TV screen sitting next to him.

Together Taylor and Adam looked at the screen where the doctor was pointing, “And that little spot right there is your baby.”

Tears streamed down my face, “Look at that honey! That’s our baby, seems pretty healthy to me.” Adam looked at the doctor for confirmation.

The doctor nodded, “Everything looks great and sounds…..what a minute.”

My heart sunk. Oh no, he has found something wrong. I looked over at Adam, pure panic in my eyes. “Calm down honey,” he looked over at the doctor, “What’s wrong?”

The doctor smiled as he looked at the two of them. “I’m sorry, I didn’t mean to scare you. The babies are fine.”

Adam felt his own heart start beating again. He was trying very hard to stay calm through all of this, for Taylor’s sake. His eyes grew wide, reality of what the doctor just said starting sinking in. He looked down at Taylor, realization must have just hit her as well, “Babies?” they spoke together.

The doctor looked between the both of them, smiling. He loved the moments he got to tell parents they were having twins, the reactions were great. He nodded. “Yes, you not only did what a doctor said would be impossible for you to do, but you showed them they were really wrong and decided to have twins.”

My hand went to cover my mouth, tears poured down my cheeks. Adam kissed my forehead, they were having twins! Neither of them could speak. What do you say in a moment like this? I placed a hand on his cheek and smiled. “I love you. Are you ready for this wild ride we are about to go on?”

“As long as we ride it together we will be ready for anything.”

Adam looked over at Taylor for probably the tenth time since leaving the doctor's office. She hadn't said a word, she just stared out her window, "Tay, are you alright?"

I looked over at him and smiled, "I'm fine, why?"

He shrugged, "You are just so quiet. I figured you would have more to say."

"I'm sorry," I reached across and placed my hand on his thigh, "Just a lot to soak in really, just thinking that's all."

Nodding Adam agreed, "Twins, wow. Twins."

"Amazing, I know. I keep saying the word in my head thinking it will make it seem more real but honestly, it hasn't helped. I still can't believe we heard him right. I almost feel like calling him and making sure we heard right."

Adam pulled the truck up into the front of the house, put it in park and turned the engine off. He leaned back in his seat and looked over at me, "I love you so much."

I laughed, he almost acts like I was the only one involved in creating these two little lives, "I love you too but you do realize we are being thrown into parenthood with a double dose right?"

Adam took a deep breath, "I'll be honest, I'm terrified. I was terrified to find out I was going to be a father of one but now, to find out we have two coming at once, wow!"

"You keep saying wow."

Adam laughed, "That's because I really have no idea what else to say it's just, wow!"

"Trust me, I understand. I think this is going to take more than a few moments for it to sink in for either one of us. Although I have to admit I'm thankful the wedding is soon. I don't want to walk down the aisle with a baby bump but I will assume that since there are two growing in here," I placed my hand on my stomach, "We will be seeing the baby bump soon." I had already noticed my body changing and my stomach seemed a little rounder but I still fit into my dress that I knew. I tried it on last week when we picked it up and it was fine.

Adam placed his hand over mine, "I can't wait to see these two growing."

"Adam, I am going to be huge. You probably aren't even going to want to look at me, I will be so fat."

"You are going to be beautiful and you are wrong, you aren't' going to be fat, you are going to be carrying my children. I can't wait to show you off."

I laughed, "You're already the proud daddy."

Adam leaned over to me and claimed my lips, both of our hands still resting on my stomach. I melted like I did every time he kissed me and my sex became wet. I wondered if there would be a time when I didn't react to him like this. I was ready to jump onto his lap and ride him right here in the truck right in front of the house, seriously, not having a care in the world of who might walk out and see us. I really needed to try and control this.

Adam pulled away, his smile reaching his eyes. "Come on, let's go tell everyone our news," he jumped quickly out of the truck. I felt a little disappointed knowing that I wasn't able to just steal him away to our home and ride him until dinner, my body was humming with need, if this is how the whole pregnancy was going to be I was in trouble. I took a deep breath to try and calm the rage building inside of me and by the time he reached my side I was out and shutting the door. He grabbed my hand and together we went in search of the family.

Chapter 16

"Twins!" Hailey and Grams said together after hearing the news.

"What does twins mean?" Bryson asked a puzzled look on his face.

Adam crouched down to his nephew's level, "Well buddy that means we are having two babies instead of one."

"Well are they boys? I sure don't want two girls to play with." Bryson had a look on his face like he just smelled something bad.

"We can have two boys, two girls or actually one boy and one girl, we are not sure yet," Adam explained to him.

"As long as there isn't two girls I don't care," Bryson put two fingers up to indicate the two he was talking about.

Adam laughed and rustled his nephews hair, "We will do our best little buddy."

Bryson smiled and nodded his head satisfied with his Uncle Adam's promise then left the living room and headed up to his own room.

Ryan placed a hand on Adam's shoulder, "Come on let's go outside and enjoy a beer. You look like you could use one."

Adam laughed and nodded his head, he took a deep breath and sighed, "A beer sounds real good right now actually."

"Well I have supper to start preparing for," Grams gave Taylor a hug and a kiss on the cheek, "I am so happy for you two, I just can't wait."

"Thanks Gram," I watched as she disappeared into the kitchen.

"Come on, let's go out and sit on the porch swing." Hailey lead the way outside.

We were both sitting on the porch swing lightly swinging back and forth. We could see the guys out at the corrals deep in conversation. Hailey looked over at Taylor, now she could ask all the questions. "So the doctor said everything was good? Babies seem to be healthy?"

The only answer I gave was a small nod of my head, then I just went back to lightly pushing the swing with my toe. Hailey watched her for a moment, "Taylor, what is the matter? I would have figured you to be more than excited."

"Oh, I am excited, just a lot to grab onto that is all. Come on, look at the short amount of time that has passed since I arrived. I have fallen in love, became pregnant, am getting married, and now having twins. It's just a lot to take in that's all."

Hailey sat there for a moment longer once again examining her best friend. "I will agree it has been a busy and rather quick couple of months but I know something else is bothering you. I know you way to well and I know you have something else going through that pretty brain of yours so, out with it."

I looked at my friend for a moment, sometimes it wasn't such a good thing to know each other as well as we knew each other. I knew Hailey wasn't going to leave me alone about this until I talked to her. My hand went to my stomach, my eyes back on the man who had changed my life, "I found out today that the doctor in Napa wrote in my files that pregnancy could not happen."

Confused Hailey looked at Taylor for moment, "Alright, so the doctor was wrong."

"I know but he never told me there was no way. I was always told there was a possibility that I couldn't become pregnant, what if I hadn't…."

"Alright Taylor stop," Hailey interrupted her, "You have to stop with the, what ifs. You weren't supposed to live either, trust me, I remember when we were told that news in the hospital. Look here, not only are you alive but you are healthy and with the exception of a couple scars, which I fully believe bother you a lot more than anyone else, you are in great shape and now to top it all off you are pregnant with twins. It's like you are being given the second chance and even though you lost your first pregnancy you were meant to be a mother of two."

Hailey sat quiet for a moment waiting for a response but only tear filled eyes looked back at her, "Taylor, you have been through a lot, there is no denying that, but please don't take this wrong but, it is time to move on. Your past and Mike are behind you now. I'm not saying you have to forget it because you never will but you need to stop living it every day of your life. In a couple of weeks you are finally going to get the wedding you have always wanted, a man who loves you exactly the way you are, and two babies on the way to care and live for. It's time to put the past behind you and enjoy the future and the fact that you were given a second chance to live."

Hailey reached over and traced one of the scars on Taylor's face, "You will always have these scars to remind you but you should look at these scars and be proud and thankful. These prove how strong you were and are, Tay. You lived, Taylor, and you were given a second chance at a life that you completely deserve to have. It's time for you to move on."

I looked from Hailey back out across the yard to where Adam stood. Hailey was right, I did need to get past the "what ifs". Why I couldn't get past the facts of what the doctors said, I couldn't figure out, I should be jumping around with joy. These past few years I had only thought about how Mike had destroyed my life, maybe I should look at it as a chance at a new one. It was my way out of my miserable life I was living and given a chance to be happy and loved. I traced the scar that Hailey had just traced. "You know I never told anyone this before, well no, I take that back, I did tell Adam this when I told him everything, but there were so many days after I got home from the hospital that I would stare in the mirror and just wish that I had died." I heard the gasp that Hailey took from hearing me admit to wanting to die, I hated that I sounded weak to her. I didn't look over at her, I didn't want to see the disappointment in her eyes that I knew was there, I just kept my eyes on the man across the way. "Then I would become more upset at myself for not being strong enough to not feel that way. I never really looked at myself as someone who was weak, but then I met Mike and even though I knew our relationship wasn't good and he was destroying everything about me, I stayed. I figured I could change him, I became one of those women who let her husband abuse her and to take away everything that made me who I was. I hate that I sound so weak now. It drives me crazy that everyday something from all of that gets in the way. Trust me it drives me crazy that I can't just be happy that everything is great right now. I have a great guy and two amazing miracles on the way, I still sit here feeling sorry for myself. I cursed Mike over and over again for doing what he did to me. I wondered what terrible thing I had done to deserve that kind of punishment. Why didn't I die? Was it so that I would have to look at myself every day of my life and be reminded of it?"

"Taylor," disbelief etched Hailey's voice this bringing Taylor's attention away from Adam and she looked over at her.

"No really, many times I thought about this. For hours I would just stare into a mirror. I wondered how I was going to face the public, would they just think I did something to deserve it, would they figure out what Mike had done to me. Would they look at me weak, I couldn't even protect my unborn child. So you see I never thought of myself as strong only weak. Trust me every day since your brother said he loves me I wonder what I did to deserve him. Trust me I know how lucky I am, he has had to deal with a lot from me. No matter how many times I wallow in self-pity he stands there and listens to me and then he tells me how much he loves me and how amazing I am. I don't deserve him, but I thank god every day for giving him to me."

I wiped at the tears running down my cheeks and smiled, "Right before I found out I was pregnant I didn't think I was ready for marriage. The thought that I lived with him still scared the crap out of me. I was afraid I was moving way to fast, I'm not even sure if I was completely ready for him. Now however, I can't wait to be married to him, to start this family with him. You are right, it's time to move on. I promise you I'm done with the, what ifs. I won't promise I won't have my days that I won't slip back a little but I'm done wallowing. Thank you for always being there the way you are. I love you more than I will ever be able to put into words." I wrapped my arms around Hailey in a tight hug, together we cried.

Hailey had a lot of questions but decided maybe it was best to leave them alone. Taylor had confided in her and told her more then she had ever told anyone. She could feel that this was her way of closing that chapter in her life and Hailey was happy for that. "Well, if you slip back we will all be here to slide you back up and lead you ahead Tay. I love you too."

Chapter 17

"You know I have been thinking," Ryan said sitting on their bed later that night looking at the closed bathroom door, "Bryson is pretty excited about having his new cousins on the way, well, as long as they are boys. He is five and we have always said we wanted more children. Maybe it's time to start thinking about that."

Hailey came out of the bathroom tying the belt of her robe. She walked over to where her husband sat and straddled his lap. She was a little surprised he brought this conversation up. Sure they had talked about having more children but usually she was the one starting the conversation not him. It must be all the talk today about the twins, "I am so happy you think so."

Here her man sat, no shirt on, only in his boxers, and sexy as hell. This isn't exactly the way she wanted to tell him her news but so much for planning. She bent forward and ran tiny kisses from one side of his neck and then nibbled on that ear. She felt the belt of her robe give way and he smiled when he found she wore nothing underneath. His hand cupped one of her breast, his finger massaging her nipple to life, "Shall we start practicing on that?" he asked as he claimed her lips.

The kiss was hot and passionate. Hailey's blood ran faster and all seemed to meet at her sex. She felt Ryan's erection grow hard up against her, the only thing separating them was the thin fabric of his boxers. She was already wet with need for him and she slowly began to rotate her hips up against him. She dropped her arms from around his neck to her sides to allow her husband to slide the robe down her arms and let it fall in a pile on the floor.

Her hands went into his hair and she pulled his head to her chest his tongue found the peaked nipple that ached for some attention. He circled her nipple with his tongue slowly at first. Hailey moaned, her head fell back and her finger nails dug into his scalp and she pushed his head harder to her breast he took her breast into his mouth and sucked. Her head came up and she smiled, "No practice needed."

Ryan stopped and looked up at her, "Are you saying...?"

She smiled and nodded, "That is what I am saying."

He claimed her lips in a kiss that had a mixture of happiness, shock, delight and love. He stood up and she kept her legs wrapped around his waist. He turned them around then laid her down onto the bed. She unwrapped her legs and Ryan quickly discarded the only article of clothing he was wearing. Starting at her toes he ran his tongue up her ankle past her knee and then into the inner thigh where he kissed one thigh then the other. Hailey inhaled sharply as his tongue found her wetness between her legs, his tongue flicked her and her hips pushed forward driving his tongue deeper inside of her. She was starting to feel herself lose control and she wanted him inside of her for that. She grabbed his shoulders and puller him away, he took the hint and he started to slide up her body his lips stopping at her belly where he lightly kissed, "I love you."

She smiled, "I love you," and then she was lost again when his mouth claimed one of her breast.

Hailey ran her hand down his side to his leg and then came around and found his hard erection. She wrapped her hand around him and began to stoke him slowly at first. His tongue on her nipple began to twirl and tease her a little faster now and she matched that with the strokes of her hand, she heard him moan and she smiled. She parted her legs wider, she wanted him in her now. Ryan left her breast and reclaimed her lips about sending her over the edge. She quickly guided him into her wetness and then wrapped her legs around his waist. He could feel her body pulse around him with every thrust into her he made. Faster and deeper until her body convulsed around him, pulling him in deeper and deeper and finally his release came. Hailey cried out and squeezed her legs tighter around his waist as his seed poured into her.

Ryan stroked Hailey's back as she nestled up against his chest, "When did you find out?"

"Day before yesterday. I have been trying to figure out when and how I wanted to tell you but when you mentioned it tonight, I figured this would be a good time."

He tightened his arms around her. "You have no idea how much you mean to me woman."

"Well if it's even half as much as I love you then I have a good idea."

Both laid there for a moment without saying a word, Hailey thought maybe he had fallen asleep,
"Ryan?"

"Hmmm."

"I don't want to tell anyone until after the wedding. This is Taylor and Adam's time right now with the wedding only a couple of weeks away and them just finding out they are having twins. I want them to enjoy this time, they both deserve it."

"I understand but it's going to be hard. Adam reads me pretty well some times and the smile on my face may give me away."

Hailey laughed, "I am sure he will be preoccupied trying to get use to the idea of two babies and a wedding around the corner, to pay too much attention to your smiles."

"I love you woman more and more every day."

"I love you too."

Chapter 18

"So you thought you could hide from me? I should have warned you that is next to impossible when I really want something."

That voice rang in her ears. She had only gone to work and then home the last couple of weeks. She stayed far away from the bar, she had even called Tom the owner and asked him to spread it around that she had left town for a while on business. Nice thing about small towns, news travels fast. Now here she sat in the diner, eating alone and he happens to walk in. So much for hoping he had left town.

Lindsay took a deep breath and then as she turned she placed her very well practiced smile on, "Mike, whatever do you mean?"

He studied her for a moment, "Where have you been?" He came around and sat down across from her at the booth.

Lindsay narrowed her eyes at him. Who did he think he was, demanding to know her whereabouts? She forced herself to eat one of her fries, hopefully she appeared a lot calmer than she actually felt. "I had to go out of town on business. I just returned the day before yesterday as a matter of fact."

"What kind of business?"

She was starting to get a little mad now. How dare he question her! "I believe that really isn't any concern of yours." Mike glared at her, he wasn't buying any of it, she was almost sure of that. She was thankful the place was crowded, he wouldn't cause a scene in front of everyone at least not if he was trying to keep a low profile about being in town.

"I don't believe you were out of town, Lindsay. I think you have been trying to hide from me," his eyes never blinked, he just continued to stare her down.

Lindsay knew he was waiting for her to crack, to show any sign that she was lying to him. "Wow! You have a pretty high impression of yourself to believe I would alter my life so much just to stay away from you." She grabbed her sandwich and took a bite. She had to keep reminding herself to act normal, like him sitting across from her was no big deal.

She swallowed her bite hoping not to choke, "I'm sorry to disappoint you but my life doesn't revolve around you, Mike." She shrugged her shoulders, "I mean, don't get me wrong, we had a couple of great nights together but nothing more. I needed to take care of business and I didn't think of a need to call you about my travel plans."

"Well then, since you are home, you are free tonight!"

It wasn't a question it was more of a demand, "Sorry, no, I have already made plans for tonight."

Just then a friend came and sat down next to Lindsay, "Lindsay, who is your friend here?"

Lindsay had to stop herself from wrapping her arms around her friend Rebecca and holding her at the table maybe then Mike would leave, "Rebecca, this is Mike."

"Rebecca it is nice to meet you."

Lindsay watched as Mike completely changed his demeanor in front of Rebecca turning to his charming and very dangerously handsome self. You would have never thought that just seconds ago he was staring her down with the coldest stare she had ever seen. She wondered how many other women succumbed to his charm and then was hurt. She looked over at Rebecca, she was just staring, not even attempting to hide the fact that she was in awe of him. "So Rebecca what's up?"

It took Rebecca a moment to react to Lindsay's question but finally she remembered herself and looked at her, "Well you will never believe the news that is flying around town!"

"What gossip did you happen across now?"

"Well, as you know, Taylor Kennedy has come back to town and well, it seems her and Adam Kageen are getting married next week, but wait, there is more."

Lindsay tried to will Rebecca to stop talking, she had noticed the change in Mike the second Taylor's name had been mentioned. He was starting to get that same crazed look in his eyes that he had the last time they were together. "Rebecca, really you shouldn't spread gossip."

Rebecca stared at Lindsay like she had all of a sudden grown a second head, since when did Lindsay not like to hear or spread gossip.

"Oh no, please, I would like to hear what else she had heard." Mike's voice brought both ladies heads around to look at him.

Rebecca smiled, "Well, the best part is, not only are they getting married but she is pregnant with twins."

Oh god, Lindsay thought to herself, she looked over at Mike. She might not care for Taylor a whole lot especially after coming back to town and grabbing up the only single guy worth anything in this town but she was terrified for her at this moment. She was pretty sure Rebecca somehow completely missed Mike's reaction to the news but she hadn't and she hadn't missed what he said either, "This time I will kill her," he had whispered to himself.

Getting up from the table Rebecca looked back at Lindsay, "Well I saw you were here and just had to tell you, I guess I will see you later."

Lindsay wanted to grab her hand and pull her back down into the seat and make her stay with her but she knew she couldn't. She smiled and nodded and after Rebecca left she looked back down at her plate. She needed to figure out how to deal with this mess she managed to get herself into. She knew that now that he had found her he was going to make sure she kept her mouth shut. At that moment an image of Taylor flashed into her head from that night she had seen all of them at the dance hall, she had commented on the scars on her face, oh god Mike did that. "This time I will kill her." Mike's words ran through her head once more.

Mike heard Lindsay gasp, he studied her for a moment, she was staring down at her plate. He had to do something about her because he couldn't afford for Taylor to find out he was in town now. This woman wasn't going to destroy his plans now, not being this close to getting his revenge. "So again, I say you are free tonight!"

Lindsay looked up, she had to get out of here before she screamed. She had to get away from him! "I will meet you at our location if my other plans change." She lied to him, she just wanted to leave get out from those eyes that kept bearing down on her. She tried to, as casually as she could, get up from the table and walk to the counter to pay for her meal. She prayed her legs wouldn't give out under her. She turned to walk out the door when a hand grabbed her arm and not gently, Mike's voice was in her ear, "It wasn't a question and if you try and say anything to anyone..."

He let the sentence hang. Lindsay looked around, no one was in hearing distance of them.
She looked back at him, she slanted her eyes as she stared back at him, "For one, I could care less about Taylor and your relationship and for two, don't threaten me. I don't care for it. I'm not your wife. I'm not even your girlfriend. You may be able to control Taylor but don't you dare believe for a moment I'm going to take you threatening me. So like I said before, if my plans change tonight you may or may not see me."

Mike didn't like being talked to like he wasn't being taken seriously but now was not the time to make a scene, too many people were around. He tightened his hand around her wrist and pulled her in real close, "That wasn't a threat, it was a promise!"

Lindsay tried not to react to his words but her heart was racing and she was pretty sure he could feel her pulse quicken in her wrist. She pulled out of his grasp and without another word she turned and left the diner. She didn't look back as she walked towards her car, she knew he was watching her, she could almost feel his eyes blazing into her back. She quickly got into her car and locked the doors. Her hands were shaking so much that she couldn't put the key in the ignition, tears welled up in her eyes. "Come on damn it, pull yourself together," she lectured herself. Finally the key made it into the ignition, she threw the car in reverse. It took everything she had in her not to push the gas pedal to the floor, she began to pull out of the parking spot. As she drove out of the driveway she glanced into her rear view mirror and was relieved to find that he hadn't moved which meant he wasn't following her home. She took a deep breath and tried to relax a little.

She drove straight home, pulled up into the driveway, quickly threw the car into park and ran into her house locking the door behind her. She threw her purse onto the couch and went straight to her room pulling out her suitcase and began to pack some clothes. She had some vacation time at work. She saw that look in Mike's eyes, he was crazy. If he would attempt to hurt his own wife she knew for sure he wouldn't even think twice about making sure she didn't say anything to anyone. She knew she had to warn Taylor! She wanted no part in his plans or for anyone to find out she had known about it and hadn't said anything. She might not care much for Taylor but no one deserved what Mike had planned for her.

She quickly finished packing and then grabbed her purse off the couch as she ran back out of her house and to her car. She threw her suitcase into the back seat and got in. On her way out of town she would stop by the ranch and talk to Taylor and Adam. Hailey's husband was a cop. maybe he could do something to help her. Her mind made up, she pulled out of her driveway and headed to the ranch.

Chapter 19

"Well it sounds like everything is ready to go. What shall we do until Saturday?"

I looked across the table at my parents, they arrived earlier today and I was extremely excited that they had finally made it. My brother was flying in on Thursday and I couldn't wait. I looked over at Adam. We hadn't told my parents about the twins yet, we were waiting for them to get there to tell them in person. I looked around the table, the dishes had been cleaned away and everyone was just sitting around in conversation. Now would be the perfect time.

"Well mom the wedding plans are all good for now, but there is something you can start helping me with on planning. How would you like to help me decide on how to decorate the babies' nursery?" I smiled over at Adam and then added, "With needing two of everything, I want your opinion on how we should place everything."

"Well, of course honey, I would love....," Sandy stopped mid-sentence as Taylor's words sank in, instant tears sprang into her eyes, "Two of everything?" she repeated back.

I nodded, "We had our doctor's appointment early last week and well, we found out we are having twins."

Through all the screams and excitement the doorbell sounded in the room, "I will get it." Adam stood and left the dining room to answer the door.

As Adam walked down the hallway he noticed Lindsay standing outside the screen door, "Lindsay, what are you doing here?"

"I hope I'm not bothering you guys but I need to talk to you and Taylor, it is important."

Puzzled Adam stared at her for a moment, then he opened up the screen door and stood to the side to let her in, he noticed the expression on her face, "Is everything alright?"

Lindsay stepped in and stopped in front of him shaking her head, "Honestly, no."

Adam didn't like the sound of that. What could Lindsay be here about that would be bad? He led the way back down the hallway into the dining room.

"Lindsay, what are you doing here?" Hailey asked the second they appeared in the room surprise written plainly on her face.

"Hailey, mind your manners, that was pretty rude." Grams scolded her.

"Sorry, I didn't mean to sound rude more surprised is all," Hailey apologized.

"I'm sorry to interrupt," she looked over at Taylor's parents, "Mr. and Mrs. Kennedy, it is nice to see you again. It has been a long time."

"Nice to see you Lindsay," Sandy answered back. She remembered Lindsay. She and Taylor never really got along, "We are here for the wedding."

"Lindsay, you said you needed to speak to Taylor," Adam reminded her.

"To me?" I pointed at myself a little surprised that Lindsay would have anything to talk to me about. I stood up from my chair when Lindsay nodded her head, "I guess we can go into the other room and talk."

Lindsay held her hand up to stop her, "Actually what I need to tell you maybe everyone should hear." Lindsay watched as Taylor sat back down in her chair.

Adam pointed at one of the empty chairs around the table, "Have a seat," then he himself took a seat next to Taylor.

Lindsay sat down and looked at Bryson across the table then at Hailey, "Bryson dear why don't you go ahead and go up and play in your room," Hailey picked up on what Lindsay was thinking.

"Okay mommy," and he was more than happy to jump out of his chair and run upstairs to play.

Lindsay watched as the little boy left the room and then she turned her attention back to the table where she found every single person staring at her waiting for her to talk. "First off I just want to say I am very sorry that I have waited so long to make you aware of this." She took a deep breath and continued, best to start from the beginning. "About a month or so ago I met this guy at the dance hall. He started asking me a bunch of questions about how long I had lived here, if I knew everyone in town that kind of stuff. He started telling me how he was here looking for his wife because she was here with some guy. She had stolen all of his stuff and he just wanted to get what was his back. After a night together, which I'm not proud of but anyway, I found out that wife he was looking for was you Taylor."

Gasps around the table were heard but Lindsay continued, "To make a very long and very embarrassing story short that guy is named Mike, your ex-husband, and he knows where you are and he knows about the wedding and about the twins. He is coming after you and he said this time he is going to kill you. I'm very sorry I didn't come sooner. I was scared and I still am. He has threatened me that if I was to tell you he would come after me. I came here first and now I am heading out of town. He is crazy. Taylor, Adam I'm very sorry."

I couldn't speak. He was here and had been for quite a while it sounded like. He knew where she was, he knew about Adam and her getting married, and he knew about the babies.

"We should have known," Robert spoke up.

My wide eyes went to my father, "What are you talking about dad?"

"Well, we found out Mike had left town but we figured he never would have found out where you were. We just thought he left because basically everyone in town shunned him."

"Dad, you guys still should have told me. I had the right to know."

"Taylor, calm down," Adam tried soothing her, but he had to admit his heart was down in his feet right now.

"What is going on?" Grams asked before anything else could be said.

Hailey looked between Taylor, Adam, and then Ryan. They had never told Grams about why Taylor had really come to visit, "Grams, we didn't want to worry you but Taylor didn't just decide it was time for a vacation. She found out Mike, her ex-husband, the one who almost killed her was being released from jail so I guess the best way to explain it is Taylor came here to hide."

I looked over at Grams, she didn't look worried she actually looked a little pissed, "Grams, I'm so sorry. I know we should have told you but I didn't want you to worry. I didn't mean to put your family in danger either."

"Taylor, my family is strong, I'm not worried about them but I am upset that you guys thought to keep this from me. I may be old but who do you guys think raised this family to be a strong as they are? You four should never have kept something like this from me."

I looked down at my hands, I have never had Grams mad at me and I didn't like that she was now. I looked over at Adam, "Grams, we should have told you and we are sorry," Adam apologized for all of them.

I should have known coming here wouldn't have kept Mike from finding me. I should have known that he wasn't going to come out of jail and just leave me alone and move on. I had put him behind bars, he would be looking for me again to punish me for that alone. Now I had even brought that danger onto Lindsay, "Lindsay, what are you going to do now?"

"I have some vacation time at work, I figured I would leave town for a while."

"No, you are coming with me to the station. We will have you tell me everything you can to help us stop the bastard and then you will be put into a place and under police protection until we can find him and put him behind bars, for life this time. I'm still trying to figure out how the hell that man didn't get more jail time for the first time," Ryan had been trying to figure out how a case like Taylor's got so little jail time. That man should have been in prison for years for attempted murder! How in the hell did a lawyer get that man so little time?

Lindsay thought about it for a minute, maybe doing this Ryan's way was a better idea and hopefully with the information she could give them about where he was staying could get him found and this whole mess cleared up with very quickly, "Alright I'll go and tell you what I can," she turned to Adam and Taylor, "I'm so sorry guys for all of this mess. I should have come and said something to you right from the start. I am just glad he hasn't tried anything. I will admit, shamefully, but when I first found out who he was looking for I just figured it would be an easy way to get you out of here and away from Adam. I'm not proud of what I did and I know what kind of danger I put you in because of my jealousy. I just want to say I am very sorry and I hope everything is worked out soon."

I knew Lindsay wasn't happy about my relationship with Adam, but because of her jealousy she put herself into harm's way, "Lindsay, we are not mad. I too am very happy nothing has happened to anyone."

Ryan stood up, he needed to get down to the station. "Lindsay, let's get going to the station, I will follow you back to your house and you can drop off your car there."

Lindsay nodded then started following Ryan out of the room but they were stopped when I spoke. "I am leaving as well!"

All eyes swung over to me, "Over my dead body you are leaving!" Adam stood up and looked down at me. He didn't yell but from the expression on his face and the blaze in his eyes he wasn't happy.

I stood up, "Adam, if I'm not here then there is no way for anyone here to get hurt because of me. I will not stand here and let anyone in this house get hurt. He is crazy and he will not just stand off because you are between him and me. He went through some trouble trying to find me, I am pretty sure he isn't going to just let it go."

"Tay, you are getting married on Saturday," Hailey reminded her.

"The wedding is going to have to be postponed. I will not sit here and wait for something to happen."

"I'll be damned if you are leaving! I'm not letting you out of my sight and we are getting married on Saturday. I will hire security if I have to but we aren't postponing anything!" Adam was beginning to yell now.

That's when Ryan stepped in, "Adam, calm down. Hopefully with what Lindsay can tell us we can find him and put him away long before Saturday arrives."

Adam took a deep breath and then grabbed me and wrapped me up into his arms, "Honey, I will not allow Mike to ruin our day. We are going to find him, you are going to stay here and finish planning our wedding and on Saturday we are getting married."

I wrapped my arms tightly around Adam's waist, my head on his chest. I said nothing. This nightmare was never going to end was it? Right when I thought I was going to get to have a normal life with the man I loved, children on the way, a large red light shows up and stops everything again. How can one man cause so much pain? What if he came to the house? Grams, Bryson, Hailey, Ryan, her parents and Adam were all there. All the people she loved in this world were in one location and Mike could show up at any time. If anything happened to any of them I would not be able to live with myself.

“Come on Lindsay, we need to get going. The more time we spend here the more time Mike has to change his plans,” Ryan broke the silence in the room.

Lindsay nodded, “Again, I’m very sorry,” she turned then followed Ryan out of the house.

My sobs echoed in the dining room, “Taylor sweetie, everything is going to be alright, please try and calm yourself,” my mom spoke. She hated seeing all of this on Taylor’s shoulders. Her daughter had been through so much already.

I was getting tired of everyone trying to make this sound like it was no big deal. I knew what Mike was capable of. I pulled myself out of Adam’s arms and took a step back, “You all want to know something? I’m damn sick and tired of everyone making this sound like it’s no big thing. My ex-husband has already tried to kill me once. He killed our unborn child and scarred me for life. To top it off, the bastard somehow got this amazing lawyer who got him next to no time in jail for it and then to top it off he is released early because of good behavior which I find absolutely hilarious for a man who tried to kill someone. My life is the one that has been completely turned upside down and twisted because of him. I had to pick up my life more than once and start over I even moved. Now here I am starting to feel like my life was getting back to normal again and he comes in to destroy it. Please don’t tell me to calm down! I want to scream or to hit something maybe even cry until I have no tears left and I don’t want anyone to tell me I can’t or I shouldn’t. This situation is not fine! It’s completely messed up and I have dragged everyone I love right into the middle of it.” I took a deep breath looked around to everyone in the room then turned and ran out of the house.

Adam started after her but stopped and turned to his sister, “Hailey, Sandy and Robert were going to use one of the rooms at our house but could you please put them up here? I would feel better if you guys had a man in the house since Ryan is going to be gone probably most of the night.”

"Sure," Hailey nodded, "Do you want me to go make sure she is alright?"

"No I will go take care of Taylor. I don't think anything is going to happen tonight but all the same, I think we need to all stay a little more alert," Adam didn't wait for a reply from anyone, he turned and headed to his house to go check on Taylor.

Adam quickly ran over to his house. Walking into the front door he found Taylor sitting on their couch, she hugging one of the decorative pillows. He walked over to her and sat down, "Are you alright?"

"I'm sorry," was all I said in response however, I never turned to look at him.

"You have no reason to apologize, Tay." He waited for her to say something but she didn't. He placed his hand on her leg, "Tay, look at me."

For a moment he thought she wasn't listening and then her head turned, tear filled green eyes looking at him. "Do you understand how much danger I have put this entire family in? I should never have let Hailey talk me into coming here. I should have known if he wanted to find me he would. I can't even be mad at Lindsay for telling him everything that she did. I know that Mike can be very charming when he wants something. I learned that first hand."

"Listen to me, if you had never come we wouldn't have fallen in love and we wouldn't be getting married nor would we be having our babies Taylor. I'm not sorry one bit that you decided to come here and visit or hide, whatever you may want to call it. You and these two little ones," Adam pulled the pillow out of my hand then placed his hand onto my belly, "Are my world now and I'm not going to let anything happen to you, them, my family, your family or myself."

Oh god, he was thinking I regretted my move here? That wasn't what I meant, "Adam, I'm sorry I didn't mean for it to sound like I regret my decisions to move here or to marry you. You are the best thing to happen to me. There is nowhere I would rather be then here with you on this ranch. I am extremely happy. You mean everything to me, I'm just scared."

"Come here," He held out his hand and I crawled right into his lap, he wrapped his arms tightly around me cradling me almost childlike in his lap. "I know you are scared but I promise you we will all be fine. I would never allow anything to happen to you or these little ones," his hand rubbed my belly.

I closed my eyes, how was he going to be able to stop Mike if they didn't have any idea of how or when he was going to try and attack? They were supposed to be happy right now making the final adjustments that needed to be taking care of before Saturday. Her mom and her trying to figure out the best way to set up the twin's room. No, instead they were going to be on complete Mike watch.

Adam kissed the top of my head, "I love you."

"I love you too."

The night had been a long one Taylor had continually been pulled out of sleep by nightmares. Adam would finally fall asleep only to be wakened up again by a scream or her thrashing around. Around four she had finally fell back to sleep, her breathing calm now. Adam just laid there holding her, that's when he remembered back to the day he had left to pick up her engagement ring. When he was pulling out that man was walking down their dirt driveway. That was Mike, he knew he had recognized the man. He had been within reaching distance and he had no idea. It sickened him to know that he could have stopped all of this. He knew Taylor didn't blame Lindsay for any of this but he did. She should have come to them sooner. She is the one who showed Mike where the ranch was and because of her jealousy she had put Taylor back into danger.

He looked down at Taylor finally sleeping soundly in his arms. She would be his wife in five days and he couldn't wait. He would do whatever he needed to do to make sure she stayed safe. He would not allow that bastard to get a second shot at hurting her. He had to admit he was happy her parents were here and that her brother would be here soon, that meant more people around and hopefully that would keep Mike from trying anything until they could figure out a way to find him and put him back in jail.

He looked over at the clock, it was six and he knew there was no way he was going to get anymore sleep and he wanted Taylor to get as much sleep as she could so he decided he would go down and start some coffee. He carefully pulled his arm out from under her and then brought the blanket up over her shoulders. Slowly he got out of bed trying to make sure not to move the bed too much and cause her to wake up. Once out of bed he stared at her for a moment. She looked to be sleeping pretty good, she had to be exhausted.

Walking down stairs he went straight for the kitchen and started his coffee, he leaned against the counter and looked out his kitchen window, he wondered If Ryan had found anything out last night. Just then he saw Ryan pull up into the driveway, he must just be getting home, he went to the front door to go and catch him before he went into his house only to find Ryan already walking up the front steps as he opened the door, "Hey."

"Hey, I figured you would be up."

"Come on in, the coffee should be ready. You want a cup?" Adam walked back into the kitchen Ryan following right behind.

"Coffee sounds good, thanks," he waited as Adam poured two cups then turned and handed him one cup and they both went and sat down at the table. "Where is Taylor?"

Adam nodded his head towards the stairs, "Still sleeping. She didn't get much sleep last night, it was one nightmare after another. Finally around, I would say four, she fell asleep and seems to be finally sleeping peacefully. It's been one heck of a night though. The things she has been saying in her sleep are tearing me apart. If you leave her be and just listen to her you know exactly what happened that day. I would love to get my hands on the bastard and kill him myself. Did Lindsay happen to have any information at all that could help you guys?"

Ryan took a drink of his coffee and shook his head, "Not really, last night she told us everything she could to help. She told us the hotel he was staying at here along with the room number but of course by the time we got a team out there to check it out he was long gone. He did rent a car but we haven't figured out too much on that either. We are hoping to have a better lead on that sometime today."

"He probably figured Lindsay would come here and tell us."

"From what she told me on the way to the station yesterday, he had met up with her a couple of weeks ago all bent out of shape about something but he never really told her what. Anyway, she said that is when she found out he was up to no good."

"Well then why the hell didn't she come to us then?"

"I don't know, all she said is she stayed clear of him, then yesterday they ran into each other at the diner and that is when he threatened her if she said anything, and well you know the rest."

"Where is she now?"

"At a hotel in Nashville, we have a couple of suits on her morning and night until we find him so hopefully we will get something of a lead real soon."

Elbows on the table, Adam ran his hands through his hair. Ryan could tell it had been a long night for his friend, he felt pretty much the same way with getting no sleep but the worry had to be driving him crazy as well. "Well, I know for sure he knows where we live."

Ryan looked at him a little puzzled for a moment, "What do you mean? Lindsay told us she had told and shown him the ranch?"

"No, I know, but last night I remembered the morning that I left to go and pick up Taylor's engagement ring. A man was walking down our drive from the street. I stopped and asked if I could help him with anything. I thought then I had recognized the man from somewhere but couldn't figure out where at the time. He had come with Taylor to your wedding. He said he was lost and was at the wrong place, I brushed it off and left. I hadn't thought about it since, until this morning."

"So there is no telling how many times he has been out here. I have already gotten a squad out here to watch after the place until we find him so hopefully, like I said earlier, something comes up soon as a lead."

Adam was about to say something in reply when a blood curling scream sounded through the house. Both Adam and Ryan were out of their chairs and up the stairs within seconds. Adam charged into their room first finding Taylor sitting up in bed her eyes still closed and her hands were up over her face like she was trying to protect herself, "Please no more! Please stop!" she kept saying.

Adam went to the bed quickly and sat down next to her, his hands on her shoulders shaking her, "Tay, come on honey, wake up! Its ok, I'm here. You are alright."

I could hear Adam's voice in the distance of my dream. I wanted his comfort, his protection but my dream wouldn't allow me to wake up from it. I saw Mike. He was looking over my shoulder like he was looking at someone behind me, then his eyes came back to me. I could feel my head pounding and the blood running down my face. I couldn't take the pain of another blow, I had to wake up.

"You are mine Taylor and you always will be mine or you will be no ones, I will kill you both."

His words echoed in my head, I could still hear Adam's voice somewhere in the distance. Why couldn't I wake up? Then I saw him come at me with the knife, "Noooo!!" I yelled out, my eyes finally flew open and I launched myself into Adam's arms, sobbing hysterically.

Adam's arms tightened around her, his hand running up and down her back, "It's alright, I'm here. Nothing is going to hurt you, I promise." He looked up over her head to Ryan still standing in the doorway.

Silently they spoke through their eyes to one another, Ryan almost felt helpless with having no leads to go on to make sure this man never touched Taylor again. He gestured to Adam that he was going to go and leave them alone.

Adam nodded and watched as Ryan turned from the room and left. He heard the front door close, "Tay, it's alright honey. It was just a dream, everything is fine."

Ryan walked across the yard over to his house, all he wanted to do was wrap his wife into his arms and hold her. He couldn't imagine anything like what Taylor had been through happening to her. He had seen a lot of domestic abuse in his line of work but not someone so close to him.

He was exhausted. All he wanted to do was sleep for a little while and then maybe with a fresh mind he could figure out a way to catch this bastard.

To his surprise when he went into the dining room he found Taylor's parents and Grams sitting at the table with a cup of coffee each, "Where is Hailey?"

"Bryson and she are still sleeping," Grams answered.

"Were you able to find anything out?" Robert asked hopeful.

Ryan shook his head, "No, we went to the hotel that Lindsay said he was staying at but by the time we had gotten there he had already checked out. He must have figured Lindsay would come and tell Adam and Taylor."

"Sweetie you look exhausted. Why don't you go and get some sleep?" Grams could see how tired he was.

"I am tired, so I'm going to go up and get a few hours of sleep and then when I get up I will call the station, hopefully by then we will have some clues as to where to look," he ran his hand over his face and then through his hair in frustration, without saying another word he turned and headed for his room.

Grams watched as Ryan turned and walked away. Now she was not only worried about Taylor and what her ex-husband may do, but also about Ryan. He was going to take this upon himself if god forbid something happened to Taylor.

Ryan walked into his room and stood by the bed for a moment looking down at his wife and son cuddled together sleeping. He couldn't imagine what Adam was feeling right now. Wondering if at any moment someone would sneak around the protective wall they were trying to create and take his every reason to breathe away from him. He kicked off his shoes and pulled off his socks, pulled his shirt up over his head and pulled his pants off laying them in the chair next to the bed. He slid into bed molding himself to his wife's back, his arms wrapping around her waist and his hands settling on his son's shoulders, "I love you," he whispered into her hair.

"I love you," was whispered back.

After leaving the diner Mike had decided that going back to the hotel probably was not a good idea, Lindsay had been trying a little too hard to act normal but he hadn't known her that well and he may just be on edge but better safe than sorry, he couldn't trust anyone.

He had found out where Lindsay had lived, that was the one good thing about small towns. As long as you acted like a great and trusting person, people trusted anyone and would be more than happy to help with information.

He had grabbed his stuff from the hotel and then he headed over to the address his was given for Lindsay, no surprise to him she was not there and he would bet she wasn't coming back anytime soon so there was no reason to wait around. He was sure now that she went to Taylor and had told her everything, he had to get out of town for a little while just in case they were looking for him.

He had found out the date and time of his ex-wife's wedding as well when finding out information about Lindsay. It took everything in him not to laugh at the trusting store manager, but instead, he thanked him for helping a friend that was extremely excited about surprising his friend for her wedding. Leaving Lindsay's house he decided he would go into Nashville, lay low until Saturday and then put his plan into action. He hoped that once Lindsay went to Taylor and let her know that he knew where she was and after a couple of days of them looking for him they would assume he left because he knew Lindsay went to them. He knew Taylor would not be left alone right now and he had waited this long, one more week was nothing as long as he got his wife.

Chapter 20

It was Thursday and I felt like the week was crawling by. It wasn't like there was any down time, there was so much to finish before Saturday and I was never alone. I felt like if I wanted any time alone I had to excuse myself because I had to use the restroom. Thank goodness I was pregnant, it was the perfect explanation for having to pee all the time but, honestly, I used the excuse just to have a few minutes to myself. I knew Adam and Ryan were worried and didn't want anything to happen but sometimes it was just a little too much. I smiled down at my stomach, I rubbed my hand across the very little mound that I now had, seemed kind of funny, women that I knew who were already mothers always said the only time they had alone was when they were in the bathroom and even then the kids always needed something the second you sat down on the toilet. The babies weren't even here yet and that was where I was trying to hide.

I pushed the porch swing slightly with my toe, right now I was actually enjoying a little time alone not in the bathroom. My mother, Grams, Hailey and I had been going over the to-do list for Saturday. It seemed endless and after a couple of hours I just needed some air. My mother had said she would go out with me but I promised I wouldn't leave the porch and with them in hearing distance and Ryan out with Bryson in the barn I assured them I would be fine.

Looking down the driveway I was now waiting for Adam and my father to get back. My brother had flown in today and I was extremely excited to see him. I had begged Adam to let me go with them but he asked me to stay at the house with Ryan. Since Lindsay had come to the house telling them about Mike and them finding his hotel room empty they hadn't seen one clue that he was still around. I hoped that meant he figured out they had found out he was in town and he gave up but I knew it wasn't that easy. I knew Mike he wasn't giving up, it was just a matter of when now.

They hadn't told Mathew anything yet. I knew if my brother knew Mike was in the area he would have been on a plane earlier in the week, but I didn't want him to worry and had begged my parents not to say anything until he got here. I knew Adam and my father were going to tell him everything I just hoped he wasn't too mad at them for not telling him earlier. I laid my head back against the swing, they should be here shortly and just as I closed my eyes I heard the truck coming down the drive. I quickly stood up and walked down the stairs, I watched as the truck pulled up to the house and I ran to the passenger back door, my brother barely making it out of the truck to catch me into his arms. I hugged him, "Mathew I can't believe you are finally here."

Mathew and I have always been very close. I may be the older sister but he has always treated me like I was the youngest of the family. We were only fourteen months apart in age, our mom had always teased that it was like having twins and he had always been very protective.

Mathew squeezed her tightly then quickly released, "Have to be careful, don't want to squeeze my little nephew or niece too much," he looked down at my belly. "You look amazing. How are you feeling?"

I looked over at Adam, "Did you tell him yet?"

Before Adam could answer Mathew did, "If this is about Mike yeah, they told me but I don't really want to talk about that right after getting here, you look to happy to talk about something that is just going to piss me off completely. I would rather talk about happy stuff for a little while."

Adam saw the smile on Taylor's face when she had asked the question. He knew she wasn't talking about the Mike issue, she was talking about the babies, "No we didn't say anything, I knew you would want to be the one to tell him."

Mathew threw up his hands, "Wait there is more news?" His face look worried. "Is the baby alright?"

"The babies are great!" I smiled up at him watching his face expression wondering if he was going to actually pick up on what I said but of course, he was a guy.

"Good," he took a deep breath, then looked between his sister and soon to be brother in law, "Then what other news do you need to tell me."

"Mathew, we are having twins," I simply stated and watched my brother as he registered what I had told him.

Mathew looked down at my stomach like he could see the babies through it. "Wow! Twins, really?" He hugged me and patted Adam on the back, "Good job man."

Adam laughed and shook his head, "Thanks," he grabbed my brother's bag out the back of the truck and grabbed my hand, "Come on let's get you settled in. I'm sure Grams will be calling us for dinner shortly."

"No girlfriend yet little brother?" I asked as I passed him the plate of chicken.

"For your information, yes, I am seeing someone," he didn't even look at me he just smiled, placed a piece of chicken on his plate and passed it to our mother.

My eyes grew wide with shock. "Why hadn't anyone told me about this and to top it off you didn't bring her, why not?"

"We tried to talk him into inviting her she is a sweet heart but you know your brother and how he can be," our mom informed the table.

"Again I ask, why didn't you bring her with you? I would love to meet the woman who finally got my brother to stop switching women every week."

Mathew rolled his eyes, "Really I'm not that bad," he spoke to the table trying to not sound like a complete player. "We haven't been going out that long and I felt like if I invited her to my sister's wedding she may think we are moving too fast. I don't want to scare her away."

"Wait, mom and dad already met her so what's the difference if she met me?" I looked hurt. "How long have you two been together?"

Mathew, her parents, and Adam started laughing, "Calm down Tay, I am just messing with you. She is flying in on Saturday morning. She couldn't get off work any earlier than that and she was excited about meeting you. I spoke to Adam and asked if you guys would mind me bringing a date." He pointed his spoon in his mother's direction, "Honestly I didn't really have a choice, mom invited her for me."

I glared over at Adam and playfully punched him in the arm, "You knew about this and didn't say anything to me?"

"Yep for about a week now," he laughed.

"And you didn't think to tell me?"

He pointed over at Mathew, "He told me not to tell you."

I glared at him for a moment longer then turned my attention back to my brother, "What's her name? Where did you meet? Come on! I want some details."

"I'm eating," was all my brother said and then shoved a spoonful of mashed potatoes into his mouth and smiled. My glare told him I wasn't letting this go and he better start talking. Swallowing, he set his spoon down and gave his full attention to me, "Fine, her name is Riley. We met through friends and the rest you two can talk about once she gets her." He picked his spoon back up and shoveled another bit of potatoes into his mouth.

"Sweetie, you are going to love her. Your dad and I fell in love with her right away. She keeps your brother in line too. She says jump, he says how high. It's great!"

Mathew began to choke, "Whatever, it's nothing like that mom."

"Mathew, stop. Man its ok, all the men at this table know how it is, trust us we all have a woman in our life. We understand the 'yes dear' statement," Ryan bailed him out. Of course his reward was a glare from his wife. He smiled, leaned over and placed a small kiss on his lips, "I love you!"

"Um hmm I love you too! After dinner you can give Bryson his bath."

"Yes dear," was all he said then looked at the others at the table with the 'I told you so' look on his face, the table coming alive with laughter.

After dinner the ladies quickly cleaned up and then went into the living room to go over what was left to finish before Saturday. All the men went outside, staying out of the women's way. Sitting around Adam's porch out of hearing distance for the ladies, "Alright now that we are away from my sister, let's finish our earlier conversation." Mathew took a seat on the porch railing, his dad and Ryan sat down on the porch swing and Adam was leaning up on the corner rail of the porch, "Do we have any idea where the bastard is yet?"

Ryan shook his head, "We have a bunch of dead ends is all we have right now. Honestly, we don't think he is town right now, so I'm figuring he is laying low for the time being. Even a chance, a small one at least, that he has left for good and gave up?"

"If he has been here as long as Lindsay says he has I don't think he would just give up," Adam rubbed his hands over his face, this waiting and not knowing was driving his nerves crazy, "I don't know the man but I would think that he has some plan. I think he is just laying low and hoping we begin to think he has left so that we relax on the whole thing."

Adam's right," Mathew agreed, "He isn't going to just give up. He is crazy and stupid. He is going to try something it's just a matter of finding out what and when."

"The wedding," Adam, Ryan and Robert all said at once.

"Do you really think he would try something that stupid?" Mathew asked then realization crossed over his face. "Never mind, the man is that stupid. He doesn't want her happy and that is every woman's happiest day. He knew that Taylor always wanted a wedding, I believe he talked her out of it with him because he knew she wanted it so bad. He also knew she was head over heels for him and would do anything to make him happy."

"He thinks that everyone is going to be too busy that day to notice him. There are going to be a lot of people, he will just lay low until he thinks he has his perfect opportunity," Adam looked at each of the men with worried eyes then turned and looked out into the darkness. All Taylor wants is this perfect wedding. Her wedding that she has dreamed about since she was a little girl. He knew Mike had talked Taylor out of her dream wedding, she had told him that. That was why no matter what, he was going to make sure that this wedding was everything she had dreamt about. Now Mike was in the picture trying his damnest to make sure this day was ruined for her as well. This man had taken so much away from her already. Adam pictured Taylor, the scars that were constant reminders of what Mike had done to her and what he had taken away from her, the life that she had carried inside and had ripped away from her. All of this because of one man's jealousy.

Adam could be thankful of one thing though, even though she was put through hell by Mike it did get her away from the man and into his arms.

She was now going to have the child she has wanted, or should he say children. She was back on the ranch which he knew she loved, you could see it in her eyes and face every time they were out riding or when she was with one of the horses. He knew she had given up a lot with her photography, leaving her other home and staying here but she was booking sittings quickly. He had no doubt in his mind she was soon going to become very busy here in her new home as well. First though they had to get rid of this threat, this man who seems to think that if he cannot have her then no one is going to have her.

A hand on his shoulder brought him out of his thoughts, he looked over his shoulder to Ryan, "Adam the department is going to make sure nothing goes wrong on Saturday. We have already thought about Saturday being the day he would try something. We have five of our guys who will be under cover as guests at the wedding, we have two guys who will be at the front of the driveway with a guest list making sure everyone who is driving in is invited. I have a man who will be with the women at all times while they are getting ready."

Adam said nothing he just nodded. He knew Ryan and the department were doing everything they could to make sure the wedding had no problems. If this day wasn't so special to Taylor he would be suggesting that the two of them go off somewhere and just get married. However, he knew that she would never be happy with that.

Mathew looked over at his soon to be brother in law, he was happy for Taylor, Adam was a great guy. He had always liked Adam and he knew that Adam would take very good care of his sister and Taylor deserved someone who would put her first no matter what. "Adam I have already allowed that bastard to hurt my sister once. I will never forgive myself for allowing her to get hurt that way, but I will be damned if I am going to allow it to happen again. Even if he doesn't show his face at the wedding I have taken a leave from work and will be staying to help keep her safe. "

"Matt you didn't allow anything to happen to your sister." Adam couldn't imagine what Taylor's parents and Matt had gone through when they had learned what had happened, “Mike was her husband and there was no way you could have protected her from that.”

He turned back around so that he was facing all the men, “Taylor has no idea about the extra guest we have this weekend. She is aware of the two who will be checking the guest list as everyone arrives but nothing of the undercover cops. The police officer who will be with her when she gets ready is actually a female and a good friend of Hailey’s and Ryan’s. Taylor hasn’t really spoken about any of this lately, she has only had the wedding on her mind. I’m not saying she has forgotten because I’m sure she hasn’t, but she is trying to push it aside. I want to make sure her wedding day is perfect for her.”

Everyone nodded in agreement and understanding, “Man does this mean we don’t get to give you a bachelor’s party tomorrow night?” Ryan asked trying to lighten the mood a little.

Smiling Adam shook his head, “Sorry man, Taylor and I have already decided we are taking everyone out to dinner tomorrow night to show our thanks to you guys. If she can’t go out for a wild night than neither can I.”

Chapter 21

Hair and makeup finished, I looked over at the clock next to the bed. Thirty minutes and I would be Mrs. Adam Kageen I couldn't help but smile. I thought back, not even a year ago my life was so different, I would have never imagined this is where I be. If someone would have told me that I would have been marrying Adam my best friend's brother I would have laughed in their face. Not only was I marrying Adam, I was pregnant with his children. My hand went to my slightly rounded belly, twins! Who would have ever imagined? It was all a little overwhelming at the moment. Yet I knew this was right, all of it. I was alright with leaving my home and career behind. Although I had to say I was quickly becoming known here in Tennessee, the calls for photo shoots were coming in daily. Only real problem has been that since Lindsay had informed us that Mike was hanging around I have either had to cancel photo shoots or take someone with me. That was driving me a little crazy although I knew it was completely useless to try and argue so I just took a deep breath, smiled, and prayed everything would settle very soon. Although I was able to help on the ranch on the days when I wasn't shooting, of course my dear husband to be would watch me like a hawk making sure I didn't overdo it. A knock at the bedroom door brought me out of my thoughts. I watched in the mirror as Hailey stood from the bed and went and answered it.

The familiar face on the other side of the door had me up and across the room, "Levi I am so happy you came."

"Do you honestly think I would have allowed anyone besides myself to photograph this amazing day for you?"

Levi was one of my closest friends from back in California. We had met in photography class in college, he had been through everything with me when I was married to Mike. Actually he was one of the only friends that stayed around when I was with Mike, although we always had to be careful of meeting each other because Mike was so jealous.

"By the way, just met the hubby to be. I do believe you have picked a good one."

"I think so," I turned to Hailey, "Hailey, this is Levi. Levi, this is my best friend Hailey."

"It's great to finally meet the girl behind the name. Taylor talked about you all of the time, I feel like I know you already."

"Nice to meet you, she has talked very highly of you as well."

"Well as much as I would love to sit here and get catch up you, I have a groom waiting and I have to get set up. Love you, see you in a few."

As he opened the door Mathew and a girl were just about to knock, "Holy cow, it's like grand central in here right now," Hailey pointed at my dress, "You have about fifteen minutes before you are supposed to be down stairs."

Laughing I turned my attention to my brother, "Don't mind her she seems to forget they can't start anything without me."

"Tay, I want to introduce you to Riley. Riley, this is my sister Taylor."

I looked over at the petite brunette standing next to my brother, she was beautiful. "Riley, it is great to finally meet you."

"It's nice to meet you Taylor. Your brother has talked about you a lot. I'm sorry we interrupted you, I know you need to get ready. I told him this could wait until later."

"Absolutely not, I'm glad he brought you up."

"Well thank you very much for inviting me! Sorry I couldn't get her any earlier."

"Please don't apologize, I am just glad you made it. We have plenty of time to get to know each other after the wedding."

"We are going to head down to our seats before Hailey throws us out," Mathew kissed his sister on the cheek, "You look amazing and the dress isn't even on yet."

"Thank you, love you!" I watched as he and Riley left, closing the door behind them. I turned back to Hailey, "Alright, I'm all yours my dear! Let's get this dress on so I can go marry your brother."

Together Hailey and I worked at getting my dress on, Hailey had been at every fitting to make sure she knew exactly how to tie and button me up, "Tay, you look amazing, I can't believe that you are going to be my sister, I knew this would work between you two."

"What do you mean you knew this would work between us?"

Hailey grabbed my veil and gently placed it on my head, "I knew if I could just get you out here that the two of you would hit it off."

"Oh really? So there was a plan behind the invitation?"

"Absolutely!" Hailey smiled, "No need to thank me."

Again a knock at the door, I smiled and shook my head as I watched Hailey answer it, "Oh my goodness! Taylor honey, you look beautiful," Sandy swept into the room and straight to her daughter.

"I will go and make sure everything is ready to go and give you two a moment," Hailey quickly left the room giving mother and daughter some time.

"Thank you mom, for everything you and dad have done and gone through with me. This time I am doing it right."

"Honey, your father and I have always been so proud of you. Adam and you will be so happy together he will take very good care of you and my grandbabies, I have no doubt about that."

I looked down at my hands, my engagement ring now on my right hand. Once my wedding band was placed on my left hand I'll place my engagement ring back on the left figure. When I looked back at my mother a single tear was falling down my cheek, "Mom I'm scared that Mike will show up today."

Sandy's heart broke, she wrapped her daughter into her arms. The fear in her daughter's eyes made her heart hit the floor. Taylor hadn't spoken about Mike at all lately. She knew everyone hoped that the wedding was keeping her from thinking about it. How could any of them think she would have forgotten about him? She pulled away from her daughter and placed her hands on her cheeks, "Honey everything will be fine. All you need to worry about today is enjoying yourself. Don't let that man ruin this for you. Mike may be a very stupid person but I do believe he has enough brains to know that there are a ton of people her today and for him to try anything today would be a death sentence for him."

Another knock, I turned to the mirror and gently wiped my eyes as my mother answered the door, "Taylor, are you ready? There is a very impatient man waiting outside for you and I am afraid if we don't get this wedding rolling he may come up here, throw you over his shoulder, and run away with you."

I turned and smiled at my father. My mother was right, Mike would be beyond stupid to try something with all of these people here. If there was anything she had learned about Mike it was that no matter how mad he had become with her in public he never showed it until they were alone. Making scenes were never his way, "Yes dad, I'm ready."

Sandy gave her daughter a hug, "I am going to go to my seat. I love you sweetie."

"I love you too mom."

We walked out behind my mother, slowly making our way down the stairs through the house to the back door. Once outside we walked across the porch and down the stairs. My dad stopped and turned to me, "Tay I am so very proud of you. I know you have a man who is going to keep my baby girl safe and happy. I love you honey."

My eyes once again filled with tears. We were standing at the beginning of the aisle, rows and rows of people turned around to watch. I looked over and saw Adam, standing proudly next to the pastor, Ryan to his left. Hailey had just taken her spot. The music began, I heard the pastor ask for everyone to stand, I looked back at my dad, "I love you so much daddy and I will always be your baby girl."

I turned back towards the front, looped my arm into my father's and we began the walk down to the man I would spend the rest of my life with.

The day had gone in a blur now that I was thinking back. I remember the walk down the aisle, only seeing Adam. I faintly remembered hearing the pastor ask who gave this woman away and my father answering, "Her mother and I do." I remembered the strength in Adam's hand when my father placed my hand into Adam's, his eyes as he looked down at me and whispered, "You are beautiful."

I looked down at my now wet left hand, covered slightly with bubbles, and admired my wedding set. The whole ceremony was a slight fog, although I could still feel the ring as it slipped slowly onto my finger as Adam repeated his vows. "I now pronounce you man and wife. Adam, you may kiss your bride." That kiss spoke volumes. I felt every emotion Adam felt through that one kiss and could remember hearing the cheering of our friends and family.

Our first dance, I cried as Adam held me tight and whispered, "I love you. I can't believe you are mine. We are going to have a beautiful family." Then the one I don't think I will ever forget him whispering,

"Please don't ever stop loving me Taylor for you will forever have my heart." Tears filled my eyes even now as I remembered those words.

The father daughter dance I had always dreamed about, and then the dance that had everyone in tears, Adam had danced with Grams. Cake in the face and the laughter while trying to clean it up. The toast and all the great stories that people shared along with a very moving speech for Hailey that, yes, once again had me in tears. I could blame all the tears on being pregnant but I knew they were from pure happiness and the perfect wedding. This day was everything I had dreamed about since I was a little girl.

It was now finishing off perfectly, Adam had the bathroom decorated in burning candles. A table set up next to our oversize bathtub with two glasses and a plate filled with chocolate covered strawberries. He was running the water and pouring in the bubbles when he realized that the bottle of sparkling cider had been forgotten. He was determined to make everything perfect telling me to get in and relax, he would be right back. He helped me out of my dress and tore himself away from me to run back to the other house for the bottle. My laughter filled the bathroom as I thought back to his reaction when I told him the doctor had said I could have a glass of Champagne that one would be alright. Adam was shaking his head no before I had finished my sentence. He was having nothing to do with anything that could possible hurt the babies. That just made me fall that much more in love with him if that was possible.

Head laid back, eyes closed, smiling at myself, I ran through the day over and over again hoping to burn it into memory. The sound of footsteps brought my head up, but the smile quickly fading, "Hello Taylor."

My nightmare raced through my mind. I started to stand up but quickly remember I wasn't wearing anything so instead sank further into the tub hoping the bubbles covered me. "What? Are you not happy to see me? You look a little surprised. Are you telling me that you didn't know I was in town?"

My eyes traveled down to the gun in his right hand and the robe he held in his left. I had to stay calm, I had to keep him calm. I took a deep breath and looked back up at him, "How did you find me?"

Laughing, Mike took another step into the bathroom, "That actually wasn't very easy. No one knew where you had gone but one day I had manage to find out where you were living in Napa. As my luck had it, when I got there the moving crew was there packing the house. I told the nice guys I was a friend and it didn't take much for them to tell me the state into which they were moving the stuff too. As soon as I was told Tennessee I remembered you and I coming here for that friend of yours wedding. Now once I got here that was easy, I'm sure Lindsay told you the rest."

He held the robe out to me without saying a word, I shook my head, "Not a choice here Taylor. Get out of the tub. Honestly, I'm not sure why I'm being so nice to even let you put the robe on, I have seen it all before."

Standing slowly, I knew I didn't want to do anything to piss him off. I stepped out of the tub and grabbed the robe from his hand, my eyes going to the gun and then back up. I could feel his eyes on my body so as quickly as I could I put the robe on and tied it around my waist, "What do you want Mike?"

"Funny question really. At first I was going to come here, get you, and go home, that's where you belong with me. I'm your husband."

Shaking my head I argued, "Mike we haven't been married in years. How could you even think I would want to be married to you after what you did to me?"

"After what I did to you?" he yelled waving the gun at me. "You were pregnant with another man's child."

"It was your child Mike. Why didn't you believe me on that?"

The question was never answered, "Then I found out after getting here that you have already slept with another man and are getting married so now, why am I here? Well I am here to have you watch me kill your husband and then I am going to kill you."

I had to think fast and calm him down, "How did you get in here?"

"That was actually quite easy, a couple of weeks ago while the family was all having dinner over at the other house I came in here and became familiar with the layout of the house, you guys should really lock your doors when you leave your house, you never know who is going to get in." He gave me a smug smile and then continued, "I knew today there would be a ton of people around but they would all be in back with the ceremony and watching you two. After the ceremony was started I was able to walk onto the property and into the house. I watched everything from the bedroom window, you got your big wedding. Anyway, after this room was put together I waited for them to leave, came in, grabbed the bottle and took it knowing that man you just married wouldn't just let that go. I just waited until I knew he left the house and I'm sure you can figure out the rest. Now we just wait for the third member of this party to arrive."

A movement in the bedroom caught my attention, I tried not to make it obvious that someone was there but Mike caught me looking into the room. The gun came up and pointed straight at my chest, "I suggest you don't make another move or I swear I will kill her."

I watched as Mike turned his head to see behind him and before I knew what was happening first one shot went off and then a second one.

Adam watched as Ryan came into the room first, his gun drawn. He was followed by one of the other officers who just so happened to have still been there because he was talking to Ryan about the day and how no signs of Mike had been seen. When Adam had walked back into the house from grabbing the bottle of Champagne from next door he had heard Mike's voice once he was at the top of the stairs. He knew he had taken a chance with leaving the house again to go get Ryan but he had no other choice. He knew Mike would be armed and he had his gun in the room.

Now his worst nightmare was happening right in front of him and all in slow motion. Ryan had entered the room first, the second officer going in and placing himself next to the bed to the left of the bathroom. Ryan yelled for Mike to drop the gun and turn around. Mike turned to his left which placed his left shoulder outside of the bathroom the other officer next to the bed saw the opportunity and took the shot that was the first shot. The second was from Mike's gun which shot straight into the bathroom. Mike fell to the floor and Adam looked in just as Taylor fell to the floor as well.

Adam ran into the room, pushed past Ryan and jumped over Mike's body landing onto the ground next to Taylor, there was blood on the floor and the robe she wore red now. He felt for a pulse feeling one in her neck, "Ryan call 911, hurry!" he cradled his wife in his lap, "Come on Tay, hold on, stay with me honey."

From a distance he heard someone yell to call 911, he even heard the scream from a woman but all he could think about was his wife in his arms. "Don't do this Tay! Don't you die on me, come on sweetheart the babies need you to keep breathing, I need you to keep breathing."

Chapter 22

Taylor had insisted on framing this goofy picture of the two of them and putting it on her nightstand next to their bed. He remembered the day she saw it and laughed so hard he thought she was going to fall over. His sister had taken it with her phone. One of those moments where you were caught with a terrible expression or your eyes half closed, in this case both. Taylor had loved it and how was he supposed to tell her no after hearing her laughter. It was the best sound to his ears.

He placed the picture back on the nightstand and looked around, making sure that he had grabbed everything he was told he needed. The last couple of days had been a blur, everyone trying to help out. He looked into the bathroom you would never know that two days before it had been covered with the blood of his wife. He hoped that one day he would be able to look into that room again and not see his wife's lifeless body lying on the floor. He turned back to the bed, grabbed the bag, and walked down stairs. Walking into the kitchen to grab his wallet off the counter, passing the refrigerator he stopped and looked at the only thing on the door, the ultrasound of their twins. He remembered the panic he felt when the doctor first showed them two babies and not just one. He could still see Taylor's eyes go so large from hearing the news and then both of them just stared down at her belly like the babies were going to jump out. He stood there and just stared at the words, Baby 1, Baby 2, their babies.

A hand on his shoulder made him jump, "Sorry, I didn't mean to scare you. I called your name a couple of times but you didn't answer."

Adam turned away from the picture and straight into his sister's arms, "They are my everything!"

She pulled away from him, a tear escaped and rolled down her cheek, "I know."

Looking back at the picture, "It should have been me, not her."

"Adam, Taylor would have done anything to make sure Mike didn't hurt anyone else. This isn't your fault."

"Adam, I hope you know we have gone over and over the actions from that night to ensure that the actions that Sean took were the right ones," Ryan explained.

"I don't blame anyone for this Ryan. I know Sean was doing what he thought was best."

Ryan told Adam yesterday morning that Mike hadn't made it through the night. Mike was no longer a threat to anyone, if anything Sean had ensured that Mike wouldn't harm another person.

"Come on guys we have to go," Hailey said heading to the door.

Adam stared at the picture for a moment longer, took a deep breath, and then turned and grabbed his wallet off the counter and the bag he brought down from the bedroom and followed his sister and Ryan out of the house and out to Ryan's truck.

Standing in front of door number 216 his life had changed so much in the last two days, he would never take anything for granted any longer. Hailey and Ryan had waited out in the car knowing it wouldn't take long. He opened the door and looked around. No one was in the room, he looked around, the sound of the door to his left caught his attention and he turned dropped the bag just in time to wrap his wife in his arms, she smelled so good, she felt even better in his arms.

He was careful not to squeeze her too much, her right arm held against her chest in a sling. When Mike had turned to look behind him his arm had rotated with him causing the gun to go from her chest. When he fired it the bullet had gone into her shoulder and straight out the back. He remembered sitting in the waiting room with all of the family, along with her friend Levi from California, waiting for the doctors to come in with any kind of news. He felt like they had waited for hours and then finally the doctor came in and announced that she would be alright but they were keeping her for a couple days to monitor her and the babies.

"Did you bring me everything I asked for? I need to get out of this hospital gown."

"Everything you asked for," he kissed me on the forehead, picked up the bag, and handed it to me.
"Why don't you go get changed while I go take care of paper work and then we can go home."

I took the bag, pushed up onto my tippy toes and kissed my husband, "I love you so much."

Looking down at me he smiled, "I love you too."

Two pair of bright blue eyes, two heads full of dark brown hair, both babies wrapped up in receiving blankets, one handed to mom and one handed to dad, "Congratulations mom and dad! You have identical twin boys."

The idea not to know the sex of the babies was all mine. It took a lot of convincing on my part to have Adam go along with it. He kept trying to find out at every ultrasound we had. I looked over at Adam, "We have boys."

"How are we supposed to tell them apart?"

I laughed, Adam had been worried about this for the longest time. They would be lying in bed and he would just come out with the most random situations, "Honey, don't worry! We will not mix them up, plus, we have already decided one in blue, one in red."

A nurse with two tiny hospital bracelets came over, "Alright who is Trevor," she held the bracelet up with Trevor's name on it and waited.

I looked down at the bundle in my arms, "This one."

The nurse put his bracelet on and then turned to Adam, "This little one is Austin then."

I watched as the nurse finished with the bracelets then looked up at Adam, he was running his finger over Austin's little cheek, if you ever wanted to see a grown man cry then just hand him his child for the first time. My heart swelled looking between the men in my life. How lucky can one woman be? The door opening brought my attention away from my husband. Standing there was Hailey, Ryan, Bryson, Grams and my parents. My brother should be here shortly with Riley, they jumped on the first plane they could once they heard I had gone into labor.

"Are you guys good with having some visitors?" mom asked from the doorway.

"Of course," Adam answered, "Come meet your grandsons."

Bryson started to run towards Adam, but Hailey caught him by the arm, "Honey, don't run. The babies aren't going anywhere." I laughed as Hailey waddled quickly after her son.

"I have to see! I have to know, are they boys?" Bryson came up to the side of the bed and stretched his head up to see.

I laughed, "Yes buddy, they are both boys," Adam answered, "That one there that Aunt Taylor is holding is Trevor and this is Austin."

“Yes!” Bryson pumped his little fist into the air, “At least they are boys.” He pointed over his shoulder with his thump at his mom’s belly, “That is a girl.”

Laughter filled the room. I looked around and tears filled my eyes. How I had become so lucky I will never know. I did know however that I wasn’t going to take one day for granted. Life had taught me that it is great in so many different ways. I have come to understand the whole saying “Everything happens for a reason”. I may have wondered for many years what those reasons were but looking around today I could give you multiple reasons and I wouldn’t change a one!

About the Author

I live in Southern California with my husband and two daughters. I own a hair salon and a photography business and during my off time I coach both of my daughter's soccer teams and referee. This brings me to how I started writing, when I needed to relax and have a little down time, I would sit down and start writing, my husband was the one who convince me to share my stories with everyone.

I fell in love with romance novels back in High School. I have always loved a story with a crazy way two people meet in the beginning, a little fun and adventure between the two people in the middle, and a happy ending.

I hope you have enjoyed reading about Adam, Taylor and the family. I would like to hear back on any thoughts you as the readers may have so please feel free to contact me at:

AuthorTonyaClark@gmail.com

Or go on Facebook and like my page at:

Facebook.com/AuthorTonyaClark

You can even follow me on my Authors page at:

Amazon.com/author/tonyaclark

Twitter @AuthorTonyaC

19873520R10153

Made in the USA
San Bernardino, CA
17 March 2015